Praise for Tell Me No Truths

'Powerful and impressive. An outstanding piece of writing.'
Tim Bowler, author of *River Boy* and winner of
fifteen awards, including the Carnegie Medal

'Gill Vickery has the enviable knack of introducing us right
at the start to characters who will interest and intrigue us.
This novel moves between the present and the war-time past
in Italy, bringing both periods to life most enjoyably.'
Adèle Geras, Author of *Troy*, *Ithaka* and *Dido*

'Intrigues and captivates in equal measure. A winner!'
Celia Rees, award-winning author of *Witch Child*,
Sorceress, *Pirates* and *Sovay*

'A compelling YA novel for our times. The past explodes
upon three teenagers amid the glories of Florence and the
Tuscan countryside. These vividly-drawn young characters
uncover the horrors of fascism and war through their
personal quests to untangle mysteries and hidden histories.
A shocking yet sensitive story to make young readers think.'
Julie Bertagna, author of the *Exodus* trilogy

Also by Gill Vickery

THE IVY CROWN

Tell Me
No Truths

Tell Me No Truths

GILL VICKERY

The Greystones Press

First published in Great Britain in 2018 by

The Greystones Press Ltd
Greystones
37 Lawton Avenue
Carterton
Oxfordshire OX18 3JY

A CIP catalogue record for this book is available
from the British Library

ISBN 978-1-911122-23-4

This book is a work of fiction. Names, characters,
businesses, organizations, places and events are
either the product of the author's imagination
or used fictitiously.

1 3 5 7 9 10 8 6 4 2

Designed and typeset by Nigel Hazle

Printed and bound in Great Britain by Clays Ltd, Elcograf S.p.A

Contents

To Jane Weller, friend and much-loved godmother, and in memory of Sergeant Malcolm Griffin who cherished the flag of Villagrappa school for sixty years.

The brimstone is back
in the woken hills of Tuscany,
passing the word
from speedwell to violet
wood anemone to celandine.

From 'Primavera' by Robin Robertson

Disegnia Antonio, disegnia e non perder tempo.
Draw, Antonio, draw and don't waste time.

Michelangelo: written on a drawing by his pupil,
Antonio Mini, c.1524.

I can recall nothing after the boy burst into the room and shot me in the head. To be more accurate, I have pieced together my own remembered fragments of the massacre while friends who were also there have filled in the gaps. Only one memory still eludes me: what happened immediately after the Black Brigade boy turned his shotgun on me? I know that something was said, something vital, but what it was I can't remember.

The day had started well. It was Easter Sunday, 9th April 1944, deep in the hills of Northern Italy. The farmer's wife, her daughter Tecla, and daughter-in-law Elena, were preparing a feast. Today it would seem an ordinary meal but in that year Italy was close to starving and the prospect of real food was at the forefront of all our minds. There was to be the usual chestnut polenta that had sustained both the farmer's family and the motley collection of partisans, escaped prisoners of war, and myself, a British agent of the Special Operations Executive, through a bitterly hard winter. In addition to this staple, there were to be eggs, a chicken and vegetables, and wine, all of which had mysteriously found their way to the farmhouse. There was even a bar of American chocolate. No one asked where any of the food had come from. Anticipation of full bellies had made us less alert than we should have been; besides, who would attack on such a holy day?

When dinner was ready I went to collect Jerzy and Henryk, two Polish POWs, who were sharing a rare cigarette in the courtyard, their stolen German weapons leaning against the well. At that moment a young girl, a partisan courier called Ilaria, burst through the trees shouting, 'They're coming – the Black Brigade! They're coming!'

Jerzy and Henryk immediately took up a defensive position, crouched behind the well with their rifles, while I ran up the steps to the farmhouse door and gave the alarm. The partisans leaped to their feet sending chairs and benches crashing to the floor, grabbed their weapons from a stack by the door and scattered around the farmyard. The farmer hurried his wife, daughter and granddaughter away. Before we could do anything else, the Black Brigade screamed up the track in their vehicles and into the courtyard.

I'd left my weapons in the stable where I slept. Cursing myself for my stupidity, I was about to run for them when Gaetano, the farmer's son, called to me from the kitchen at the back of the house. His terrified, pregnant wife, Elena, was there and he wanted my help to get her outside and into the relative safety of the woods. As we made our way to the door gunfire began blasting from the front of the farmhouse, followed by yells, screams and the ping of bullets bouncing

2

off stone. The kitchen door swung open. It was Ilaria, the partisan girl. 'This way!' She beckoned to Elena who stumbled forward, Gaetano supporting her, myself following. Too late, we heard the unmistakable sound of a weapon being cocked and a voice ordering, 'Stop!'

Ilaria didn't hesitate: without looking back, she pushed Elena and Gaetano out onto the hillside, slammed the door after them, leaned her back defiantly against it and faced the intruder. Her eyes widened in shocked recognition.

That moment of recognition is the last thing I remember of the massacre at the farmhouse.

CHAPTER I

WHEN THE TAXI dropped Nico and his family at Via del Corno he felt a deep sense of disappointment. It was nothing like his fantasy of a Florentine street: it should have been a row of square but graceful houses with shady trees casting shadows over two stone steps leading up to the front doors. This was a narrow, flagged alley with blocks of very tall buildings stretching along each side. At least the one they were going to stay in did have an imposing wooden door with the two stone steps he had imagined in his dreams, but even they were spoiled by having Mum's latest boyfriend, James, standing on them.

Nico's scowl twitched to a grin as another taxi stopped at the house and a man bounded out, ran up the steps past James, pressed the entry phone and announced, 'Mr and Mrs Thompson and girls.' The box on the wall squawked and the door clicked open. The Thompsons picked up their jumble of cases and bags and went into the house. James sent an exaggerated sigh in their direction, hefted his black leather suitcases and nodded to Nico's mother. 'In you go, Hattie.'

'After you, you've got the heavy cases,' Mum said.

'Ladies first.'

Oh, make up your minds! Nico thought. They could be here all day while James and Mum tried to outdo each other with thoughtfulness. Nico decided for them and marched into the house in a swirl of black coat. Mum followed and James came in last, dropping the cases in the lobby. Mrs Thompson was talking in rapid Italian to a sturdy young woman standing by the open door to a ground-floor flat. One of the Thompson girls turned and smiled at Nico. 'This is Ornella. She says we've all got to come inside and meet the landlady.'

Nico couldn't help smiling back. 'Right.'

'Andiamo,' James said in his best holiday Italian.

Nico rolled his black-rimmed eyes in exasperation. Why couldn't the muppet James just say 'Let's go', like everybody else?

'Dio mio!' Ornella stared with fascinated horror at Nico's kohl-edged eyes. He blinked once – slowly – then stared back steadily. Ornella bent her fingers into the sign against the evil eye. Nico was impressed; he'd never had that effect on anyone before.

'Come on,' Mum said. Nico tramped forwards, his boots thudding over the marble floor. Ornella guided them into a large room hung with photographs and

5

ornately decorated certificates in gold frames. An elegant old lady sat at a huge table covered in a crisp white cloth.

James ushered Nico and Mum to the table and as Nico tugged at a hefty chair he somehow grabbed a handful of the damask cloth and almost pulled it off the table. The maid sniggered. The Signora spoke sharply to her and Ornella disappeared into another room.

Mum patted the cloth back into place. 'Sorry,' she said.

Nico slumped into the chair. What did she think she was doing, apologising for him? It was humiliating. They'd only been here five minutes and she was already making him look a fool.

'It does not matter,' the old lady said. 'Let us introduce ourselves. I am Signora Minardi and,' she turned to the Thompsons, 'you are Mr and Mrs Thompson from Derby, no?'

'That's right,' Mr Thompson said. 'I'm Kevin, this is my wife, Luisa, and these are my daughters, Jade and Amber.'

'Luisa, that is an Italian name, no?'

'It can be English too,' Mrs Thompson said. Nico thought she spoke sharply considering the question was perfectly reasonable.

'But you speak Italian perfectly!' The Signora's eyes were round with admiration. Nico thought they were

6

also shrewd and inquisitive. He glanced at the girl who'd spoken to him in the lobby, Jade. She had an odd, closed look on her face.

The Signora went on, 'I heard you speaking to Ornella – so perfectly, so politely.'

Nico noticed that though the old lady's voice was warm and her smile kindly, her bird-like old hands were clenched tightly and her knuckles were white.

'And your daughters too, spoke to Ornella in Italian.' Signora Minardi turned to Jade and Amber. 'How is it that you speak the language fluently?'

Nico could see Jade struggled not to smile and tell the Signora what she wanted to know. He wondered why Jade was hesitant; the old lady's question was harmless. Jade's sister said bluntly: 'Our granddad, our nonno, he was Italian and we learned off him.'

'How charming.' Signora Minardi's eyes flickered from one sister to the other: 'You are twins!'

Nico was annoyed he hadn't noticed something as obvious as identical twins. But then he'd been too busy looking at Jade to look properly at Amber. Besides, they were dressed differently and had different hair – Jade's was shorter than Amber's and spiked up.

Signora Minardi smiled at Luisa and Kevin. 'It is a beautiful thing to have children,' she said and then with a disconcerting switch, 'You are Mr and Mrs Crozier from Brighton?' she said to Mum and James.

'Yes,' Mum said, though it was only half true. 'I'm Hattie, this is James and this is Nicholas.'

'I'm Nico,' Nico said.

Polite 'hellos' echoed round the table. Nico risked another glance at Jade. They exchanged small, cautious smiles. The other twin – Amber – stared at him suspiciously.

The maid came in and put a tray of refreshments on the table. The Signora gestured graciously and said, 'You will all take coffee? And the children perhaps fruit juices?'

The Signora was too authoritarian, Nico thought as he defiantly chose a tiny cup of coffee and sipped. Instantly he wished he hadn't. The bitter brown sludge sat malevolently in the bottom of its little white cup like a dose of poison. Nico drank it in one agonising gulp. Why weren't there any biscuits to take the taste away? He looked hopefully towards a bulky sideboard but there was no sign of biscuits, only a silver-framed old black and white photograph of a young man and woman sitting in a field of flowers.

'Now we do the informations,' the Signora said. She passed pamphlets down the table. 'Here are maps and directions to the important places, also the emergency services.'

Nico knew his mother was going to take careful note of those.

The Signora went on, 'I have indicated the best restaurants . . .'

'Restaurants?' James interrupted, his loud voice drowning out the old lady's.

Nico turned away in embarrassment and saw Jade looking at him sympathetically.

Signora Minardi went on, 'I can recommend to you a restaurant in a small town, only half an hour's drive away.'

'What's the town called?' James asked.

'Borgo Sant'Angelo.'

Nico's mother drew in a sharp breath but he was too fascinated by the Thompsons' reactions to pay attention. Mrs Thompson's mouth was pressed into an angry line and Mr Thompson squeezed her hand in what Nico thought was a comforting gesture though he wasn't sure: it might have been a warning. He couldn't make sense of the twins' reaction at all: they seemed to shrink into a kind of frozen watchfulness. The family masked their reactions so quickly that Nico was sure only he and the Signora had noticed before James boomed, 'What's the name of the restaurant?'

'Il Nido,' the Signora said.

'You know it well?' James thundered on.

The maid laughed softly as she poured more coffee for James.

'Oh, yes,' Signora Minardi said. 'I have a house in

Borgo Sant'Angelo. I divide my time between there and Florence.'

'This Borgo Sant'Angelo,' Mum said, 'it's not the model for E. J. Holm's Montebosco, is it?'

Signora Minardi nodded. 'I believe so.'

'I knew it!' Mum said, beaming.

'Who's E. J. Holm?' Jade asked.

'He's a crime writer,' Nico said. 'His detective, Alessandro Lupo, lives in Montebosco and fans are always trying to find out if it's based on a real town. Mum's done her research – she thinks it's Borgo Sant'Angelo.'

'She's a fan then?'

Nico nodded. He wasn't going to confess that he was as well, not after hearing the disbelief in Jade's voice.

'You must all visit there,' Signora Minardi said. 'In fact, you shall be my guests at Il Nido. Shall we say, Tuesday? It will give you three days to settle in. We shall have dinner at 7.00. And now . . .'

The arrangements were made so suddenly that no one had a chance to disagree before the Signora was passing keys down the table and starting up a whole new topic for James to complain about. Nico's heart clenched as James frowned at the label on his keys. 'This says first floor. I booked the ground floor. There's been a mistake.'

'There is no mistake,' the Signora said.

'It says ground floor on our booking forms,' Luisa said, *'piano terra.'*

'We don't mind swapping, do we, Lu?' Mr Thompson said.

'I don't see why not. What do you think, girls?'

The twins nodded in unison like a pair of metronomes perched side by side on top of a piano.

'The apartments they are identical,' Signora Minardi said. 'You may exchange without a problem but please decide now before Ornella brings your suitcases from the hall.'

'All right,' James said.

You might've asked us, Nico thought resentfully as James swapped keys with Mr Thompson.

Jade and Amber leaned over the balcony outside their bedroom and looked down into the tiny garden. It had a lot packed into it in a haphazard sort of way: at the far end there was a table with a striped umbrella and four chairs shaded by some lush trees while the few bushes and flowers looked as though they'd arrived by chance and survived by not giving any trouble.

Jade read the guidelines she'd found in the flat. 'It says you can hang washing in the garden.'

Amber tugged at a looped rope slung on pulleys between the balcony and the wall of the opposite apartment. 'This rope thing must be the washing line – it's got pegs on it.' She leaned even further over the balcony and tugged again. The pulleys squealed and the pegs jerked towards her. Jade didn't bother to warn her about the danger of dangling five metres above the ground; it wouldn't do any good: Amber always acted first and thought later.

Amber straightened up. 'Those Croziers that nicked our apartment, they've got a patio outside their back doors and the washing line's right over it.'

Nonno would've said, *Amber, it is 'stolen' not 'nicked'*. He hated slang. Jade forced herself to stop thinking about her grandfather. 'The Croziers didn't nick the apartment,' she said. 'You know we swapped because Mum thinks ground-floor flats are too noisy.' All the same, Jade couldn't help grinning at the thought of James Crozier trying to relax on the patio with a line of dripping underwear dangling over his head.

'They think they're better than us,' Amber said. 'They're snobs.'

'How d'you know that?'

'They've got snobby voices and an attitude.'

'The dad has, I'm not sure about the mum and you can't tell with the Goth boy . . . what's his name, Nico?'

'Nicholas!' Amber mimicked Hattie's cultured tones perfectly.

It was a pity Amber always assumed that people like the Croziers were snobs, Jade thought. Nico was interesting and she'd like to get to know him but

Amber would make trouble if she decided to hate him.

'Let's go out,' Jade said. 'It'll give us something to do while the olds are unpacking – you know they always take forever.'

Mum thought it was a good idea too. 'Your dad's having one of his naps and I'll be glad to get some peace and quiet to myself'.

Jade took a purse and a list her mother had hastily scribbled down. 'It's just the basics – I'm not cooking tonight. We'll eat out – we can afford it now.'

Nico heard James call to Mum from the paved area outside their bedroom: 'We could sit in the garden – the trees give plenty of shade. I think we've done all right for ourselves.' James could be so smug.

Nico crashed back on his bed and wondered how he was going to survive being cooped up with the muppet James for two weeks. He groaned. He was a prisoner.

No he wasn't! He had a plan, a secret one, and he wasn't going to be able to carry it out if he didn't make a stand from the start. He sprang up and marched out to his mother. 'Mum, I'm going for a walk.'

'Not on your own,' she said, exactly as Nico had anticipated. He suppressed a groan; just because he'd been ill with meningitis last year, frightening his mother half to death, was no reason for her to carry on treating him as though he were made of glass.

'I'll be perfectly safe,' he insisted. 'I've got the Signora's instructions, I won't get lost – you can't get lost in Florence anyway, it's too small.'

'The instructions aren't very clear.'

'Only in the English bit. It's more detailed in the Italian part. We've done directions at school, it's not hard,' Nico blagged confidently. His mother had no way of knowing he'd hardly understood anything. Mr Mowatt, the language teacher, hadn't bothered to change textbooks since about 1950 and Nico thought he was probably learning to speak Italian the way people in bad historical novels spoke English – accurately but quaintly.

'I'll stay in touch,' he said firmly.

Mum hesitated.

'He's sixteen, Hattie, not six,' James said coming in from the doorway.

For once Nico felt grateful to James.

'If he goes out . . .' James slipped an arm round Mum's waist and smirked suggestively, '. . . it'll give us a bit of time to ourselves.'

Nico stopped being grateful. 'I'm going,' he said.

'All right,' Mum agreed, slapping James's hand away. 'Be back in an hour.'

Nico thought the slap was very half-hearted. 'Two hours,' he said firmly and left.

In the street, he hesitated. He couldn't believe it; his mother had hardly argued about him roaming alone in a strange city – a strange *foreign* city. He looked at the map again. Now, which way should he go?

CHAPTER II

NICO GOT LOST.

He turned right down Via del Corno and walked randomly, happier than he'd been for a long time but then, how could he not be happy in the city of his dreams? He sloped down busy streets and across piazzas swirling with tourists. He walked on, accidentally coming across places he knew from books. He didn't stop. He was in Florence for a fortnight; he could explore the famous places later. Now it was enough just to be here.

Walking made him hot in the bright Easter sun and when he turned into a small square and saw a gelateria he decided to stop and have an ice cream. The shop had a tiny frontage with two doors; *Bar Vivoli* shone in fluorescent lighting over one and *Gelateria* over the other. Nico wanted authenticity and the people going in and out seemed to be Italian rather than tourists so here was his chance. Silently rehearsing in Italian, *I'd like a large pistachio ice cream please*, he sauntered across the flagstone street and into the ice cream parlour.

Nico was too anxious about his Italian to take in the subdued lighting shining off polished wood and brass fittings. He couldn't get Mr Mowatt's strangled accent out of his head. He pointed at a swirl of pale green in a metal container and said, 'Vorrei un . . .' Before he could finish, the man behind the counter said, 'You want pistachio eh? What size?'

'Um, large. Grande, per favore, signore,' Nico mumbled.

'OK, grande,' the man agreed and grinned.

The ice cream was a lot more *grande* than Nico had bargained for. He decided he didn't care. He paid up, went to a table at the back of the gelateria and sat under a lurid fresco of Florence at sunset. While he ate he looked round at the grey marble walls and waist-high wooden panelling. Mirrors reflected warm golden light from two globes topping a floor lamp writhing from its base like a cast iron plant. Nico liked the Bar Vivoli Gelateria. He liked it a lot. He switched his phone off, took his sketchbook and pencils from a deep pocket inside his coat and began to draw.

Jade and Amber knew exactly where they were going: to the SITA bus station. After they'd collected timetables they left without discussing what they'd done or what it meant. They walked in silence, not going anywhere in particular now they'd started to put their plan into action. They went with the flow of tourists, taking in the warm stone of the tall buildings; the iron lanterns set high up; the green window shutters half open like drowsy eyelids; the shops and churches and statues and houses all blending effortlessly into one. 'It's not like Derby, is it?' Jade said, breaking the silence.

'What?'

'I mean, there's no concrete blocks or burger bars – not that I can see anyway. Everything matches.'

Amber stared around. 'I never noticed till you said.'

They linked arms and wandered on till they reached a huge cast iron and glass market. 'The shopping!' they yelled, then dived into the noisy hall and went from stall to stall buying cheese and meats and bread and fruit and salad.

'It's weird, isn't it? Everybody talking Italian all the time, not just us and Nonno and Mum.' Jade found her eyes mysteriously prickling with tears. She'd thought she was over the hurt; it was a year since Nonno had died.

Amber marched silently out of the market. Jade didn't take it personally. Like Mum, Amber managed pain by ignoring it and refusing to think about it.

It'd be nice to have someone to talk to about how I feel for once, Jade thought and trudged after Amber, her sense of loss weighing like a small stone lodged in her chest.

They wandered down a maze of streets that opened

onto a small square with people sitting on stone benches or standing around talking.

Amber pointed one of her shopping bags at a tiny, glass-fronted ice-cream parlour. 'That looks good,' she said.

'Bar Vivoli Gelateria,' Jade read. 'Let's go in.'

Inside the cool little shop Amber ordered two regular cups of strawberry.

The man behind the counter grinned. 'For such beautiful sisters I give extra for free, no?'

'As long as it's free.'

While Amber paid, Jade looked round. The only available seats were at the far end where she saw Nico drawing intently in a small book. She wasn't sure if he really was concentrating on drawing or just pretending he hadn't seen them.

She went over, 'Can we sit here?'

Nico stood up. 'Of course.'

No one had ever stood for Jade before; she was impressed. Amber came up with the ices and stared in open astonishment as Nico got up for her too.

'How long are you staying in Florence for?' Jade asked.

'Two weeks.'

'Same as us,' Amber said licking her strawberry ice slowly and looking at Nico through her long eyelashes. 'We saw you at the airport. You and your mum were reading. Your dad was organising stuff.' Jade knew Amber was trying to find out what sort of boy Nico was and not being subtle about it.

'James Crozier is not my father. My dad lives in the States with his second wife and my name's Collier.'

'Right.' Amber went on staring.

'James is on a trial holiday with us to see how we get on together. If it works out he wants to move in with us.'

'D'you like him?' Amber asked.

Is she dumb or what? Jade thought. It was obvious Nico couldn't stand James.

Nico shrugged. 'He's better than some of the boyfriends Mum's dragged home. I don't see much of him normally; I'm away at school.'

'Away? Like at boarding school?'

Nico nodded.

'Like Hogwarts?'

Nico sighed. 'No.'

He must've been asked that a million times and was sick of it, Jade thought. 'What about the Goth thing? You can't be a Goth at school,' she said. For a wild moment she had an image of a school full of white-faced, black-uniformed pupils treading silently up and down endless stone staircases.

'No, it's got a strict uniform policy, you can't customise it at all or you get an imposition.'

Imposition? What was that? Like a detention or something, Jade supposed.

'I dress like this because I made a bargain with my parents. Mum was wrecked when my father walked out. I said I was going to leave school and live with her but my father said I had to stay on for my own good. I knew I couldn't win and I agreed not to kick off about going back if I could do what I wanted when I was at home.'

'What's that?' Amber asked.

Nico smiled, a bit maliciously Jade thought. 'Paint and draw all day,' he drawled, 'wear whatever I like.'

'Did it work?' Amber said.

'Absolutely.'

'Your mum didn't mind the Goth thing?'

Nico shrugged. 'What could she do? Dad promised to let me exercise my self-expression. If I make him put up with it when I'm with him, she has to go along with it too.'

Hattie Crozier – Hattie Collier – seemed so uptight she must've freaked out the first time she saw Goth Nico. Jade started to laugh. Amber joined in. Nico cracked a smile, and then laughed out loud.

He's nice when he laughs, Jade thought.

'How about you?' Nico asked. 'Are you here to visit relatives?'

'Not really,' Jade said at exactly the same moment as Amber said, 'No.'

If Nico thought that was odd he must've been too

polite to say so. 'You speak Italian really well, and your mum – I just kind of assumed you had people here.'

'Like we told the Signora, we learned off Nonno, our Italian granddad,' Jade said.

'Was he from Florence?' Nico asked.

'He lived in the countryside just outside the city, till World War II. He was a partigiano – a resistance fighter – for a bit then he was forced to go on the run. He escaped to England right at the end of the war.'

'Impressive.'

'Yes, it was,' Amber said, glaring at Nico as if he were disagreeing with her. 'He was shot in the leg defending an English spy. It left him with a bad limp.'

'Poor guy,' Nico said.

Amber was still glaring. She thrust her right hand out, fingers splayed. 'And the enemy sliced off two of his fingers.' She folded down her index and second fingers.

Trust Amber to go the whole nine yards, Jade thought, though she had to admit, it did have an effect on Nico: he dropped the languid pose, whistled softly and said, 'He must've been treated like a hero when he went back.'

Please shut up! Jade thought. Nico didn't know it but he couldn't have said anything worse.

'He never went back to Italy,' Amber snapped.

'That's tragic – why not?'

22

'Family stuff,' Jade said quickly and turned the questioning in Nico's direction. 'Why are you in Florence?'

Nico's kohl-rimmed eyes glittered. 'Mother and I agreed that James's trial had to be here . . .'

Apparently James hadn't had any say in the arrangement. Jade felt a bit sorry for him.

'. . . because we like art and because we have this thing about a detective series set in Florence.'

'The one your mum was talking about to the Signora?'

'That's right. My mother wants to do a pilgrimage to all the places Alessandro Lupo – that's the detective – goes to in the books.'

'Places in Florence?'

Nico nodded. 'And places roundabout – Lucca, Siena, Torre Del Lago.' His sly smile turned mysterious. 'Me, I want to do something else, something that Mother knows nothing about.'

'What?' Jade and Amber said.

'I'll tell you if you keep it to yourselves because I don't want Mother to know about it.'

'OK,' Amber said immediately.

Jade hesitated. Why would Nico tell two people he'd only just met a secret he needed to keep from his mother?

'OK,' she agreed, partly because she wanted to know the secret and partly because she couldn't think of a reason to refuse.

Nico leaned forward and spoke softly, 'E. J. Holm, who writes the Alessandro Lupo books, is a recluse. All his fans are mad to know more about him. I think he lives near Florence and I'm going to find him.'

'That's the big secret?' Amber said. 'You want to find out where some writer lives?'

'If my mother knew she'd want to do it with me and she'd be so embarrassing I'd want to top myself.'

Jade bit her lip to stop from laughing. It *was* a bit sad being tied to your mum like that though Jade had seen enough of Hattie Collier to know she was a complete control freak, which was hardly Nico's fault. 'Why d'you think this E. J. Holm lives in Florence?'

'Because he writes as if he knows every corner of it. I don't think he could do it that well unless he lives here or . . .' Nico tapped his black fingernails thoughtfully on the table top, '. . . unless he lives nearby. A village called Montebosco appears in all the books and the Signora said it's modelled on Borgo Sant'Angelo. You remember? The village she said had a great restaurant that she's invited us all to?'

Jade nodded.

'I think E. J. Holm might be based in Borgo Sant'Angelo and I'm going to be spending a lot of time there, exploring,' Nico said.

Jade stood up abruptly. 'We need the loo.' She grabbed Amber and they fled to the lavatory, slamming the thick wooden door behind them. There was no chance Nico could hear them in here.

'What are we going to do now?' Amber said. 'If he sees us poking around in Borgo Sant'Angelo he's going to start asking questions.'

'We've just got to tell him.'

'Are you mad or what?'

'We've got no choice! He might tell his mum he's seen us there and she might tell our mum. And if *she* finds out . . .'

'What's to stop him telling his darling mummy anyway?'

'Because if he tells our secret, we tell his.'

'It's hardly the same thing, is it? If *our* mum finds out she'll be devastated, if *his* mum finds out she'll be a bit mad.'

Jade clutched her sister's hands. 'I still think he really, really wants to get away from her and that James,' she wheedled. 'I don't think he's going to risk us telling on him.'

Amber shook her hands free and glared at Jade. 'I suppose – but I'll kill him if he tells.'

'I'll help you.'

Jade hugged her twin, knowing she'd hug back. It always happened after they'd argued; it made them feel one again.

'How much shall we tell him?' Jade asked.

'Only enough to shut him up, not the whole thing about Nonno.'

'Course not! D'you want to tell him?'

'No, you're better at that stuff than me.'

Jade led the way back; there was no point in messing about, she came straight to the point. 'Look, our nonno lived in Borgo Sant'Angelo.'

'Wow!'

Jade waved Nico's excitement away. 'He had some sort of quarrel with his family during the war and that's why he never went back after it ended. He died last year and Mum decided now's a good time to come to Italy to find out a bit about her heritage. 2005 is sixty years since the war ended and Mum doesn't think there's much chance of anyone being left who'd remember Nonno.'

'OK.'

'She wants to visit Borgo Sant'Angelo, to see where Nonno came from, but she doesn't want to talk to any of the relatives because of the quarrel. We want to, though. We're going to try and find his family, to explain his side of things.' Jade's eyes filled with tears. Although she hadn't meant it to happen she decided to make use of it. She let a tear trickle down her cheek. She heard Amber sniff and grope noisily in her bag for a tissue. Jade let another tear fall.

'I'm sorry,' Nico said.

'Mum doesn't know what we're doing. She gets all

upset at the thought of Nonno's Italian family quarrelling with him. We've got to find them without her knowing, or Dad, obviously. And then, if we do find the family, Mum'll never know but we'll have done what we have to, for Nonno.'

Jade glanced at Nico through her tear-damp eyelashes. 'You won't say anything if you see us in Borgo Sant'Angelo, will you?'

'No,' Nico said, 'of course not.'

'How do we know that?' Amber said.

'I just wouldn't. Anyway, you know my secret – I'm not likely to risk giving away yours when you could give away mine, am I?'

Jade smiled, tremulously. It was going exactly as they'd hoped.

CHAPTER III

THE SIGNORA'S DOOR was solid enough to withstand a siege and Nico's firm knock sounded feeble against the thick slab. He heard footsteps approaching from the other side of the door and a loud clicking of deadlocks and rasping of drawing bolts. The door opened a crack and Ornella peered suspiciously out. 'Sì?'

Nico did his best to explain that Mum and James had gone out taking the only key and he needed to borrow a spare. Mr Mowatt's lessons hadn't catered for emergencies like this one and Nico got nowhere. Ornella shut the door firmly in his face.

Now what was he supposed to do? He could only see two choices: sit outside the apartment until Mum and James came back or ask the Thompsons for help. He opted for the Thompsons.

Mrs Thompson was very sympathetic and made him a cup of tea and a sandwich. Nico was surprised he had room for it after the giant pistachio ice cream. While he munched away and chatted to Mrs Thompson Amber went downstairs to ask about the pass key.

'Have you phoned your mum?' Mrs Thompson asked.

'Yes. She said she went to look for me because I was late back and my phone was turned off. She's right on the other side of the river – it'll take her a bit to get back.'

'You can stay till then if you like,' Mrs Thompson said.

Nico shook his head. 'Thanks, but I'd better be there when she gets back. She gets a bit anxious about me.' That was the understatement of the year, Nico thought. 'If I could have a couple of tea bags I can make her a cup of tea to . . .' Nico stopped; he'd been going to say, to calm her down.

'I can do better than that.' Mrs Thompson piled a tray with food. 'The girls bought far too much this morning. Take this so it doesn't go to waste. You can make your mum and James afternoon tea.'

Nico noticed that Mrs Thompson didn't say 'your mum and dad'; the twins must've told her about the relationship with James.

Since Nico's hands were full with the tray, Jade came down to the apartment with him to open the door. 'Come and inspect the flat,' Nico said.

'It's exactly like ours,' Jade said, 'except you've got the garden.'

'Sorry about that.'

Jade laughed. 'It doesn't matter – Mum doesn't like ground floors. They're too noisy. Just wait till James hears Amber stomping around upstairs like an elephant.'

29

Nico's phone rang with the dirge he'd set for Mum's texts. 'My mother's having hysterics.'

'Why?'

'She gets worried.' He texted back while Jade poked about in the cupboards. She took out a tablecloth and some dishes. 'Let's give your mum something better to think about.' They soon had the table set and food laid out. Nico even found a silver candlestick and a white candle to finish the setting off.

'You need flowers,' Jade said.

They picked sprays from a creeper and wound them around the candlestick in a cascade of green leaves and pale violet flowers. 'I wonder what they are?' Jade said.

'Wisteria, there's a lot of it in Italy.'

Mum's tune weebled from Nico's mobile again. 'She's going to be about half an hour.'

He texted back, yet again, then stuffed his mobile deep into a pocket. 'Honestly, Jade, my mother's going to drive me to murder one of these days.'

Jade looked at Nico with a strange expression.

'I didn't mean literally,' he said.

Jade laughed. 'I know you didn't, it's just . . .'

'What?'

'I was thinking, it's nice you always know for sure I'm me and not Amber. I mean, you know I'm me now – obviously – but you didn't get me and Amber mixed up

30

when we were in town. People do, even when we make ourselves different.'

'You're not completely identical.'

'Oh?'

Nico switched on his artist's eye and scanned Jade's face in a dispassionate way. 'Your eyes are a bit almond shaped – Amber's are more round.'

'And?'

'Your face shapes are different – you've got a classic oval, Amber's got a slightly more pointed chin.'

'Anything else?'

What more did Jade want? And why was it important to her? Nico spoke carefully, weighing his words, 'Your voices aren't the same, yours is a bit deeper.'

Jade frowned a little and Nico went on hastily, 'Your styles are different – Amber's kind of . . . pink.'

A brief grin flashed over Jade's face. Encouraged, Nico went on, 'And you're more individual, more funky.'

Jade's grin was open now. Nico had obviously said the right thing. He was glad. He liked Jade.

'I'd better get back,' she said. She picked up the tray and Nico showed her out which she seemed to find very funny for some reason. 'Hope you don't get too much grief,' she said before she ran up the stairs. *So do I*, Nico thought as he went back inside imagining Mum storming in saying that he'd caused her unimaginable torments of worry and how could he do this to her?

Nico picked up his book and flopped into a chair by the open doors to the garden. He turned to the chapter where the detective, Commissario Alessandro Lupo, was at a wedding in Montebosco when he was called back to Florence to investigate a particularly brutal murder.

As Nico read the familiar words he found himself wondering if Borgo Sant'Angelo really was 'Montebosco'; the Signora had seemed very sure of it. The minute she'd told them of the connection Nico had realised two things: firstly, that the Signora wanted them all to go there for some reason and secondly that Borgo Sant'Angelo had some major significance for the Thompsons. He'd been proved right about that when the twins told him about their grandfather. It had been risky letting Jade and Amber know he planned to visit Borgo Sant'Angelo but he'd wanted to make sure that if they saw him there they wouldn't let it get back to Mum. He was determined to start shaking himself free of his mother while he was in Florence. He didn't need to feel guilty about it; she'd got James to look after her now.

Nico read on. The sounds of the city – bells, voices, traffic – muffled by high walls surrounding the garden, were background music to the dark story of Semiramide and her death among the glittering mirrors of the shop in the Road of the Silver Unicorn. She was Alessandro's lover and the call he'd received at the wedding in Montebosco was to tell him she'd been murdered. *The Shattered Mirror* was Nico's – and Mum's – favourite Alessandro novel. James didn't understand their obsession with E. J. Holm's books and Nico was glad. He didn't know what the books represented to Mum but, for him, Alessandro filled the absent space Dad left behind when he walked out. In his imagination Nico had followed the detective as he trod through Florence and stopped with him at every landmark along the way till he felt he could walk the routes in reality – sometimes he dreamed he did. He began to leaf slowly through the book, savouring its familiar words. He had to be sure of every detail, every clue if he was going to find the books' elusive author. The mild air billowed the lace curtains like the draperies of goddesses in Nico's favourite painting. I wonder what the Italian for French windows is? he thought before he lost himself totally in the book.

Jade rolled over on to her back. 'I can't believe we're really going to start looking for Nonno's people,' she said.

Amber was sitting on the other bed painting her toenails sugar pink. 'Me neither. It's so cool.' Amber was always confident. That was another thing about them that was different: she never saw the problems that came at Jade from every corner.

'Amb, are you sure this is going to work?'

33

'Course it is.' Amber squinted at her nails. 'We've already started – we've got the bus timetables to Borgo Sant'Angelo – we can go anytime we want.'

It was true. 'I hope Nico can get away as well.'

'He can't come with us!'

'I know that, obviously. I meant, it's sad he can't get away and do stuff by himself, away from his mum and James.'

Amber stopped painting her toenails. 'You don't *like* him, do you?'

'He's all right. He's funny and he's polite which makes a change from most boys. He even escorted me to the door like a butler when I took the tray down! And I really like the Goth thing.'

Amber snorted. 'You would.'

Jade had gone out with a Goth boy a couple of times and Amber never got tired of taunting her about it. 'Nico's not a real Goth – he's a Baby Bat.'

'True – he probably doesn't know any actual Goths. He's only doing it to annoy his mum remember, he doesn't have to get it right.'

'I suppose.' Amber swung off the bed and padded over the cool stone floor to the balcony to wriggle her wet pink toenails in the late afternoon sunshine.

Jade closed her eyes and daydreamed of drifting away over the red-tiled city and out to hazy green hills beyond. She imagined drawing closer to them, walking in them, finding the places she'd envisaged for so long – the woods, the pool, the stony track, the house among the chestnut trees.

'Nico!' Mum flung her arms round him, then grabbed him and held him at arm's length. 'Where've you been?'

'Walking, looking, thinking.'

'All this time?' James said. He dropped into a chair and disappeared behind his copy of *Intensive Italian for Discerning Travellers*.

Nico shrugged off Mum's iron grip. 'I stopped for an ice cream with Jade and Amber. We were perfectly all right. Luisa didn't mind how long they were out – and they're girls.'

'They're not my responsibility and anyway they're more . . .'

'More what?'

'Streetwise.'

Nico knew Mum had been going to say something much more uncomplimentary than that and it annoyed him. He liked Jade and Amber, and their parents. 'Streetwise? I'd be streetwise if you'd let me out *onto* the streets occasionally.'

'How did you get in?' James asked from behind the guidebook.

'With a pass key.'

'Good thinking,' James said.

'It was better than sitting on the steps waiting for the search party to come back.'

'Nico! I was frantic!' Mum wasn't going to back down.

'At least he had the sense to get food on the table,' James said.

Mum blinked like an owl dazzled by sudden daylight. She stared at the table covered with bowls and dishes overflowing with green salad, olives and tomatoes, cheeses, meats, butter and bread and glasses of ruby wine.

'Nico, this is a real treat!'

'I thought I'd make good use of my time.' It was nice to be appreciated, Nico thought, but why did it have to be James who'd noticed first, not Mum?

CHAPTER IV

NICO PRESSED THE button on the automatic blinds and they folded upwards, slam, slam, slam, like a series of steel doors closing one after the other. He opened the French windows and stepped into the pale morning sun. Luisa Thompson was pegging washing on a rope contraption slung between the flats. She caught sight of him. 'Ciao, Nico.'

He waved. 'Ciao, Signora Thompson.'

Luisa added a pair of lacy knickers to the line. 'They should be nice and dry by the time we get back from exploring Florence. What are you doing today?'

'We're going sightseeing as well.'

'Might bump into you later then. Ci vediamo.' She waved cheerfully and went back inside.

Florence – Firenze! The very name sent a bolt of excitement through Nico. Then James's face swam into his mind's eye and he scowled. James was an embarrassment, waving his guidebook around and lecturing at the top of his voice. *Today*, Nico vowed, *is going to be different.*

He started by taking fresh coffee to Mum and James, made exactly the way James liked it. James, in a short robe and towelling slippers, was wincing at the bedroom blinds crashing and pleating their way upwards. Nico prodded his mother's shoulder. She stayed obstinately under the covers. James took his coffee without a thank you, opened the French windows and strutted outside.

Nico heard, 'Ciao, Signor Crozier,' chiming from above James's head. He smirked as James stumbled back inside as fast as his dignity and his slippers allowed.

'It's like a squat out there,' he snarled.

'What?' Mum's tousled head lifted from the pillow.

'Out in our garden – those Thompson girls are spying on us and there're panties flapping on a washing line.'

'Where else would they put wet knickers?' Mum yawned. 'Stop stressing.'

'Yes, James, stop stressing,' Nico said. He felt Mum's foot jab at him warningly.

'I'll go and get ready,' James said.

'We want to go to the tourist office,' Jade said. 'It's in Via Cavour.'

'Is it?' Dad opened his guidebook and looked at the street map.

Amber waved down a narrow lane, packed with stalls selling tourist things. 'We go down that way, turn left and left again and we're there.'

'You might get lost,' Dad said.

He's turning into Nico's mum, Jade thought. 'No we won't,' she said, 'you can't get lost in Florence, it's too small.'

'We'll still stick together,' Dad insisted, 'just till we get our bearings.'

'Let's do the markets before they get too crowded,' Mum suggested.

'I could do with a new footie shirt.'

'Dad!' Jade and Amber groaned.

'You've got enough already,' Jade said. 'You've got . . .'

'. . . wardrobes full of Rams' strips,' Amber finished.

'I haven't got any Juventus ones though,' Dad said.

'Come on.' Mum the peacemaker led them down the crowded street looking at stuff they'd seen before and stuff they hadn't: T-shirts with bits of famous paintings printed on them; umbrellas made to look like the cathedral dome; calendars for the still far away next year; plaster statues of David; tiny models of Vespas and bigger ones of Lancias; leather handbags and belts and shoes.

Abruptly the street opened onto a huge square. Jade and her family stopped and let the crowds flow round them as they gazed at the soaring white and green and pink marble buildings. 'It's a bit different from Derby,' Jade said, taking in the cathedral, the slender bell tower and the baptistery with its shining golden doors.

'Suits me, Derby,' Mum said. She turned her face

and marched away just as the sun moved to light up the marble and polish the golden doors. By the time Jade and Amber and Dad caught up with Mum they'd left the marvellous buildings behind and were in a broad road lined with shops.

'Why don't you two find that tourist office,' Dad said. 'Me and your Mum'll get back to the markets. Keep in touch and we'll meet up later.'

Jade felt Amber's arm slip into hers. 'She was sad,' Amber said.

'I know.'

'I didn't know what to say.'

What could anyone say to console their mother? Nonno was dead and visiting his long-lost homeland was Mum's pilgrimage; a way of honouring his memory and finding out about the country he had come from. Despite that, she had to live with the knowledge that his family had threatened to kill him if he ever returned. Jade pulled her sister close, though which of them it was meant to comfort she wasn't sure. 'We've really, really got to make sure Mum doesn't find out what we're doing.'

Not far now, not far now, Nico silently chanted as he followed Mum and James through the packed streets. *Not far now, not . . .*

Why was James stopping to stare in a shop? Nico caught up. It was a music shop, *Dischi Norberti*, with a window display of James's favourite old bands. He'd gone on about them till Nico knew their names by heart even though he hadn't wanted to: East of Eden, Black Widow, Atomic Rooster, Van Der Graaf Generator, Xtreme Measures . . . and more – lots more. Nico groaned. If they went inside it'd be hours before they got out again. He stared pointedly at Mum who didn't look too happy either.

'James!' Mum said. 'Our tickets are for ten o'clock – if we don't get to the Uffizi by then they won't let us in – you know they're really strict about timing.'

James didn't budge. 'In a minute.' His eyes roved greedily over the display.

Nico felt as though he were going to explode with fury. He was in Florence, which had more art treasures than any other single city in the entire world, and James wanted to stop and drool over tragic old heavy metal music. 'Mum!' he ground out.

Mum took a firm line with James. 'Come on!' She grabbed him by the arm and pushed him up the road.

'Not far now. Not far now,' Nico grimly intoned, not caring about the startled tourists who took one look at his set white face and hurriedly backed away. The road ended. The Duomo rose before Nico in all its shining beauty. Even James looked dazzled and stayed silent.

Jade wrapped her arms round her knees and felt the sun gently warm her skin as she sat on the stone steps of the loggia running down one side of the Piazza. The square was already full of day-trippers admiring the sculptures and the fountain, taking photographs of the palazzo and the horse-drawn carriages. She and Amber were out of the tourists' way and only a stone lion looked down on them as they pored over the information from the tourist office.

'It's all here!' Jade said. 'The names Nonno told us about – the Rondine river, the Piazza della Fontana . . .' The names brought back memories in a rush – Nonno's beloved voice telling them stories of his orphaned childhood in the little town where he grew up – Mum giving way, as she always did, letting Nonno tell them 'just one more story' before bedtime.

'Now we've sorted out the buses we can go when we like,' Amber said.

'I'm worried about getting Mum and Dad to leave us alone for long enough.'

'We're alone now.'

'Only till lunchtime. We can't do everything we want in half days – look how Dad wanted us to stay together today. And we'll have to go out with them sometimes or they'll get suspicious if we keep disappearing for no reason.' Why didn't that cross their minds at home when they made their plans? It was so obvious now they were here.

'Think of something we can do in Florence they

42

don't want to do but they don't mind us doing,' Amber said, as if Jade hadn't been worrying away at that ever since the weakness of their plan had dawned on her.

'It'll have to be educational,' Jade said.

'OK – what?'

Jade had no idea.

A shadow fell over her. 'Hi.'

Jade squinted up, shading her eyes. 'Hi, Nico, what're you doing here?'

'We've got tickets for the Uffizi gallery, just down this arcade.' Nico waved down the length of the loggia.

'You're going to an art gallery?' The horrified scorn in Amber's voice made it sound like Nico was going to an abattoir to watch the mass slaughter of baby animals. Jade kicked her surreptitiously, warning her to shut up; she'd had an idea that would solve all their problems and she didn't want Amber sabotaging it.

'I remember – you told us yesterday you like art,' she said to Nico. 'So do I – can we come with you, to see the pictures?'

'Not without tickets, unless you don't mind queuing. See that line there? Stretching all the way down to the river and back? That's the queue for the Uffizi.'

'No chance!' Amber said.

'Nico!' Jade saw Hattie waving from the other end of the loggia.

43

'Sorry,' Nico said, 'I can't wait. Mum's on edge – James doesn't want to go to the gallery.'

'Why don't they split up then?' Amber said. Jade kicked her again.

'Can you get me some books and cards and stuff?' she asked Nico. 'Then at least I can read up.'

'Yes, of course.'

Jade gave Nico a bunch of Euro notes. 'It's for a project. We need loads.'

Nico tucked the money into a wallet he fished from another pocket in his long black coat. 'What are you interested in most?'

Across the square the gigantic statue of David looked at Jade. It was one of the few pieces of art she recognised. She even knew who the sculptor was. He was famous. 'Michelangelo,' she said.

'OK. You might want to try the Accademia gallery for information as well, and the Casa Buonarotti.'

'We'll do that.'

'Nico!' Hattie's voice rang down the loggia again.

'I'd better go. See you later and give you the cards?'

'Sure. But – don't tell anyone what you're doing for us will you?' Jade said.

'Why not?'

'Tell you after.'

'Nico!' Hattie's voice was shrill.

'See you.' Nico tramped away.

'What was that all about? You're not interested in art,' Amber said.

'Yes I am. We're going to explore Florence discovering stuff about Michelangelo. It's for coursework.'

'We're not doing him in Art.'

'We are now.'

'We're not and even if we were I'm not working on holiday. Why should I?'

'To keep Mum and Dad happy like we were talking about, right? Nico can get evidence to convince them we've been to galleries and palaces and museums but really we'll be going to the Villa dei Fiori. Simple.'

'OK,' Amber said slowly. 'What if Nico doesn't want to do it?'

Jade stretched, raising her arms as if she were reaching greedily for more sun. 'I think he will – he's nice.'

Amber rolled her eyes at Jade. 'If you say so.'

'I do.' Jade lowered her arms and leaned them on her knees. 'Anyway, don't forget, he wants us to keep his secret.'

Amber understood that. She smiled wickedly and nodded. Jade hoped for Nico's sake that he kept his part of the bargain. Amber hated people who broke their promises.

CHAPTER V

NICO SCUFFED SULLENLY along a brown corridor in the Uffizi, staring through the wide windows at the river Arno curdling its brown way along the far bank. Behind him, Mum muttered into her mobile at the muppet James who'd decided to go back to *Dischi Norberti*. Far away, nestling among trees on top of a hill basking in the sunshine, was the little black and white church of San Miniato. It was so ridiculously magical that Nico instantly felt lighter, as though he'd leaped out of his boots and gone barefoot.

Mum squeaked into the mobile, 'If that's what you want, James, that's fine.'

Nico ground his teeth. If Mum didn't let go of James, Nico might just have to kill them both to get a bit of peace and quiet. He was nearly at the room; the one he ached to see and he didn't want the experience spoiled. Mum put the mobile away. 'We're meeting James for lunch,' she said.

'OK.'

'I'd still have liked him to share this experience with us,' Hattie said.

'You can't force people to like what they don't.'

'I suppose not. James is lovely but I didn't realise he doesn't like art at all. He never said.'

Nico knew it wouldn't do any good to remind her that the main purpose of this trip was to find out what the three of them had in common and what they hadn't and whether they could cope with the differences. 'Have you got the book?' he asked.

'Of course.' It was in her bag, all marked up with comments from the Reading Group.

Amber opened her sparkly new notebook and balanced it on her knees. 'Where did he say those other Michelangelo places were?'

'Casa Buonarotti and the Accademia,' Jade said.

Amber's pink pen scribbled busily. 'I don't know how you remember all that stuff.'

'It's a gift,' Jade said. *And another difference between us.* She watched the crowds while Amber wrote. The piazza was more packed than ever. How many people flowed through it in a day, a month, a year? Did they feel as amazed as she did by what they saw? What was it about this city that made her ache with a strange kind of longing?

Amber finished writing. 'That's a start. One – project:

the life and work of Michelangelo. Two – places to visit'. She chewed the end of her pen. 'D'you really think Nico's going to back us up?'

'Probably. Like I said, he's nice and anyway, he'll enjoy the research.' In her mind's eye she saw Nico's kohl-rimmed eyes glowing as he talked about art. She nudged her sister. 'Get writing again – I've had another idea.'

'What?'

Jade told her.

As Nico and his mother arrived at Room 14, a group of Japanese tourists filed out of one door and a group of Americans out of the other. Amazingly, Nico and Mum had the picture to themselves. Nico gazed at the painted figures in their enchanted woodland glade while Mum softly read out the passage from *The Shattered Mirror* that they both knew almost by heart: 'Commissario Alessandro Lupo knew as much about Botticelli's *Primavera* as anyone and more than most. He knew that the picture is painted in tempera on board; that it is over three metres long and two metres high; that it depicts – from right to left – Zephyr in pursuit of the nymph Chloris, Flora the goddess of spring, Venus the goddess of love, the three graces and Mercury the messenger of the gods, all set in a grove containing over 500 species of plants. He also knew that it was connected in some way with the deaths of at least five people and was probably going to be responsible for more to come.'

'It's incredible, Mum,' Nico said as his mother closed the book. He'd dreaded being somehow disappointed in the picture when he saw it in real life but he wasn't: the faces were beautiful, the figures elegant as they danced among flowers that bloomed in eternal spring and never died.

'I can't see it,' Mum said. 'I can't see why Alessandro thought it was so marvellous. It's all wrong.'

'Wrong?'

'Venus's eyes are on different levels, and the nymphs' shoulders are too sloping – the anatomy's not right. And look at Mercury's flying boots – they've only got one wing between them and there should be four.'

'Is there anything you *do* like?' Nico asked bitterly.

Mum pointed to the cupid above Venus's head, blindfolded and aiming a burning arrow at the three Graces. 'That cherub's so hefty it's a miracle Botticelli got it airborne, but I like it.'

'Why?'

'It reminds me of you as a baby.'

Behind Nico a passing tourist sniggered.

Amber stopped at a shop. Jade recognised the light in her eyes. 'We're not going in there!'

'Why not? It's a free country.'

49

Because we're not billionaires, Jade thought. Even though Granny Grace's trust fund had brought Mum sudden unexpected wealth after Nonno's death, Jade worried that the legacy had gone to Amber's head. Her allowance would be all used up if she insisted on shopping in places like this. Jade stared in horror at the simple black façade of the shop and its window display of a single shoe all spot-lit and sleek. 'It's too . . . exclusive.'

'You're just scared.'

Too right she was scared. 'Can't I just take your photo by the window?' Jade lifted her camera hopefully.

'You're so sad sometimes,' Amber said and marched confidently through the sleek black door as though she shopped at Armani every day.

Mum went on rubbishing the *Primavera*.

'There's hardly room for those dragons on Mercury's wand; they're clinging on by their claws.'

'It's not a wand, it's a caduceus,' Nico said, 'and they're snakes not dragons.'

'They look like dragons.'

'It's symbolic, Mother – that's how they painted them in those days.'

Mum lost interest in the *Primavera*. 'I want to go and see the Michelangelo paintings.'

Though Nico wanted to keep looking at Botticelli's

masterpiece and he wasn't that keen on Michelangelo's paintings, he had promised the twins he'd get some information for them and Mum's suggestion gave him an idea. 'I'm going to the gallery shop,' he said. 'See you later.'

Mum looked taken aback at being left by herself. Nico didn't care; it was her own fault for dissing the *Primavera*.

'Look at that!' Amber clutched at Jade's arm and pointed down the pedestrianised street.

Not another shop, Jade thought. She liked shopping but not this much.

'It's Segways – they're hiring out Segways! I've always wanted a go on one.'

A young man was guarding six of the grey vehicles parked at the side of the road. Next to him, a woman was trying to persuade a pair of elderly tourists wearing inappropriate shorts to book a trip.

'Florence SEGWAY excursions,' Jade read from a sign. 'It's €80 for a three-hour tour. Too much and too long.'

'Let's go and ask if we can just have a quick go.'

The twins grinned at each other and walked towards the man, chatting as they went about how nice it would be to go on a tour if only the Segways were safe.

'D'you think they're hard to ride?' Amber said.

The man turned and flashed a smile. 'It's very easy.' He motioned for Amber to step onto the Segway and showed

51

her how to grip the handles. 'You lean forward to make it go, and back to make it reverse or stop.'

'Is it safe?' Jade asked.

'Oh yes,' the man said. 'You come and try it too.'

Jade tentatively stepped up. 'Won't it fall over? It's only got two wheels.' She hoped she wasn't overdoing the stupidity.

'No. Always it stay under you. It is very stable, very easy to ride.'

Jade jiggled a bit, as if to test it. The man watched her intently. Amber jiggled in unison and the man practically went cross-eyed trying to watch them both. *It's going well*, Jade thought happily. Amber should be ready to pounce at any moment.

'What's it like when it's going?' Amber asked, wide-eyed.

'I show you.' The man turned a yellow key in the ignition and the Segway whirred softly.

The woman talking to the tourists looked up. 'Hey, Daniele, what are you doing?' she called in Italian.

'It's OK, Mamma,' he called back, also in Italian. 'I'll convince them to take a tour, don't worry.'

Jade looked up at Daniele. 'Italian sounds so lovely,' she cooed. 'I wish I could speak it.'

Nico bought a selection of material on Michelangelo for Jade and Amber and some books for himself. Then he wandered through the shop, riffling idly through trays of postcards. He came across a portrait of a dark, dour-faced man who looked as if he was hiding a tragic secret. He was exactly like E. J. Holm's descriptions of Alessandro Lupo. Nico bought the card and went back to the gallery door ready to re-visit the *Primavera* without having to listen to Mum's stupid comments. The guard wouldn't let him back in. Nico showed his ticket. It didn't make any difference. The guard insisted that Nico had left the gallery and now he was out, that was it. Nico glowered at the guard and gave up arguing. He texted Mum to say he was going to explore and would see her later at the cafe where they were meeting James for lunch.

Outside he climbed over a group of German students cluttering up the loggia steps and plunged into the slew of tourists. They swept him along like a piece of flotsam until he found himself in a street near the cathedral.

Jade really enjoyed the Segway; it was a breeze to ride, like gliding around on a small stage with a scooter handle at the front. It was as quiet as a wrinkly's electric buggy though not as dangerous because it was easy to swoop round pedestrians. Jade swept between two tourists and back again in a figure of eight. She came face to face with Nico. She ran over his foot.

'Oh my God! I'm sorry, Nico!' She leaped off the Segway. 'You surprised me!'

Nico hopped around clutching his foot. 'Not as much as you surprised me.'

Amber zoomed up. 'You all right?'

'I ran over his foot,' Jade snapped. 'It's probably broken!'

'No it's not,' Nico said. 'Honestly.'

'It doesn't hurt because the wheels are so wide,' Amber said. 'It distributes the weight evenly.'

'I didn't say it didn't hurt, I said it isn't broken.' Nico limped a few steps.

Daniele ran up and glowered at Nico as if the accident was his fault. 'There is a problem?'

'No, it's OK,' Jade said quickly.

'We need to make the list of the customers,' Daniele said. 'You will pay for the tour now.'

'No thanks, we've decided against it.' Amber hopped off the Segway.

'I say, you pay for the lesson,' Daniele insisted.

'I don't think so,' Jade said in Italian. 'It doesn't say we have to on your poster.'

Daniele took a step towards her. Nico squeezed between her and Amber and stared right in Daniele's eyes. 'We're going now,' he said.

Daniele backed off and Jade, Amber and Nico walked off down the road leaving Daniele to explain to his mother why the girls hadn't booked a trip after all.

'How's your foot?' Jade asked Nico.

'Killing me if you really want to know.' Nico sat on the step of a nearby church and nursed his foot.

'I'm really sorry,' Jade said. 'It was seeing you suddenly like that – it made me forget to stop.'

'If I promise not to do it again will you promise not to run over me?'

Jade laughed. 'Want to come for a Coke and a slice of pizza? You can sit and rest your foot.'

'No thanks, I've got to meet my mother and James for lunch.' He stopped massaging his foot and stood up. 'It's not too bad now.' He took a few experimental steps.

'We've got a plan,' Jade blurted out.

'And we want to talk to you about it,' Amber said.

'Oh?'

'It'd help you too,' Jade said.

'OK. Why don't you get your mum and dad to come to the restaurant we're going to? That'll give us a chance talk about it.' Nico told them where the restaurant was and then walked haltingly away.

'He's not limping much now,' Amber said. 'I bet it's not that bad.'

'You haven't got a heart, you've got a swinging brick.'

It was true; Amber was tougher than her – that was yet another difference between them, Jade thought. Strength had its uses but sometimes a softer approach worked better. That was why she was phoning Mum and Dad now and not Amber – she'd have no problem getting her parents to do what she wanted.

The restaurant tables spread out over the edge of a small piazza tucked away behind the Mercato Nuovo. They were covered by a green awning supported on tall straight poles, spreading above the diners like a canopy of leaves. It reminded Nico of the glade in Botticelli's picture.

James seized the menu card as soon as they sat down. He pointed. 'I'll have that,' he said and passed the card to Mum. 'I'm off to the lavatory. Order for me if the waiter manages to get to you before I'm back.'

The waiter heard. He glared and moved towards a couple who'd just sat down. *It's going to take forever to get served now*, Nico thought, *and I'm starving*. He picked up a grissino and broke it in half. A sparrow flew under the awning and landed on the edge of the table. It stood poised on its matchstick legs, its calculating black eyes fixed on Nico and his breadstick. Nico pushed some crumbs towards it. It hopped warily forward and pecked at the food. Nico got out his book and pencil and began to draw.

'Vermin!' A waiter swiped a napkin at the sparrows and they darted away. 'You do not encourage them,' the waiter said. He flicked the breadcrumbs from the table and stalked off. Nico knew the wait for lunch was going to be very, very long. 'Sorry,' he mumbled to Mum.

'Don't apologise, Nico, they're adorable. And you're not the only one who likes sparrows, look.'

Mum was right. The waiter was busy cracking his napkin and telling off another group of diners. The sparrows were ahead of the game, appearing on tables like magic. 'I wonder if sparrows can give you bird flu?' Mum said. Nico ignored her and carried on drawing.

'There's Nico,' Jade said and steered Mum and Dad to where Nico was sitting with Hattie.

'Hello, Mrs Collier,' Jade said politely, trying to make sure she got into Hattie's good books. 'Have you had a nice day?'

'Yes, thank you, Amber.'

'I'm Jade.' She hoped Amber wasn't going to get in a strop about the mixed-up names or she might start cheeking Hattie in the broadest Derby dialect she could manage, which was pretty broad, and she'd start muddling up her grammar on purpose. She always did that when she thought posh people were being patronising.

'I'm sorry, Jade, please excuse me,' Hattie Collier said. She sounded sincere.

'It doesn't matter.'

'That's very gracious of you. I think it would annoy me!'

Nico stood up and drew out his chair for Luisa. 'Would you like my seat, Mrs Thompson? I can sit with

Jade and Amber and you and Mr Thompson can sit with Mum and James.'

It was like a politeness competition, Jade thought, except that it came naturally to Nico, he'd been trained.

'Sweet,' Jade said as they found another table, 'we can talk here without them hearing.'

'And it means I don't have to sit with the muppet James,' Nico said.

'Is he that bad?' Amber asked.

'Yes . . . no . . . sometimes. It's complicated.' He piled cards and booklets onto the table. 'I hope these are what you wanted.'

Jade glimpsed white marble limbs and a bright saffron cloak as she gathered up the material and pushed it into her bag. 'They're great. Now, about this plan.'

'Yes?'

'You know we want to find Nonno's long-lost family in Borgo Sant'Angelo?'

Nico nodded.

'Well, we hadn't sorted how to get off on our own for long enough to do it. Mum and Dad are only OK about a few hours and we need to be sure of having all the time we want, when we want it.'

'I get that, but how does it affect me?' Nico asked.

'We want you to take us round all the Michelangelo things in Florence and show us his art and where he lived and worked and that.'

'For an imaginary art project,' Amber added.

Nico's black eyebrows pleated in a puzzled frown. 'How's me giving you a guided tour going to help?'

'We won't really be going round Florence,' Jade said. 'We'll start off together then split up and do what we want on our own.'

'Why would your parents let you go off with me?'

'Because you're posh and clever,' Amber said.

Jade glared at her sister. 'She means you're polite and well-educated. Mum and Dad respect that.'

Nico didn't seem to mind. He laughed. 'It might just work. You're fluent in Italian so there wouldn't be a communication problem if we got into trouble.'

'Why would we get into trouble?' Jade said.

'We won't – it's just that my mother sees disaster lurking round every corner but if she's convinced we'll stay together she might go with it. I could give her an itinerary and keep in touch by mobile. We can let them see us together in Florence then split up and report back together when we've finished. How about that?'

Jade couldn't see any flaws in the plan. She nodded towards the adults' table. 'I bet they'll be all right with it.'

James and Dad were deep in conversation over the CDs from Dischi Norberti.

'Does your father like heavy metal?' Nico asked.

Jade and Amber groaned. 'He used to be a roadie with Xtreme Measures,' Jade said.

'They're James's favourite band!'

That explained the sudden, unlikely friendship. *But what about our mums?* Jade thought. The two women were leaning over *The Shattered Mirror*, Hattie waving her arms about and being animated and sparkly. Amazingly, Mum looked fascinated.

'They're all friendly,' Jade said, 'It'll make it a lot easier . . .'

'. . . to convince them to leave us alone,' Amber finished.

Nico smiled the small, sly smile Jade was getting used to. She could tell that he couldn't believe their luck either.

Nico and the twins lounged on the steps of San Miniato al Monte. After the meal James and Kevin had decided it would be a good idea to walk to the little church. James's guidebook had described the picturesque views from this side of the hill but forgotten to mention the gradient. Even Nico was so tired he'd opted to sit on the steps and draw rather than walk around exploring the building. He could do that later – if the plan worked. For now he was content to draw Florence as it lay in the valley below him, sleeping like a golden cat curled in the hollow of the hills.

'It's very peaceful here,' Amber said.

'Not many tourists,' added Jade.

'They can't be fussed with the slog up the hill,' Amber said.

Nico laughed. 'They could take the bus, or ride a Segway.'

'How's your foot?' Jade asked.

'Fine, just a bit bruised.'

'They were good, the Segways, but too expensive,' Amber said. 'And you can't use them on the roads like a scooter. We were going to hire scooters to get to Borgo Sant'Angelo till we found out you've got to get a special licence.'

'You can ride scooters?'

'Dad's got trail bikes and we've been riding those since we were little.'

Nico couldn't imagine Mum letting him ride trail bikes; she'd see too much potential for a broken neck.

'Kids!' James called from above them. The adults had come out of the shadowy cool of San Miniato and were walking down the steps.

'We're going for ice creams,' Kevin said and led the way along the curving road to the Piazzale Michelangelo dotted with stalls and kiosks. Another statue of David was dominating the square, this one gazing down on the city.

'D'you think this is a good time to tell them about the project?' Nico asked the girls.

'Yep,' they agreed.

Nico caught up with Hattie, and saw Jade and Amber do the same to Luisa, walking one on either side of her like friendly police officers.

'Mum,' Nico said, 'we've been talking and we've had this idea.'

In order to understand what happened that day at the farmhouse I must look further back, to the lives of four young friends, Gaetano, Elena, Roberto and Ilaria. The story, as told to me, really began in 1933 with an encounter between two boys . . .

Gaetano was on his way back from the well, his bucket of water slopping as he hurried to the farmhouse, when a movement by the stable door caught his eye. He left the water and went into the stable. At this time of day it should be empty. What was making the noise coming from the far stall? He went to look. A bare foot protruded from a heap of straw in one corner. Gaetano wasn't afraid; the foot was even smaller than his and, besides, he was tough.

'Come out!' he demanded.

For a moment nothing happened and Gaetano thought maybe he should prod the straw with a pitchfork, then the heap heaved and a boy emerged.

'Roberto?' Gaetano looked at his friend in surprise. 'What are you doing?'

'Hiding.'

'Why?'

'I don't want to go to the orphanage.'

Gaetano understood that; orphanages had a fearsome reputation, though he didn't understand why Roberto would be sent away when he had a home of his own. 'Your nonna's going to send you to the orphanage?'

Roberto nodded, his eyes wide. 'She's ill and her family will take her in but not me.'

Gaetano wasn't surprised. No one wanted a bastard in the family. Roberto's mother had run away leaving her baby son with his widowed grandmother. The woman had raised him harshly, bemoaning the fate that had willed this unwanted child on her. Gaetano had often heard her complaining in the streets of the small town where they lived and seen her beat him when he annoyed her. Now he had no one, not even her.

'Are you hungry?'

Roberto nodded.

Gaetano jerked his head towards the farmhouse. 'Come on then, Mamma will feed you.'

Gaetano's mother plied the small boy with food and then sent him off to help Gaetano with tasks around the farm while she talked to her husband. After the evening meal Gaetano's father called both boys to him. He put a hand on Roberto's head and said, 'You can stay here for tonight and in the morning I'll go into town and make arrangements for you to stay permanently.'

64

Gaetano grinned at his friend. 'Now I'll have a brother to help me when Tecla bosses me around!'

'No,' his big sister said as she dumped bedding into Gaetano's arms, 'it means I will have two little brothers who have to obey my every word. In the meantime, go and make up a place for him in your bedroom.'

As the boys assembled a makeshift bed in the corner of the room, Gaetano realised that Roberto hadn't spoken since he'd been discovered in the stable, not even to say thank you to Babbo or Mamma. He'd simply looked with round eyes at whoever was speaking to him and nodded. Gaetano thought that Roberto's eyes were strange, like an old man's looking out from his thin child's face. He shivered.

'Let's get ready – I'll show you where the privy is.'

Still Roberto didn't speak, only nodded and stared. It went on that way until Mamma had said goodnight and the boys drifted off to sleep. In the night Gaetano was woken by the sound of muffled crying. He listened for a while, unsure of whether to offer comfort to his friend. He fell asleep again before he had decided. In all the years that followed, he never heard Roberto cry again.

CHAPTER VI

NICO THOUGHT HE'D feel guilty about deceiving his mother; he didn't, he was too excited at the thought of being independent. If Mum wanted to worry about his roaming Florence without her that was too bad; her new friendship with Luisa would distract her and if not, there was always James.

It didn't take Nico and the twins long to walk to the Accademia and by the time they got there he'd forgotten all about Mum. 'Let's do the photos,' he said.

He took pictures of the three of them outside the building and a few close-ups with just a glimpse of sky and stone behind them.

He snapped his camera shut. 'I'll get leaflets from here and then from the Medici Palace where Michelangelo lived. You can use them to blag to your mum and dad.'

'Thanks,' Jade said.

'You're welcome.'

The twins left and Nico went into the Accademia. He

bought postcards of Michelangelo's unfinished sculptures. He liked the sculptures much more than the paintings in the Uffizi: the prisoners looked as though they were alive and struggling to escape the rock they were embedded in. Nico wished he had time to look at them properly. *I'll come back,* he promised himself as he made his way to the Medici palace.

He turned into Via Cavour. Sudden roaring traffic spouting petrol fumes poured down it like a berserker army. He waited for a gap and loped into it. Instantly a cavalry of mopeds surged towards him and he only just managed to leap onto the far pavement before a phalanx of cars and strange three-wheeled vans thundered after them like an infantry charge. Nico didn't know why his mother feared paedophiles and axe murderers; traffic was Florence's real and present danger.

When Jade and Amber stepped off the bus in Borgo Sant'Angelo Jade felt as though she'd walked into a familiar dream. The small town was exactly as Nonno had described it: here was the old square with its central well, there was the pastry shop, the mediaeval town hall studded all over with painted stone cartouches, even the busy market with its waving white awnings.

'This is really, really strange,' Jade said and clung to her sister. Despite all their planning, things felt different now that they were really here. Even Amber, usually so sure of everything, sounded unnerved as she said, 'I don't want to look around – let's go and find Nonno's place.'

They walked quickly through a small public garden where they found another jarring memory: a bronze fountain of Arion riding a dolphin. Nonno had loved it when he was a boy and Jade knew she'd love it too, in time. Amber didn't give her the chance; Jade had to run to keep up with her sister who was walking rapidly up a steep, cobbled street with a church at the top. At the bottom, on the other side, was an old bridge spanning the River Rondine.

'Left or right?' Jade asked.

'Left.'

They turned down a narrow, unpaved road with silvery grey-green olive trees to one side and vineyards on the other, the twisted lines of vines like plaited cornrows stretching over the scalp of the land.

When they reached the wood, Jade's feet knew just where to go and they found Nonno's pool with no trouble at all.

Nico got more postcards from the Palazzo Medici shop and very nearly bought tickets to see Gozzoli's frescoes. He knew almost every brushstroke from prints and books and yearned to see the real thing, bursting with colour, sparkling with gold. *I can always come back*, he told himself. *It's more important to go to the Oltr'Arno district for now.* He set off for the Ponte Vecchio.

The Old Bridge, with its random arrangement of dusky yellow, red-tiled goldsmiths' shops jutting over the river, was a fantasy illustration come to life. Nico walked down the stone-flagged centre of the bridge leaving sightseers to crowd the pavements and peer into the shop windows. Over the hubbub of voices and the constant clicking of cameras, he heard a fragile thread of music coming from behind a knot of people on the middle of the bridge. Curious, he eased through the group. A man with a harp sat against the parapet, playing in time to the swirling of the brown river. Nico listened for a moment then remembered he had somewhere to go and walked on, the music drifting after him like mist until it faded away as he reached the other side of the river.

Jade wondered if the pool remembered Nonno as a boy, dangling his feet in its cool water as she was doing now. Did places have memories, or was it only people?

'Listen,' Amber said.

The sound of church bells came drifting up from the town.

'Don't they ring bells on the hour?' Jade said.

'Yep.' Amber was already slipping her shoes back on. 'Time to go, c'mon.'

Jade didn't want to – she liked the pool and its earthy, green smell. 'I could stay here for ever.'

'We've got to get to the house. We can't waste time or we'll miss the bus back.'

'I suppose so.' Jade pulled her feet out of the pool sending ripples shooting across it to slap like wet hands at the opposite bank. She followed Amber through the woods and fields, across the bridge and back into the town where they linked arms and set off for the Villa dei Fiori.

It was different on the other side of the Arno where the craftsmen and artisans worked: there weren't many tourists and the side streets were quieter, narrower. Nico walked down sloping lanes, through a small piazza and under an archway to the street he wanted. It was all that he'd hoped for – a tumble of workshops and houses with small restaurants and bars and bakeries here and there between them. Now he needed to find number 10. High up on a crumbling stucco wall a white enamel plaque said '4' in blue. Above that was a small, square slab of stone with a faded red '12' painted on it. E. J. Holm hadn't mentioned two sets of numbers in *The Shattered Mirror*. Which was the right one? Nico followed the blue ones.

Via dell'Unicorno d'Argento 10 turned out to be a private house with a firmly shut front door. Nico backtracked along the street and followed the red numbers, which he realised were businesses: 14 was a silversmith's and 12 was a bookbindery. Number 10, the Bottega degli Specchi, was where Alessandro's beloved Semiramide had died among the gilded mirrors of the workshop. Nico took a photo of the stone unicorn above the door. It was exactly as E. J. Holm had described it.

Jade pointed. 'It's down there.' At the top of a dirt road running between a stand of trees and a rocky stream was a sign reading, Villa dei Fiori. Underneath it, another sign advertised olive oil for sale. A fresh problem struck Jade. 'Nonno never said anything about the people who lived at the villa having a business – what if these are new people?'

As usual Jade's sister didn't see anything to worry about. 'Too late, we're here now.'

Jade had no answer to that. They walked down the path and turned behind the screen of trees to where a large, square house glowed chalky gold in the mid-morning sun. The stone roof was crocheted with an edging of yellow lichen and grey-green moss and a rambling wisteria hung like a garland over the whole front.

Jade felt the dream sensation again. This was the house that Nonno had described to them over and over; the house where his childhood sweetheart had lived and where he'd been happy. The house he'd been forbidden from entering ever again. Close up Jade could see that the wisteria's pale violet blossoms and fans of delicate lime-green leaves were covering crumbling plaster and peeling paintwork. The wooden door was cracked and bleached to a silvery pewter. 'Let's post the letter and go,' she said.

'There isn't a letterbox.' Amber knocked loudly and called out, 'Hello! Anybody there?'

'Momento!' a voice sang from inside the house.

Jade forced herself to smile. The door opened and a pretty woman who looked startlingly like Luisa smiled back at them from under a swing of blonde hair. 'Sì?'

Jade and her sister, struck dumb, could only stare.

'You are English?' the woman prompted.

Jade nodded. 'We speak a bit of Italian,' she blurted out.

'I speak a little bit English. We manage together, no? I am Caterina Biagi. How can I help you?'

'We saw your sign,' Jade improvised. 'Can we buy some olive oil – for our mum and dad?'

Signora Biagi laughed. 'I usually sell to restaurants and to the buyers from abroad but I can give you some samples for your parents.' She opened the door wide. 'Come in, come in!'

They went through a flagged hall to a kitchen where the woman gestured to a table and chairs by the window. 'I make you the cappuccino. I know that English people they like it very much.' She bustled about, clattering cups and fetching milk and coffee while Jade avoided catching

Amber's eye and concentrated on staring out of the window at a vegetable garden. Things were getting out of control. They'd never expected to be invited in. And the way Signora Biagi looked was such a shock – she was almost Mum's double.

Caterina Biagi put a plate of pastries on the table. 'You are students, travelling?'

Jade could see Amber was too fascinated by the woman's uncanny resemblance to Mum to think straight. 'We're school students,' she said quickly, 'on holiday with our family.'

'Where are they, your parents?'

'In town, going round the church,' Jade lied.

'Ah, they look at the frescoes – they are very fine and famous.' Signora Biagi smiled sympathetically. 'You are bored – too much of the art so you do the exploring.' Her smile broadened. 'It is like my girls, always the activity, the music, the clothes.' She beamed with maternal pride. 'They are *gemelle* – twins – like you. Is that not strange?'

'Yes,' Jade said, hearing Amber's echo from the right. She was probably thinking the same thing too. *No, it's not that strange; not if what we think about you is true.*

After the mirror shop, which was all he had hoped for inside as well as out, Nico decided to have a look around the bookbindery next door because that's what Alessandro had done during his investigations. The shop was also familiar from E. J. Holm's description except for the woman behind the counter who was throwing suspicious looks at him.

Nico picked up a green journal and gently fanned the pages. 'How much is this book?'

The woman told him. It was expensive; very expensive. Nico decided to buy it anyway. If you wanted something badly you had to be prepared to pay for it.

'We make all the books here in our workshop,' the woman said, folding the journal in gold tissue paper and slipping it into a bag. 'This, it has the parchment, not the ordinary paper. You have to remember that when you write in it.' She passed the bag to Nico.

'And draw.'

'You are artist!' A look of comprehension spread across the woman's face, showing that now she understood Nico's unconventional appearance: the long billowy coat, the spiky hair, though perhaps not, her expressive eyes said, the nose ring.

'You must have the correct pens and ink then you can make the good pictures. There is a shop where you can buy them in the Via del Drago d'Oro. You go there and say that Signora Gabrieli sends you, OK?'

Nico thanked her and left. He found the shop easily enough though it was even smaller than the bookbindery. The tiny room was crammed with pens: polished wooden ones with removable nibs; silver ones and gold ones, and glass ones, twisted like old fashioned barley sugar sticks, that seemed too fragile to write with.

Nico explained what he wanted to the assistant and held up the bag with its unicorn logo. 'Signora Gabrieli sent me.'

'Ah, Cinzia!' The assistant introduced herself as Signora Levi and told Nico about the shop, which was very old, her good friend Cinzia's shop, also very old, and the whole area of the Oltr'Arno, which had been home to artisans and craftsmen since the fourteenth century at least.

Nico bought two pens, assorted nibs and a bottle of the blackest ink he'd ever seen, all at a reduced price since Nico was a student and an artist. The bag Signora Levi put them in had a curly golden dragon on the front that reminded Nico of the dragon-snakes on Mercury's wand. It made him want to sit somewhere private so that he could read *The Shattered Mirror*. 'Is there a coffee place near here?' he asked.

'But of course!' Signora Levi directed him to a small cafe. 'It has the wonderful pastries and the very good cappuccino which all English people love very much.'

Nico thought English people avoided espresso because they had a strong sense of self-preservation. He sighed. No matter how authentically Italian he longed to be, he was never, ever going to like it.

*

Caterina Biagi beamed as Jade put her cup down. She was the smiliest woman Jade had ever seen. Mum didn't smile a lot. She wasn't a miserable person, only deeply solemn, quite different from Signora Biagi who seemed to view the world as an endless source of joy. 'It is nice to have visitors. My husband he works in town and my children they are away for the holidays.'

Jade pointed towards a display of photographs on the wall. 'Are they your children?'

'Yes, they are my girls, Lia and Valentina, and my son Dario.'

'And that one must be you and your husband?'

'Yes, that is Carlo and me on our wedding day.'

'Who's the man in the other picture?' Amber asked.

Trust you to pick out the most good-looking guy, Jade thought. She stared more closely. Whoever he was, he was *really* good looking.

'It's my brother, Matteo,' Signora Biagi said. 'And you, you have brothers and sisters also?'

'No,' Jade said, 'there's just us.'

'And your parents, who you must go back to or they will be worried. First, I will go and fetch you the sample of olive oil I promised.'

She bustled out, still smiling. Jade whispered, 'She's so like Mum!'

'She has to be one of Nonno's people,' Amber hissed back. 'Why are we whispering?'

76

'Because she might hear us and we're not ready to talk to her about Nonno yet, are we?'

'Suppose not.' Amber wriggled in her chair. 'Now what?'

'We come back. The day after tomorrow, like we planned.' Jade took out the letter they'd written the night before, explaining who they were and what they were doing. She wrote in Italian on the envelope, *Thanks for the delicious snack. It was nice to meet you. We will come back on Wednesday.* She chewed the pen for a moment then signed her name.

She put the letter on the table where it lay, white and stark except for black lines of writing across it. She got up. 'C'mon, let's go before she comes back and sees the letter.'

At the front door, Caterina Biagi gave them a leaflet and a jar of olive oil. 'Perhaps I will see you again,' she said. 'And meet your parents?'

Not much chance of the last bit, Jade thought. She said, 'Ci vediamo,' which meant, we'll see each other again, to avoid lying outright. Caterina Biagi's smile blossomed. 'That will be very nice.'

Jade hoped this lovely woman would still feel as happy once she'd read the letter.

When Nico checked in his novel he discovered that the cafe was the one Alessandro had stumbled into after he'd found Semiramide's body. He'd walked blindly from the *Bottega degli Specchi* along the winding roads of the Oltr'Arno until he fetched up in the little trattoria and began trying to work out who'd done this terrible thing to him. Nico even managed to sit at the same table where Alessandro had slumped with his grappa and his cigarette, not showing that he was dying inside. It was Mum's favourite bit of the book and she'd cried when she read it out at the reading group. Nico didn't do crying but he had felt his guts twist as he read the passage. He took a photo of the trattoria before he left.

E. J. Holm has to know the area well, Nico thought as he strode back over the Ponte Vecchio. *Who knows, he might be passing me now.* There was no way of telling: Nico didn't know what the writer looked like; nobody did. There wasn't even a blurry picture on the inside back flap, only the same bit of basic information repeated in each book – *E. J. Holm has lived in Italy for many years* – followed by a list of his novels. Some of the books mentioned the crime writing awards he'd won, none of which he'd ever turned up to collect in person.

Nico went to the Casa Buonarotti and took a picture of it. Then he texted Amber to remind her they were supposed to be visiting the house which Michelangelo had once owned. His second text was for Mum, keeping her up to date with his imaginary adventures. He had a bit of time left and decided to go to the church of Santa Croce, to visit Michelangelo's tomb and buy more postcards for the twins' invented project. He winced as he set off. His feet were blistered; tomorrow he might change his heavy boots for shoes.

Gaetano and Roberto grew close as the years went by and came to see themselves as brothers. They worked hard on the farm, went to school and church together and played in the hills together. Their favourite place was a pool in the woods which they kept secret from everyone.

In time the two friends became four; as peasants, the boys weren't encouraged to play with the children of professional families but nevertheless, two girls joined them: Elena was the daughter of a local landowner and Ilaria's father was a lawyer. In summer the children roamed the countryside together and, despite far-away wars and political discontent, the days were long and golden and the four friends were happy. So it was a surprise one day when the boys found Elena sitting crying by their secret pool.

'What're you doing here?' Gaetano demanded. 'No one knows about it but me and Roberto.'

'Ilaria and I do – we follow you sometimes,' Elena whispered. 'We just let you think it's a secret. I wanted to be on my own. It's too sad at the villa.'

Roberto sat next to her. 'What's the matter?

'My brother . . .' Elena choked on her tears.

Gaetano sat on her other side. 'Cristiano? What about him?'

'He's been killed in Ethiopia.'

'I'm sorry.' Gaetano awkwardly patted Elena's hand. Her fingers curled round his for a moment then let go.

'I'm sorry too,' Roberto said. 'But you shouldn't cry – Cristiano was a brave soldier who died for our country and for the Duce.'

Gaetano snorted. 'My babbo says it's a waste – why do we need colonies in Africa? It's so far away.'

'Mamma cries all the time,' Elena said. 'And Babbo is angry – he hates the Duce.'

'My babbo does too,' Gaetano said.

'They're wrong,' Roberto insisted. 'The Duce is a good man who only cares for his people.'

Gaetano rolled his eyes. 'You're an idiot.' He kicked a stone into the pool.

Roberto ignored him. 'Don't be sad,' he said to Elena. 'Be proud.' He laid his hand gently on her shoulder and she smiled at him.

Gaetano scowled and said nothing.

CHAPTER VII

THE WINE MUST have mellowed James, Nico decided as he wafted a sparrow off the cafe table. Either that or he'd had a terrifically good day talking about Xtreme Measures with Kevin. James swirled his wine round his glass, leaned back and looked at Nico almost sympathetically. 'Maybe they wouldn't let you go round the church because of the way you're dressed. A transparent top might've been too much.'

'It wouldn't have been seen as respectful,' Luisa agreed.

Nico wasn't sure if she was being critical; it was hard to tell with someone as serious as her.

'It's only a matter of adjusting to different customs,' she added and Nico knew she wasn't being judgmental after all.

Nico plucked at his black mesh top and squinted critically at it. 'I didn't realise it would be a problem.'

'The girls should've told you to button your coat up.' Luisa shook her head at the twins.

'We got split up,' Nico lied. 'They were at the back of

the queue and I was sent out before they realised what was happening.'

'It's because Italians are more traditional than we are where religion is concerned.'

'We? Don't you see yourself as Italian at all?' Nico's Mum asked.

'Not very – although my father was Italian my mother was English and I was born in Derby and lived there all my life. I'm a regular Englishwoman.'

'Surely you feel Italian too? You speak the language so well.'

'Only because my father made us all speak it at home. After he'd had his first stroke – a long time ago, before the girls were born – he said he couldn't understand English any more.'

No wonder the twins were fluent, Nico thought. They'd spoken Italian all their lives.

The waiter arrived with the bill and a flick of his napkin for the sparrows. It finished off the conversation and James and Kevin started up a debate about who should pay the bill. In the end they went inside the cafe still arguing.

'Where are you going this afternoon, Mum?' Nico asked.

'To a flea market in Piazza Ciompi. Do you three want to come?'

Nico didn't and he could tell from the girls' expressions

that they didn't either. 'We thought we'd do a bit more on the Michelangelo project. We wanted to try the Medici gardens where he studied sculpture, didn't we?'

Amber waved her pink notebook, fattening nicely with the cards and pamphlets Nico had passed on when they'd met up again before lunch. 'Yep, and there's loads left to research after that isn't there, Nico?'

'Uh huh. Michelangelo was a very busy artist.'

'I thought you preferred early Renaissance art,' Mum said. 'Isn't Michelangelo High Renaissance?'

Nico often accused Mum of taking no notice of his opinions and now she had it was a nuisance. 'You have to experience it all,' he said, 'everything's interesting if you understand it.' OMG – he sounded exactly like James!

'You're going to look at more art!' Luisa said to the twins.

'We might shop as well,' Amber said.

Nico smothered a sigh but thought maybe he'd look for black shoes; his feet were still aching in his heavy boots.

The shops in Florence turned out to be closed for the afternoon and when the girls dithered about what to do next, Nico suggested they go to San Marco together. He was pleased when they agreed; he liked them, especially Jade, and he was curious about what they'd done that morning. They'd been subdued when they met up at the Accademia to take more photos for their parents and he hadn't bothered them with questions. Maybe now was a better time.

'Did you find your village?' he asked as they walked up Via Cavour.

'Yes,' Amber said.

'Did you meet any relatives?'

'Sort of,' Jade said.

Nico knew it still wasn't the right time.

It was peaceful inside San Marco, which Nico supposed was how monasteries – even ex-monasteries – were meant to be. On the first floor, tiny cells, with windows overlooking the courtyard below, lined each side of a long corridor running round in a square. They reminded Nico of honeybee cells, with rounded corners. And each white-walled cell had its own exquisite fresco painted by Fra Angelico. Photography wasn't allowed and Nico kept stopping to draw.

'This is boring,' Amber complained. 'Hurry up!'

Nico ignored her. He wasn't going to stop drawing because Amber was in a sulk. Vaguely he heard Jade say, 'There's a cafe over the road; we'll wait there.'

'OK,' Nico said and went on drawing.

'I still don't get it,' Amber said, sipping her drink. 'I mean, those pictures were good but why's he so mad on them?'

'He just is.' Jade didn't know how to explain to her

sister that the paintings were magic to Nico. How could she when she didn't get it herself? She checked the time on her phone. How long was Nico going to spend in San Marco? She got through another drink before he joined them.

'What kept you?' she asked.

'I was looking for Michelangelo's sculpture school for your project,' he said.

That made Jade feel mean, which made her snappy. 'Did you find it then?'

'No, it's not in the monastery.' Nico wafted a leaflet. 'The guide told me where it is and gave me this map. It's not far. D'you want to come?'

'May as well,' Jade said, thinking it was a good job Amber was finishing her orange juice and could only grunt instead of moaning.

On the way out they passed a line of scooters stretching down one side of the road. Jade stopped by a sleek black Yamaha T Max. 'Shame we can't hire one of those.'

'We can TWOC,' Amber suggested.

Jade could see Nico wasn't sure if Amber was joking or not. She put him out of his misery. 'She's having a laugh. We don't really rob stuff.'

'Not often,' Amber added.

'Ignore her,' Jade said. 'Where's this garden?'

'There.' Nico pointed at a massive door set into a wall.

'That's one weird door.' Jade squinted at a carving of a monkey squeezing from under a huge shell crowning the lintel. She pushed at the door. 'It's closed – how do we get in?'

Nico consulted his leaflet. 'I don't think we can, it's a court house now.'

Jade noticed a scruffy sign by the door. 'You're right. It tells you here. That's all it is now – a rubbish sign and a closed door with a squashed monkey.' Her feet were hurting with all the walking they'd done and she wasn't bothered when Nico took a step backwards from her sarcasm.

'Try and imagine it like it was when Lorenzo de' Medici was alive and all the boys were learning to be artists and sculptors in his garden academy . . .'

'We know all that,' Jade said.

'You do?' She watched Nico's black eyebrows arch in surprise.

Amber joined in. 'We read those pamphlets you got us yesterday. We can read you know – we're not totally stupid.'

'I never thought you were.'

Jade saw a standoff forming between Amber and Nico and felt a bit guilty. 'We read up on Michelangelo just in case Mum and Dad started to ask us questions, didn't we, Amb?'

Amber shrugged.

'We felt sorry for Michelangelo when his dad beat him for wanting to be an artist instead of a lawyer,' Jade babbled on.

'Like my Mum,' Nico said.

'Hattie beats you!'

'No, of course not! I meant she's always nagging me about what she calls a "real" job. She doesn't think art can earn me a decent living – as if that's the point.'

'You've got to eat,' Jade said.

Nico snorted. 'True.'

'Ignore your mum,' Jade said. 'Michelangelo took no notice of his dad.'

'I do,' Nico muttered.

Jade could see he didn't like talking about Hattie and wasn't surprised when he switched topics. 'Did you read about how the boy Michelangelo made a copy of an old marble faun . . .'

'Lorenzo de Medici saw it,' Jade said. 'He told Michelangelo it had too many teeth for an old man.'

'So Michelangelo knocked them out,' Amber added.

'Only some of them,' Jade objected. She hopped from foot to foot. 'My feet are killing me with all this walking – let's go back to the flat.'

'Good idea,' Nico said. Jade noticed Nico limping and remembered the Segway. She felt guilty again, though not much.

*

Nico began his new journal. He wrote, *In Search of E. J. Holm* on the title page and inside an account of his exploration of Oltr'Arno. He added some drawings then opened his copy of *The Shattered Mirror* at the page where Alessandro found his lover's body among the broken glass of the Bottega degli Specchi. He copied a passage into his journal:

> *Semiramide's twisted body lay among glistening shards covering the workshop floor. As Alessandro forced himself to walk towards her, the glass under his shoes splintered like fragile bones. He looked down at the corpse. The light glittering from fragments of glass encircling Semiramide's serene and lovely face made a perfect halo. But the eyes that looked up at him were not the eyes of an angel, they were the eyes of death: opaque, dark, empty. And the mouth that had smiled often and generously at him was distorted by something thrust between the lips.*
>
> *Alessandro stooped and gently pulled it out. It was a rose – a scarlet rose.*

Even though the late sun lingered over the balcony, Jade shivered. 'I still can't get over the way Signora Biagi looked so like Mum. What d'you think she'll say when we go back?'

'How should I know?'

'You do still want to go back don't you?'

'Of course I do. She's got to tell us what they think Nonno did and we've got to put her right.'

'Maybe she doesn't know. Maybe she doesn't even know Nonno was supposed to have done something. Maybe she's never even heard of Nonno.'

'We'll find out on Wednesday, won't we?'

'But . . .'

'Stop going on about it.' Amber glared at Jade. 'You know how Nonno felt. You know how much he wanted to come back here and they threatened to kill him if he did. How can you excuse that?'

'I'm not – and I don't think they really meant "kill". Everybody says that – Nico said he was going to kill Hattie if she didn't stop pressuring him but he didn't mean it, did he? It's just an expression.'

With a pitying look Amber pushed past Jade and went inside.

There was no point in talking when she was in a mood. Jade stayed where she was and looked down into the darkening garden. Why did things have to be so complicated? Jade had imagined that she and Amber would just tell the Italian family what Nonno was really like and convince them he was a good man. But what if they were wrong? What if Nonno *had* done something terrible after all?

CHAPTER VIII

IT HAD BEEN a weird afternoon, Nico thought. James and Kevin had parked the hire cars in Borgo Sant'Angelo and the two families split up. Even the muppet James had enough common sense to leave the Thompsons alone. Luisa had looked very pale when she set off but was her usual self by the time they all met up again at the cafe bar in town and sat in the sunshine with their drinks. Even so, she was quieter than usual and seemed to find it a relief to listen to Mum cheerfully rabbiting on about all the similarities she'd discovered between Borgo Sant'Angelo and E. J. Holm's Montebosco. Kevin and James simply picked up their on-going conversation about Xtreme Measures. What everyone was careful not to do was ask Luisa what it was like to visit her dead father's childhood home.

Nico noticed that the adults skirted round the topic by discussing what they were going to do the next day. In the end they agreed to go to the walled town of Lucca. It was Mum's idea: she wanted to locate another of Alessandro's crime scenes and Luisa agreed. They were getting on well. So were James and Kevin; they didn't seem to mind what anybody did as long as they could talk music.

Nico and the twins sat to one side where they had a good view of the busy piazza. Nico concentrated on drawing leaving Jade and Amber to talk softly about deceiving their parents. Nico thought Jade had a point when she said, 'Amb, you tell a lie and it leads on to another and another. How many more are we going to tell before all this is over?'

'As many as it takes.'

'Doesn't it bother you?'

'No. What does it matter if we tell a few lies that don't hurt anybody if it means we find out why Nonno's family told a massive lie that really hurt him?'

Amber turned to Nico, the topic of lying clearly over. 'Is your mum going to take those books everywhere?'

Mum, pink with excitement, was flourishing *The Shattered Mirror* at Luisa.

'Probably,' Nico said.

'Why?'

'She wants to find the places in the books and compare them with E. J. Holm's descriptions. The church here was the scene of a wedding and then a murder. She wanted to see it close up – the church I mean, not the murder, obviously.'

'Why?'

'To bring the books more alive when she reads them again.'

'She reads them twice!'

'She must've read *The Shattered Mirror* maybe three or four times.'

'Why?' Amber persisted.

'Don't you listen to music over and over, or watch your favourite films twice?'

'That's different.'

'Why?' Nico said with a grin.

Amber frowned. 'Mad.' She plugged her ear buds in and turned her back on Nico and Jade.

'Is she all right?' Nico asked.

Jade nodded. 'Those books of your mum's, you read them as well, don't you?'

'It drives James crazy when we talk about them.'

'You read them to annoy James?'

'No, that's a bonus. I read them because they're brilliant.'

'Brilliant? How?'

'You really want to know? I don't want be boring like my mother.'

'She's not boring to my mum – she likes her. Go on, what's great about these E. J. Holm books?'

Nico thought about it. What would grab Jade's interest most? There were the loving, vivid descriptions of Italy, the fascinating characters. No, that wouldn't impress her.

'You know some books are a real slog and though you're glad you've read them and you won't forget them, you know you'll never read them again?'

'Yes – like the ones you have to read in English.'

'OK, then there's the ones you know are basically rubbish but you get caught up in the plot and can't put them down?'

Jade nodded.

'E. J. Holm's books are the best of both. They've got complicated plots that move fast and pull you along and . . . there's more to them than that.'

'Such as?'

'There's the characters for a start – you end up believing they're real people.' Nico decided not to elaborate; he knew he'd rabbit on for too long. 'And there's the story arc.'

'The what?'

'You know when there's a series – it could be books or TV – you get a story in each book or episode?'

Jade nodded.

'Every book – or episode – also gives you a little bit of a longer story that stretches over the whole series.'

'And at the end the big story is all tied up.'

'That's it – that's the series story arc.'

'What's the E. J. Holm one?'

Nico rummaged in a pocket for his notebook. He flipped it open at columns and rows of notes. At the head of each column was an ink drawing of a flower. 'The series story arc is something to do with the Second World War – and with flowers.'

Jade pointed at the columns. 'What do those dates and things mean?'

'It's the order the books came out in. See? First, it's *The Leopard's Kill* and then *The Coloratura Assassin* and so on. Underneath the titles I've put the victims' names and then their ages. They were all old except the last three; there's the detective's friend Bruno and Bruno's daughter, Tania – she was only seven.'

'That's two people. Who was the third?'

'Semiramide, the detective's girlfriend.' Nico turned the page over. 'I think the main story arc is about revenge for some act of treachery by one of the partisans – they were the freedom fighters who fought against the Germans when they occupied Italy.'

'I know about partisans, my nonno was one.'

'Really? Then he was a hero! You don't happen to know his code name?'

'Code name?'

'It wasn't safe to use real names; if they got captured they could be tortured.'

'That's horrible.'

Nico nodded. 'In the books, each of the victims' bodies is left with a flower – or a painting of a flower – on it. I think it's to do with a partisan group who used flowers as code names and I think all the flowers come from a painting called *Primavera*. It's in the Uffizi, I saw it on Sunday.'

'Can I read one of your books? I want to know more about partisans.'

'Course – but don't forget, these are fiction though the history's accurate.' That was true; Nico had checked. 'I'll lend you *The Shattered Mirror*, a lot of it's set here, in Borgo Sant'Angelo.'

Amber turned and pulled out her ear buds. 'I'm bored – let's go for a walk.'

Nico wanted to stay and talk to Jade. But it was too late, she was on her feet. Nico stood too.

'Where are you going?' Mum asked.

'For a walk round town,' Nico said. 'Don't make a fuss, Mother.'

'Be back in half an hour. Dinner's at eight.'

Why could she never take a hint? 'I know.' Nico strode after the girls who'd already started off without having to put up with a warning from Kevin or Luisa.

Dusk was dimming the sky and warm light slipped from cafes and bars, old people gossiped over their drinks and younger ones sauntered along the streets or gathered in small groups to watch each other parade slowly by. Nico and the twins came in for some open staring, and comments and gestures which Nico didn't understand. 'What are they saying?' he asked Jade.

She told him.

'Charming. D'you know a lot of swearing?'

'Loads – Nonno didn't like it; it was some of the old people at his Italian Club who taught us. D'you want to know more?'

By the time they got back to the bar Nico had learned a lot of colourful language and a large collection of expressive gestures. Lessons with Mr Mowatt had never been this interesting.

'Time to get going,' Mum said.

Il Nido was on the edge of town, tucked away in a shadowed side street. Inside it was surprisingly sophisticated for a restaurant in such a small town. There were several parties and couples already seated with a particularly noisy and cheerful group near the door.

'Hope we're not going to end up next to them,' James complained, staring disapprovingly at the unruly collection of elderly men and women including a priest helping himself to wine.

Trust the muppet James to make us look stupid, Nico thought as a waiter escorted them to Signora Minardi who was sitting on the far side of the room. The priest raised his glass in an insolent salute to James's back. Nico winced in embarrassment and the priest winked at him. Nico pretended he hadn't noticed.

'Welcome, welcome,' the Signora said. James made for the best position next to a window. The Signora held up her hand. 'No, Signora Thompson she will sit here, beside me.'

Even James couldn't face down the old lady. She went on being insistent about the seating order and Nico began to think she'd planned it for some reason though he couldn't see what. She sat at the head of the table with Luisa on her right and Mum on her left. Kevin and the twins were ranged down the right-hand side and Nico and James on the left. The end of the table was open. *Pity the muppet isn't sitting there on his own*, Nico thought sullenly.

After they'd ordered, the Signora asked Luisa what she thought of Borgo Sant'Angelo.

'It's very pleasant,' she said.

'Did you discover anything of interest?'

'Not really.'

'Did you visit the church?'

'No.'

'Perhaps you went further afield, to see the countryside with some of the local farms? They are very picturesque.'

What's she up to? Nico wondered. The old lady was no fool; why did she keep pushing when Luisa obviously didn't want to talk? He decided to distract Signora Minardi. Rather him than the Thompsons, who were starting to look annoyed.

'I went to the church,' he said. 'I made notes on the frescoes.' Out of the corner of his eye he saw Jade mouth,

'Thank you,' as he passed his sketchbook down the table to the Signora.

'I only had time to scribble some drawings and notes. I need to learn more. D'you know who could tell me?'

'Yes, I do.'

Signora Minardi fired off an order to a waiter who hurried to the noisy old people and spoke to the priest. He joined the Signora, greeted her formally and smiled vaguely at everyone else.

'I have a young man here,' the Signora said, 'who wishes to know more about the paintings in San Giovanni. You must talk to him, but first let me introduce you to all my English guests.'

The Signora went round the table giving names. The priest's affable smile passed over them all though Nico noticed he looked longest at Luisa and while he did his eyes grew clear and alert.

The priest spoke to Nico in slow, careful English, as though he hadn't used the language for a long time and was trying hard to remember it as he went along. 'I will introduce you to Professoressa Mussi, Camilla, who was a teacher here for many years. She knows art history better than me.'

He beckoned towards the rowdy group though it wasn't clear who he was gesturing to and the whole tableful came forward. All six knew the Signora and each of them was introduced in turn and shook hands with her

English guests. Like the priest, they seemed particularly interested in Luisa.

It's like Bilbo's unexpected party, Nico thought, especially as most of the elderly people were wizened enough to be mistaken for dwarfs; half of them had sticks and one had a walking frame. They staggered slowly round the table, shaking hands and saying, 'Piacere,' in wavery voices. The waiters and diners were staring openly in amazement.

It's surreal, Nico thought.

The door of the restaurant burst open. It was yet another elderly man. He glared at the Signora, and the collection of aged people milling round her table. He came towards her, complaining bitterly.

The Signora stood. 'Enough!' she commanded in Italian.

The old man took no notice. He raged on, eyes wide and angry, his gaze sweeping round the table – until he caught sight of Luisa. He stopped mid-rant and stared; not covertly like the other old people but brazenly. He lifted his finger, pointing at Luisa. Kevin jumped to his feet, fists balled. A waiter grabbed the old man's arm and the priest, suddenly surprisingly spry, seized the other and they frog-marched the seething old man out of the restaurant.

James's voice rang out in the shocked silence: 'What the hell was that?' For once he'd only said what everyone else was thinking.

'Please accept my apologies,' the Signora said. 'He is somewhat, how do you say it? *Rimbambito*? A little bit losing his mind because he is old?'

'Senile,' James said obligingly.

Whatever else he was, he wasn't senile, Nico thought. The light in his eyes as he'd glared at Luisa wasn't madness, it was hatred.

'Boys!'

'Babbo's ready,' Gaetano said.

Roberto ran out of the door and down the steps to the courtyard where Gaetano's father stood by the white oxen harnessed to a cart.

'Don't be so eager to collect your uniform,' he said to Roberto. 'It won't make you a man.'

Roberto nodded, his expression blank. Gaetano knew he was trying to supress his excitement and finding it difficult. Now that the boys were fourteen they were getting rifles as well as uniforms; scaled-down rifles but real ones nevertheless. Even Gaetano was excited about that.

Gaetano clambered into the cart and sat next to Roberto. As it rumbled down the track to the nearby town of Borgo Sant'Angelo, Roberto began humming a fascist anthem.

'Shut up!' Gaetano warned and nodded towards his father who was frowning. Roberto sighed and stopped humming. He'll be happy soon enough, Gaetano thought. After they and the other young people had received their uniforms at the headquarters of the Youth Movement there'd be stirring speeches from the mayor and other dignitaries, and then there'd be singing – loud, joyful singing that Roberto wouldn't have to hold back on or apologise for. Gaetano suspected that his foster brother was already silently rehearsing the words in his head.

They reached the town and Gaetano nudged Roberto to draw his attention to the grand American car drawn up near to the Casa del Balilla, the headquarters of the Fascist Youth movement. 'Look – Elena must be here already; that's her father's car.'

'There she is!' Roberto pointed. Elena, with Ilaria by her side as usual, was entering the building. Both girls had their new black and white uniforms piled in their arms.

'Signor Tirone doesn't look happy,' Gaetano said.

At the car, Elena's parents were deep in conversation with Ilaria's. It wasn't only Signor Tirone who was unhappy: Signora Tirone was dabbing at her eyes with a handkerchief and Signor and Signora Minardi were exchanging worried glances.

'Idiots,' Roberto said and jumped down from the cart.

Gaetano glared. Though he knew his foster brother would never call Babbo an idiot, he also knew that Roberto loved the Duce too and one day he would have to choose between the beliefs of the two men. Uneasily Gaetano watched Roberto run to the Casa del Balilla. He was far too eager to begin his life as a soldier for the Duce and for the King.

CHAPTER IX

NICO WIDENED HIS eyes at the mirror by the door and drew a kohl pencil along his lids. He grinned at his reflection. Mum thought he was going with the twins to the library Michelangelo had designed for the Medici. The adults were on their way to the walled town of Lucca and didn't suspect a thing; the false project plan was going perfectly.

A booming knock at the door made him jump and he jabbed the pencil in his eye. He staggered back, pressing his palm into his streaming eye.

Knock, knock, knock.

'Wait a minute!' Nico peered through tears pouring from both eyes and fumbled the door open. It was the twins. He knuckled his bad eye. 'What?' he snorted, his nose as full as his eyes.

'We're going for the bus,' Amber said. 'What's up with you?'

'I stabbed myself in the eye with my kohl when you knocked. It's killing me.'

'Sorry,' Jade said. 'Are you all right?'

'No.'

'We can't wait,' Amber said. 'The bus goes in half an hour.'

Nico didn't care. All he cared about was the pain in his eye. 'I'll catch you up.'

'You'll have to get a move on.'

Bitch. Can't you see I'm in pain? Nico thought. 'I'll get the next bus then,' he snapped.

'Sure?'

'Yes.' Nico slammed the door shut. At that moment he didn't care if he never went to Borgo Sant'Angelo again, ever, not even for the frescoes.

'He was in a strop,' Amber said as they walked down Via del Corno.

'So would you be if you poked yourself in the eye – it hurts.'

'I think he's a wuss.' Amber wrinkled up her nose. 'Look at all the fuss he made over his foot.'

'That's a bit harsh.'

Jade ignored Amber's withering look and changed the subject. 'I'm still worried about today, about Signora Biagi. She might be mad at us.' It was old ground: they'd talked about it for half the night – the other half had been spent talking about the weird old man and the peculiar dinner at Il Nido.

'So? What's she going to do? Chase us with a kitchen knife?'

'No, suppose not, I just thought . . .' Jade was worried by what she thought. *If she's angry I'm not going to hang around the Villa dei Fiori and listen to her slagging my family off.* She argued back at herself. *No, she won't do that – she's too nice – the worst she'll do is tell us to go away and never come back.* And even if that happened at least she and Amber would have tried their best to tell Nonno's Italian family the truth about him. If it failed it wouldn't be their fault.

Nico hurried towards the station, his eye still smarting. He took a wrong turning and found himself in the Piazza della Repubblica. He couldn't resist going into the Edison bookshop to buy a new copy of *The Shattered Mirror* for Jade. In all the fuss made by the old man last night Nico had forgotten to pass on his copy and he'd thought later he'd quite like to keep his old book. He was used to it and he liked the way it fell open at his favourite passages.

It took him a while to get served and he had to run to the bus station. He bought a ticket, squinted mistily at the destination and jumped on board just in time. The bus was soon out of the city and into hilly, wooded countryside. As it swooped round a bend on the narrow road, a gap opened up in the trees and Nico saw Florence rising from the valley below like the sweetest of mirages –

lovely, tempting – its golden, red-roofed houses stretching out to the green hills that encircled it before sweeping back around the great domed cathedral, gathering up the graceful towers on their way. Nico knew he would never, ever forget that golden glimpse of his beloved city. He settled back to enjoy the rest of the ride.

The bus went up and up in reckless spirals through the woods and steep rocky hillsides, the driver hauling frantically on the wheel as the front of the bus lurched over the edge of the road and back again. Nico decided not to look out of the nearside window.

The bus swept on round hairpin bends. They passed a sign with a deer on it, and one with falling boulders. The trees got thicker and the rocks got bigger and crueller. The bus swung past a gap looking straight down into a steep, wooded gully falling away in a sheer drop. Nico's stomach churned. The tightly packed trees closed in again and the hillside grew shadowy and dark. The bus climbed steadily up, and up, and up.

This isn't right, Nico thought, *Borgo Sant'Angelo's not on top of a mountain. I've got on the wrong bus.*

He had no idea where he was going.

The door opened. 'You are here!' Signora Biagi said.

'We told you we'd come back,' Amber said.

'Come in! Come!' Signora Biagi flung the door open wide and ushered them into the kitchen. 'Sit! Sit!'

The letter lay open on the table, its folds smoothed out as though hands had stroked them over and over. Signora Biagi smiled. 'You are very brave, coming here like this.'

'We thought you might be angry with us,' Amber said.

'Angry? How could I be angry with you?'

Jade and her sister had thought of quite a few reasons – tricking their way into the house, not revealing who they were, leaving the letter then doing a runner, the letter itself dropping a bombshell into Signora Biagi's life, stirring up memories of what Nonno was supposed to have done.

'I already knew a little about Roberto – your nonno – but I didn't know he had an English family who would come to look for us.' Signora Biagi reached out and took Jade and Amber's hands.

What was she going to say? Was she going to start accusing Nonno of some horrible crime?

Signora Biagi beamed. 'We are *cugine* – cousins. You can't call me "Signora". You must call me Caterina.'

The driver took the bus slowly into a clearing in the dense woodland where a few small houses clustered in twos and threes. There was a tiny cafe as well, with a green bench in front of it. The bus stopped and the driver got out and lit a cigarette.

Nico followed him. 'Scusi,' he said, 'this bus is going to Borgo Sant'Angelo, isn't it?'

The driver shook his head. 'No, it goes to Faenza.'

Faenza? Nico had never heard of it.

'How do I get to Borgo Sant'Angelo?' Nico asked.

'You have to go back to Firenze then get another bus to Borgo Sant'Angelo.' The driver pointed to the bench. 'You wait there. In twenty minutes a bus it will come. You can use your same ticket to get back. OK?'

'OK. Grazie.'

'Prego.' The driver threw down his half-smoked cigarette, ground it carefully under his heel, climbed back on the bus and drove away. The sound of the engine vanished in the muffling forest. Nico sat on the green bench. He tried his mobile. There was no signal. All he could do was wait.

Caterina brought three photos to the table and passed a black and white portrait of a pretty, rather serious-looking young woman to Jade and Amber. 'This is Elena, who you say Roberto loved. She was my nonna, my grandmother.'

Jade noticed Caterina didn't call Roberto her nonno though he was, just as much as he was hers and Amber's. 'Nonno did love Elena,' she said firmly. After his second stroke Nonno had hurt Luisa badly by grieving loudly for Elena and his unknown child; the least Caterina could do was acknowledge he had truly loved Elena. 'And he was always sad he never knew his baby.' Caterina ought to be able to understand that.

'He didn't even know if it was a boy or a girl,' Amber said.

Caterina pointed to another photograph. 'As you see, it was a girl. Elena called her Sofia and she is my mamma. This is a picture of her as a child.'

Jade expected to feel tearful when she leaned over to look at the photo but instead she felt a fierce, hot anger. The happy little face in the picture should have smiled up at Nonno not at some substitute father. It wasn't fair.

'And this,' Caterina said, 'is Mamma on her wedding day.' She held up a colour photo. 'Here is Mamma and my babbo, Davide, with his parents next to him. And here, on Mamma's side, are her parents, Elena and Gaetano.'

Gaetano – Nonno had told them he was his rival for Elena. Amber snatched at the picture and stared intently. Jade couldn't look; she was still trying to tame the rush of anger.

'You said you know a bit about Nonno – Roberto. What do you know?' she asked.

Caterina hesitated. 'There are some things in your letter that are different from what I was told by my mamma and my nonno Gaetano.'

'Oh?' Amber snapped. Caterina flinched.

'We loved our nonno,' Jade said.

'I understand. And I love my nonno, Gaetano, too. We should share our stories and see where things have become . . . confused.'

'That's a good idea,' Jade said. 'You go first.'

Caterina rested her forearms on the table while she thought for a moment. 'This is the story I grew up with,' she said. 'Many years ago there was a young man, not much more than a boy really, named Roberto Volpe. He fell in love with my grandmother, Elena, and she with him. She became pregnant. He wanted to marry her but it was wartime and Roberto was . . .' Caterina hesitated.

'Yes?' Jade coaxed.

'He was a fascist and Elena's parents would not hear of the marriage.'

A second rush of anger mixed with shock hit Jade. When she clutched Amber's hand under the table it was as chilly as her own. *This isn't right*, she thought, *this isn't the proper story. Nonno wasn't a fascist! He was a partisan fighting* against *the fascists!*

'Roberto joined a band called the Brigate Nere – Black Brigade in English.' Caterina hesitated then continued, 'Towards the end of the war he disappeared.'

Jade, numb with shock, didn't dare look at her sister.

'It was a bitter and confused time here in Italy,' Caterina said. 'Many people were fascists, many communists; others were royalists – like Elena's family – and many, many brave Italians helped British prisoners or spies. My nonno Gaetano was one of them. One young English spy whom he helped became his great friend.'

Jade bit her lip to stop herself speaking out loud:

Caterina had just recounted Nonno's story – except for the part about being friends with an English spy. Why was this Gaetano spreading lies about Nonno?

Caterina picked up the letter. 'Now I know that Roberto made his way to England and made a life there. He married a lady called Grace who became your nonna, your . . .?'

Jade managed to smile even though she was still numb from learning that Caterina believed Nonno had been a fascist. 'Granny, that's our word for nonna.'

Caterina smiled back, rather sadly. 'What we were always told – my mamma and my brother and I – was that Roberto didn't care about Elena and Sofia . . .' Caterina held her hand up sharply as Jade protested. '. . . or, because he was far away from here, he didn't know what had happened to Elena and their baby. And you say this in your letter too. What I don't understand is why he didn't try to get in touch after the war.'

'He couldn't,' Jade said.

'Couldn't? Why not?'

'Because somebody told him he'd be killed if he tried,' Amber said bluntly.

And I bet it was that Gaetano, Jade thought. *I bet Nonno knew something about him that he didn't want anyone else to know.* Though she was seething with anger, she didn't want an ugly confrontation – it would get them nowhere and if they antagonised Caterina there was a danger they'd never solve the mystery and Sofia would never know how lovely her real father was.

'I did not hear that,' Caterina said.

Jade kicked Amber under the table to tell her to stay quiet for now. 'What happened to Elena and Sofia?'

'Gaetano also loved Elena and married her quickly to hide the scandal of the pregnancy. It was such a shameful thing in those days to have an illegitimate child that Gaetano and Elena always said that Sofia was their own child.' Caterina shook her head disapprovingly. 'Fortunately, as the years passed and times grew kinder, Elena felt she could tell Sofia the truth about her father and later Sofia told me and my brother, Matteo. We always wondered what happened to Roberto. And now you are here to tell us. I'm happy that you have done this. I hope you are not disappointed to meet me?'

'Oh no,' Jade said. Truthfully, she *was* disappointed, bitterly, though not with Caterina; it was hardly her fault if this Gaetano had told lies about Nonno for some reason – maybe to get Elena for himself? They'd put him right if they ever met him. And man, would Amber be the right person to do that!

The trees towered over Nico's head, meeting far above him like the roof of a cathedral. Roots stirred in the rocky soil. *It must be wild here in a storm*, Nico thought. He remembered the bouncing rocks sign.

He squinted through the cafe window. According to James's guidebook, by law every cafe in Italy had to let you use their lavatory. But the law was no use if the only cafe for miles had a sign reading *chiuso* hanging in its window.

Nico checked his mobile. Five minutes to go before the bus was due to arrive. If he was quick there'd be time for a pee in the woods. He jogged round the corner and up the leaf-covered ground into the trees. Undergrowth was sparse on the fringes of the wood and Nico had to scramble quite a way in before he was sure he was screened from the road. He unzipped and sighed with relief. Then he heard the sound of an engine.

'Not the bus!'

The sound grew louder. The bus swept by. Nico didn't see it, he was too far into the forest for that, he only heard it rumbling away down the road back to Florence.

Hurriedly zipping up, he ran as fast as he could to where the sound had come from. He scrambled through the undergrowth, past bushes, around trees. The noise of the bus faded away altogether. There was no sign of the road. Nico leaned against a tree trying to get his breath back. Where was the road?

'OK,' he said out loud. 'I'm going downwards. The road is going downwards. I'm going to hit the road eventually.'

It seemed a reasonable assumption if he ignored the fact that he ought to have reached the road already. The undergrowth grew denser and the trees closer together.

Nico ploughed on with the forest getting more unruly round him. He found himself following a track going upwards. When had it started doing that? Further on, the track was worn very flat as though it had been well used. By hunters, maybe? James's guidebook said that Tuscans hunted a lot though it was a bit vague on what time of year. Nico didn't think it likely he was going to be mistaken for a wild boar and shot.

Wild boar. What was it James had tried to tell him and Mum about them? Something to do with danger and unpredictability and razor-sharp tusks? Nico climbed faster up the ever-steepening track. It had to lead somewhere, maybe a hunting lodge or a house? The track became so steep and rocky that Nico was almost going hand over hand. His boots slipped on the loose earth and he was glad he hadn't bought shoes yesterday; they'd have been useless here.

At last the track flattened out and broadened a bit and the trees thinned. Nico found himself in a grassy clearing. On the far edge was a boxy, stucco building with a tiled porch over a round window. Nico knocked on the stout oak door. No one answered. It was as *chiuso* as the cafe.

'Sit down,' Gaetano said.

Roberto shook his head. He leaned against a tree and scowled down at Gaetano and the girls who sat dangling their hot feet in the pool's cool water. Elena looked up at Roberto, her sweet face solemn. 'I don't want you to end up like Cristiano and die in a stupid war.'

'I won't,' Gaetano said kicking at the water and accidentally splashing Ilaria.

While they fooled around throwing water over each other, Elena, still looking at Roberto, said, 'When you turn eighteen the Carabinieri Marshal will come looking for you and Gaetano to be drafted into the army.'

Ilaria stopped splashing Gaetano. 'Don't worry about it, Elena. My father's a friend of the marshal and Babbo knows he turns a blind eye if his friends' sons mysteriously go missing when he's out with a press gang. He thinks enough young men have died for no good reason.'

Roberto shook his head. 'You're wrong.'

'Come on.' Gaetano impatiently tugged his foster brother

down. 'We won't be old enough for a couple of years anyway. Forget your beloved Duce for now. It's too hot to argue.'

Roberto pulled off his shoes, and slid his feet into the water. 'Time will prove me and the Duce right,' he said.

'We'll see,' Gaetano watched Elena tickle Roberto's feet with her toes and smile at him. For a moment, he thought Elena's teasing had worked and then Roberto's face set in an expression Gaetano recognised all too well: the bright-eyed, fanatical look of those who fed hungrily on the Duce's every word.

CHAPTER X

NICO SAT ON the top step of the building among its debris of leaves and moss. This was his mother's worst nightmare come true: he was lost, alone, with no signal on his mobile and no one knew where he was. Nico didn't care. The building and the hunters' track meant there were people around somewhere – it wasn't as though he was lost in the Amazonian rainforest. He was content to sit and look at the sumptuous Tuscan countryside rolling around him in great green waves.

He got out his sketchbook and as he began to draw, a strong feeling of déjà vu swept over him. He took out the copy of *The Shattered Mirror* and found the passage he wanted:

> *The white stucco chapel sat foursquare in the middle of a close-cropped area of grass studded with daisies. In front of it was a clear view of the hills unmarked by roads or habitations. On the other three sides, pine trees and cypresses nodded in the wind, the forest darkening*

behind them. Alessandro trod up the steps to the door. It was ajar. He pushed it wide open.

Nico knew what came next – inside the chapel Alessandro discovered scaffolding built for a restorer working on decaying frescoes painted above the door. Hanging from the metal tubing was a body:

The corpse swung gently, like a sack of wheat waiting to be lowered into a cart. Alessandro climbed the steel ladder and walked along the planking. He leaned down and pulled a wedge of paper from between the dead man's teeth making the corpse jerk and spin. As Alessandro expected there was a drawing of a flower on the paper. This one was a ranunculus, symbol of death.

Jade and Amber, with Caterina's help, sketched out a family tree in Amber's pink notebook. The complex relationships were easier to understand once they were written down.

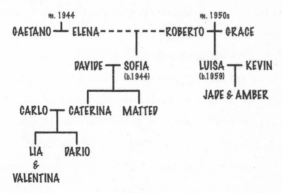

Jade looked at the names Nonno had never heard: his daughter Sofia, his granddaughter Caterina who was sitting here with her and Amber, his grandson Matteo, and his three great-grandchildren. It was cruel that Nonno hadn't had a chance to get to know them.

Coming to Italy was meant to be an end, a winding-up of Nonno's life story. Instead there were puzzles and questions, lots of them: why did Caterina think Nonno was a fascist? What part did Gaetano have to play in this new story? Was he the person who'd threatened to kill Nonno if he came back to Italy? If so, why? Jade's head was spinning. And there was another question, one Jade didn't want to think about but which wouldn't go away: what if the stories Nonno had told them weren't true after all?

From among the cypresses in front of Nico came the sound of a woman's voice singing sweetly. The figure that emerged from between the trees took him completely by surprise. It was an oldish woman, quite bulky, dressed in tweeds and tartan, prodding at the ground with a metal-tipped walking pole as she strode along. She was too intent on staring downwards to see Nico until she'd crossed the grass and reached the chapel steps.

'Sei perso?' she asked in an English accent that made Nico wonder if she'd been taught by Mr Mowatt.

'Yes, I am lost,' he said.

'You're English.'

Nico nodded.

The woman planted the spike of her stick firmly between her tan brogues and leant on it. 'Where are you meant to be?'

'Florence.'

'You're a bit off the beaten track.'

'I was on it – a beaten track – and it brought me here.'

The woman's vast bosom heaved up and down inside her tweed jacket as she laughed. 'I'm Emily Baxendall and you're on my land, sitting on my chapel steps.' She smiled at Nico. 'And you are?'

Nico told her. 'I got on the wrong bus,' he added though it didn't explain why he was stranded on top of a hill in the middle of a forest. It seemed to satisfy Emily Baxendall. She looked at him appraisingly.

'You can't stay here. Come with me and I'll help you back to Florence.'

Years of Hattie's dire warnings made Nico hesitate even though Emily Baxendall was just an old woman with a stick. She pulled the pole from the ground and tapped the spike free of soil on the step.

'You could, of course, try to retrace your steps though I wouldn't recommend it. You'd probably find it difficult and there are wild boar and the odd wolf to look out for.'

'There's wolves?'

'Yes, though I wouldn't want to raise false hope. You're much more likely to see them in winter.'

'Oh, shame,' Nico said.

Emily Baxendall missed the sarcasm. 'Yes it is, isn't it? Wonderful animals, wolves. The boar, however, are not as timid as the wolves and you should do your very best to avoid them.'

Nico decided to give both the wolves and the wild boar a miss and take his chances with the old lady. He stood up.

With a cry of triumph Emily Baxendall lifted her wicked stick and lunged forward.

Caterina put her coffee cup down. 'Why was Luisa born such a long time after Grace married Roberto? My mamma and your mamma are sisters . . .'

'Half-sisters,' Amber snapped. Jade glared at her.

'Yes, half-sisters of course,' Caterina said. 'But look, there are many years between them.'

Jade ran her finger across the line from Elena to Grace. 'Nonno Roberto married our nonna, Grace, in 1955 but she wasn't strong and couldn't have children for a long time. Our mum, Luisa, was born in 1959, five years before you.'

'Granny Grace died having Mum,' Amber added.

'That's very sad,' Caterina said. 'Roberto had to bring up your mother all by himself?'

'Yes, and it was really hard,' Jade said. 'Then, when Mum was only eighteen, Nonno had a bad stroke and she had to look after *him*. It meant she couldn't go to university or anything.'

'And how did she meet your babbo?' Caterina asked.

Jade smiled properly for the first time since she'd sat down with Caterina. She looked meaningfully at Amber and was relieved to see she was smiling too; this was a family story they'd heard over and over.

'Mum was a fan of a rock band called Xtreme Measures . . .' Jade said.

'. . . and Dad was their roadie,' Jade added.

'A "roadie" – I don't know this word,' Caterina said.

'We'll explain,' Jade said, grinning wider than ever, 'it's like this . . .'

Nico leaped from the steps and Emily Baxendall sank to her knees, stabbing the metal spike into the ground by the chapel steps. Her tartan rear-end swayed as she began to dig systematically at the thin soil. Nico went to have a closer look. Emily Baxendall dropped her stick, scrabbled with her fingers for a bit and then sat back with a plant in her grubby hands.

'What is it?' Nico asked.

'*Viperina*, Viper's bugloss,' she said with a sort of manic satisfaction. She began to lever herself up with her stick and Nico bent to take her other arm.

'Thank you, m'dear,' she said, still beaming. 'This is a real beauty for Signor Filipepi's garden. The one I had before died, poor silly specimen that it was.'

Nico didn't think Signor Filipepi, whoever he was, was going to be very thrilled with a weed.

'It's in the lower-right quadrant.'

She's mad, Nico decided, *in a harmless sort of way*.

Emily Baxendall gave the plant to Nico, pulled a camera from her tweed jacket and took several pictures of the place she'd dug the plant from. 'I should've done that before, photographed it *in situ*. It doesn't do to get overexcited but it can't be helped now. Come along, young man. We need to get this catalogued and planted out.'

She strode off, singing, her pleated tartan skirt swinging jauntily over muscled calves in ribbed brown stockings. Nico followed, thinking it odd that such a robust old woman should have a sweet, young-sounding voice.

'What does she do, your mamma?' Caterina asked, still chuckling over the story of Luisa spilling beer over Kevin at a gig in The Seven Stars in Derby.

'She's a cook,' Jade said, picking out one of Luisa's part-time jobs and promoting her from school canteen assistant.

'Do you have a photograph of your mamma and babbo?'

Jade took a small photo out of her wallet and passed it to Caterina. 'This is Mum and Dad.'

'Your mamma and me, we look like sisters!' Caterina said. 'Oh, I would love to meet her.'

'You can't,' Jade said. 'Like we told you, she gets upset when we talk about Nonno's other family.'

'Yes, I remember,' Caterina said wistfully.

'At the moment, she thinks we're in Florence doing a school project with our friend Nico while she's in Lucca with Dad and Nico's parents. We can't let her know we've found you.' And since Caterina thought Nonno was a fascist, Jade was even less keen on Mum finding out what they were doing.

Caterina patted Jade's hand. 'Don't worry, cara, I understand.' She held up the photo. 'Your father is very handsome.'

Jade and Amber laughed outright; they would never, ever, call their father handsome.

'What's his name?'

'Kevin,' Amber said.

Caterina sighed. 'How lovely. I wanted to call Dario "Kevin" – after the American actor Kevin Costner – but my husband wouldn't have a foreign name for his first-born boy. He said if I wanted a name like that it would have to be for another son.' Caterina rolled her eyes. 'I'm too busy with my business to have more boys. I'm sticking with Dario.'

The oak woods gave way to olive groves, vineyards and orchards. Above them sat a large, sprawling building, almost a castle, set on the side of a long sloping hill.

'Neat,' Nico said, admiring the golden-grey stone of the solid towers and stern buttresses basking in the spring sunshine.

'Don't let looks deceive you,' Emily Baxendall said as they reached a gravelled courtyard. 'Only fifty years ago it was partially ruined by bombs, and the owner – who'd joined the wrong side in the war – left it deserted when he fled the Allied army.'

Halfway across the courtyard Emily Baxendall yelled, 'Teo!'

The door of the main building opened and a man – who even Nico could see was astonishingly handsome – peered out. 'Sì, Signora Baxendall,' he said with a wide and charming smile that showcased his beautiful teeth.

'We've got a real little treasure to catalogue.' Mrs Baxendall waved the plant as they swept into a grand hallway with a marble floor. 'And this young man who helped me to find it is Nico Collier. Nico, this is Teo, my gardener and general Mr Fixit.'

Nico and Teo shook hands.

'Teo, stick the kettle on.' Mrs Baxendall thrust the walking pole into a stand by the door and strode into a sitting room with a huge window overlooking the hills. Nico itched to get out his drawing book.

'Spectacular, isn't?' Mrs Baxendall said. 'The Italians have a word for it: "incantevole".'

'Incantevole?'

'Entrancing.'

Entrancing – that was it. Nico felt this scene could hold him captive for ever.

Caterina came back from the home phone. 'That was my husband, Carlo. He's seeing a lawyer about selling our house.'

'You're selling the Villa dei Fiori?!' Amber said.

Caterina waved her hands in mock horror. 'No, no. We are selling our farmhouse further up in the hills. It really belongs to my Nonno Gaetano. He has no use for it and wants to sell it.'

Although it was irrational Jade was relieved. It wasn't as if she was going to come back to the Villa dei Fiori after this holiday so what did it matter to her if it was sold? *Why shouldn't I come back one day*? Jade thought defiantly. *I can always stay in touch and visit again, on my own, in a few years' time. Then I won't have to worry about keeping secrets from Mum.*

'What's the farmhouse like?' Amber asked.

'Abandoned and run-down: the windows are broken, the tiles are slipping off the roof, and there is no hot water or central heating. There isn't even a bathroom. Gaetano had no use for the farmhouse after the war. He and Elena came to live here, with her parents, and Gaetano got a job in a bank, which paid well, much better than working the land.' Caterina laughed. 'Foreigners, they like these old houses. They make them beautiful and use them for holiday homes. I have pictures.' Caterina fetched a glossy folder from the dresser.

Jade and Amber recognised the stone building with its central tower immediately. 'Nonno told us he used to play in a place exactly like this when he was a boy,' Jade said.

'Oh yes, I had forgotten. When he was orphaned he went to live there with Gaetano's family. Roberto and Gaetano were good friends then.'

Jade felt her head spinning. Nonno had lived with Gaetano and been his *friend*! No wonder he'd never mentioned the name when he told them stories about living in the farmhouse and the mischief he and his friend used to get up to there.

'Nonno said he had a best friend but he never told us his name,' Amber said coldly.

Jade recovered her senses. 'He told us his friend's family took him in and treated him like a son. He really, really loved them.'

The strangest expression flitted over Caterina's face; it was incredulous and sad together. Then Caterina was smiling again and Jade wondered if she'd imagined it.

'Can we see it, the farm?' she asked.

'I don't see why not,' Caterina said. 'I haven't seen the old place for years and I'd love to go there again. You would like a tour of the countryside?'

'Yes!' Jade and her sister chorused.

Caterina gathered up the sales brochure. 'Andiamo,' she said.

CHAPTER XI

AS CATERINA DROVE into the overgrown court-yard and stopped by a well Jade wondered how anywhere could be as romantic as this old house set in its clearing among oak trees. The stone façade had been patchily plastered over in places, the roof was missing some of its terracotta tiles and the peeling green shutters were lopsided on their rusty hinges, but the central tower was solid enough to keep a captive prince in. 'It's amazing!'

'It's really nothing special,' Caterina said. 'There were lots of these abandoned houses in the countryside.' She pointed. 'There's always a barn opposite the house, and a place for the chickens and the pigs.' She wrinkled her nose. 'The pigsties were built away from the house – and the lavatories too.'

'Can we see inside?'

'Of course – it's not kept locked – usually only my Nonno Gaetano ever comes here.'

They scrambled out of the car and up the stone steps to the first floor. 'Is it very old?' Jade asked.

Caterina nodded. 'It's mediaeval, built over an Etruscan site. The Etruscans were people who lived here before the Italians, even before the Romans.' That was exactly what Nonno had told Jade and Amber.

The steps were steep and they had to press one hand against the wall for balance. 'Why are we going to the first floor?' Jade asked.

'It's where the living area is. The stables, they are on the ground floor.'

Stables! Jade imagined horses, sleek and glossy, chomping fragrant hay in their stalls while they waited for knights to ride them on fantastic quests. She laughed at herself; according to Nonno there were never any horses here, only a mule and oxen for pulling carts and ploughs.

She stopped at the top of the steps and read an inscription carved into the lintel across the doorway:

VIVA IL DUCE
VIVA IL RE IMPERATORE

'What does it mean?'

'Long live the dictator and long live the emperor king,' Caterina translated.

'I didn't mean that exactly – I mean, why is it there?'

'It was done during the war by the Black Brigade. They came to the farm because they suspected Gaetano was a partisan and hiding a British spy here. They carved the message as a warning to others. Nonno left it here as a reminder that evil is always with us and we have to fight it.'

No, Jade thought, *our nonno said* he *was the one who hid an English spy. They couldn't both have done that – could they? Maybe it was the same spy and they looked after him together?*

'Was he really?' Amber asked. 'Hiding a British spy?'

'Yes, and when the Black Brigade got here they found other partisans too. There was a terrible fight. Gaetano managed to get the spy away, and Elena and some others too.'

'That was lucky,' Jade said, wondering who the 'others' were.

'It was, though not for Gaetano's family. They took them away for deportation – his mother, his sister and her husband, and their little daughter – and when Gaetano's father tried to stop them he was shot dead here, in front of the house.'

From dozens of TV news reports she hardly noticed any more, Jade suddenly recognised the string of small holes gouged across the face of the farmhouse wall for what they were: bullet holes.

Teo handed Mrs Baxendall her tea in a china cup before he lounged into the soft leather sofa with his coffee. As Nico leaned forward to pick up his orange juice he caught sight of familiar books lined up on a shelf. 'You've got all the E. J. Holm novels!'

'You know these books?' Teo asked.

'We've got them at home though not as many as these.' Mrs Baxendall seemed to have several different editions in different languages. 'My mother's mad on them, even more than me. She's exploring Lucca at the moment, chasing up the locations in *The Prince Without a Country* and tomorrow we're going to San Gimignano to look for sites in *Murder in the Fifteenth Tower.*'

'You have read these books also?' Teo asked incredulously.

'Take no notice, Nico, and tell me what you like about them.'

'Everything, though mainly I want to know what's going on with the serial killer and why he keeps leaving flowers with his victims.' Nico grinned. 'Mum says the books only have one flaw.'

'What's that?'

'She doesn't know why Alessandro has to be so tragic all the time.'

'What do you think?'

'Mum says it's because people like being harrowed.'

Teo was mystified: ''arrowed? What is 'arrowed?'

'Tormented,' Mrs Baxendall said. '*Tormentati.*'

'I think it's Alessandro's fate,' Nico said, 'to struggle,

to do his best to try and bring the truth to light even though it costs him.'

'I think so too,' Mrs Baxendall said.

Nico was pleased she understood: Alessandro had seen too much, knew too much about the evil human beings could stoop to. It was his fate to be a tragic hero.

The abandoned house was neat and clean inside. The huge main room, dusty and cool, had its original old table and benches, and there were more seats around the generous fireplace.

'This is where Gaetano and his family sat on winter evenings and told stories to each other,' Caterina said.

And our nonno as well, thought Jade, imagining him as boy, listening open-mouthed while everyone sat around the fire in the flickering darkness with the wind moaning outside. Jade shivered; the people whom Nonno had once sat here with had been killed or taken away to die in a labour camp.

'What sort of stories?' Amber asked.

'Tales of country life – how the peasants worked and worked without stopping – there were chickens and cows and oxen to look after, and the land. They even made sugar from beets and used the leaves of the mulberry trees to feed silkworms.'

'Did they tell ghost stories?'

'Yes, they did! If we have time I'll tell you one some day. For now, let me show you round.'

The rooms off the main hall were empty and desolate except for one with a winding staircase behind its door. 'Where does this lead to?' Jade asked.

'The top of the tower,' Caterina said.

'Whoa!' Amber raced up the stairs. Jade and Caterina went more cautiously. At the top Jade breathed in the scent of the honeysuckle and wild roses scrambling up the sides of the tower. A strengthening wind lifted her hair like a caress. She was almost happier than she'd ever been in her life. If only Caterina hadn't said that Nonno was a fascist.

Mrs Baxendall wanted to plant the viperina as soon as possible. She walked Nico through the garden, down a path leading to a hollow filled with tumbled boulders covered in ancient moss, squeezed past a vast stone head with ferns sprouting from it like wild green hair, and went into a wood.

'Is this all your land?' Nico asked.

'Father's and mine. He bought the land as well as the house after the war.'

'The Second World War?'

'That's right.'

The woodland came to an end on the edge of a small, perfectly circular grove fringed with trees. Garden flowers and wild flowers grew together in the grassy centre. It felt eerily familiar to Nico.

Mrs Baxendall stopped in front of an oddly shaped shrub, fished a trowel out of her pocket, slit the turf and dropped in the viperina. She tamped down the soil and folded back the grass. 'Let's hope it survives.' She stood up and they walked back. By the time they reached the stone face Mrs Baxendall was far away in the past. 'In between making the garden and restoring the house, Father set up the farm. It was hard at first, even when I was old enough to help out. Father was never an easy man and the war did him no favours. When he grew too frail for heavy work, I engaged Teo as our estate manager. He's a treasure.'

'I thought Teo was the gardener.'

'I say that to tease him – he enjoys it. And he does have *pollice verde* – green thumb in English, green fingers as we'd say. He actually manages our land as well as the oil- and wine-bottling plants. He's very good at it – don't let the looks and the charm fool you.'

'Your father, where's he?' Nico asked, hoping he was being tactful. Mrs Baxendall's father had to be ancient – maybe dead or senile as the elderly man at Il Nido was supposed to have been. Though, Nico reminded himself, that was only what the Signora had said. He hadn't been so sure; he thought the old man had simply been enraged about something and lost it, big time.

'He's gone off gallivanting with a friend,' Mrs Baxendall said. She glanced at the sky. 'A storm's coming on. I hope he has the sense to come back before it breaks.'

'It's going to rain,' Caterina said.

Jade peered out of a window. 'How do you know?'

'It usually starts like this, with the wind, and the sky darkening. Soon there'll be a storm. We should go.'

'Can we see the stables first?'

Caterina shook her head. 'We need to get back – we can return another time, if you'd like to.'

'Oh, yes please,' Jade said.

They closed up the house and went out to the car just as the first sizzle of lightning and a huge bang of thunder collided overhead. Amber dived into the back seat.

'Chicken!' Jade said getting in the front. A warming sense of satisfaction spread through her as they drove out of the courtyard and down the stony path through the trees. Amber was the brave one, the strong one, except where thunderstorms were concerned. She'd lie on the back seat all the way to the Villa dei Fiori, arms over her head. Only pride would stop her from shrieking. Jade, on the other hand, wasn't scared at all.

'How long will it last?' she asked Caterina.

'Oh, for a long time, two or three hours maybe.'

There was a moan from the back seat. Jade smiled and

settled back to watch lightning dart around the purple hills.

Mrs Baxendall explained her obsession with flowers. 'As a way of supplementing my income I write about life in Italy. At the moment I'm researching Tuscan flora, which is why I'm busy collecting plants.'

'You have to write for Mrs Bax where you found the viperina,' Teo said.

'Why me?'

'Each flower and plant I find,' Mrs Baxendall said, 'has its own biography, including where and how it was located. And whoever discovers it has to write the account.'

Nico was doubtful; he'd not really discovered the plant, the viperina had simply been flowering next to his foot as he sat on the chapel steps. It was Mrs Baxendall who'd spotted it.

Teo was looking at Nico sympathetically. 'You have to do it. She make me write about the cornflower I find when I fall over the gate helping her to run away from the sheep.'

Teo turned to the old lady. 'You 'arrow me, you 'arrow him.'

'It's fine, I want to help,' Nico said. He liked Mrs Bax and Teo and wanted to keep in touch. He looked at his phone. With a jolt, he registered the time.

'I can't do it now – I have to get back to my mother.' He'd forgotten all about Mum. 'I can write it when I get back to the flat and bring it the day after tomorrow if you like?'

'Then so you shall, caro,' Mrs Bax agreed. 'We're out of the way of buses as you know,' she said. 'It might be easiest if I collect you and it'll be useful for me – I've someone I need to meet in Florence. Shall we say at about ten?'

'Yes.' Mum and the others would be well gone by then, on their way to Torre del Lago to soak up the seaside atmosphere of *The Coloratura Assassin*.

Still, he ought to explain the situation at home to Mrs Baxendall and that meant explaining about the twins too. Nico gave an edited version of the truth saying that Jade and Amber were visiting relatives in their grandfather's home town and he'd meant to join up with them in Borgo Sant'Angelo but couldn't because he caught the wrong bus.

'Who are these relatives?' Mrs Baxendall asked.

Nico thought that was an odd question at the same time as he realised he'd given away information about the twins' secret. Truthfully, he said, 'I don't know.'

'So, your parents aren't aware that you and your friends are roaming around Tuscany on your own?' Mrs Bax said.

'It's for the best really, our mothers get worried, especially mine. She thinks the world's out to get me.'

'What the eye doesn't see the heart doesn't grieve over. You're protecting your mother while stretching your wings and flying freely on your own.'

'I suppose.' It was a generous interpretation; Nico only wanted the stretching wings part. Mum didn't need any protecting now: she had the muppet James.

Jade and Amber helped Caterina chop vegetables for lunch. They weren't used to it. Amber was slicing a courgette into large random lumps. 'We get our food from the supermarket.'

'In Italy we do things the correct way,' Caterina said firmly, taking over the courgettes and dicing them neatly.

Jade couldn't help laughing as she hacked at a pepper. Her family were all for short cuts and ready meals and chips and kebabs. 'Nonno had an allotment,' she said to show they did actually eat fresh food, sometimes. 'Mum still goes there.'

'What is "allotment"?' Caterina asked.

Jade explained about Nonno's little plot down by the railway line and how they used to go there together, especially when they were small.

'You were so close to your nonno?'

Jade nodded. 'I suppose because we lived in the same house. Dad moved in when he married Mum and they looked after Nonno together.'

'Gaetano is very old and we want him to move here

with us but always he says, Not yet. It was good that your family helped each other.'

'It was hard for Mum,' Jade said.

'We loved Nonno telling us about Italy – how he missed it,' Amber said, waving her knife. 'He made us speak Italian to him – then he felt less homesick.'

'Dad wouldn't even try and learn Italian,' Jade added. 'Mum said he didn't have to. It never mattered because Nonno could speak English all right, he just wouldn't.'

'He definitely forgot his English after his second stroke,' Amber recalled. 'He hardly said anything, in any language.'

'That's true.' Jade turned to Caterina, trying hard to turn the conversation around and stop Amber getting even more angry. 'But before it he told us what it was like when he was a boy here. Yesterday we found the pool where he used to swim and it was exactly like he'd said.' Jade stopped chopping her peppers. 'It's weird though – the Villa dei Fiori isn't like he described it.'

'The outside is,' Amber said, 'it's the inside that's different.'

'The house changed,' Caterina said, 'because things are different from when your nonno was a boy.'

'He's your nonno too,' Jade said.

Caterina nodded. 'I know, cara.' She added the vegetables to a sauce simmering on the hob. 'It was the war and its aftermath that brought changes. My nonno and nonna – Gaetano and Elena – left the old farmhouse with its sad memories and came to live here. After Elena's parents died, she inherited the house. Gaetano worked hard and paid for the house to be improved. Nonna Elena was so proud of this kitchen!

'When my mamma, Sofia, married, she and my babbo moved in. Soon my little brother and I arrived and it was then that Nonno and Nonna decided to move to a flat in the town.' Caterina sighed. 'Things changed again and Nonna Elena died and then my babbo. Now I live here with my husband and our children, and my mamma of course.'

Caterina leaned forward and stroked Amber's face gently. 'Cara, try not to be angry. I'm glad you came to us. My brother and I have talked about Roberto – who, as you said, is our nonno too – we wondered what he was doing in England and whether we would ever meet him. We thought it was too late. And then . . .' Caterina's smile blossomed. It was impossible to believe she wasn't truly glad. '. . . you and Jade came with your letter.'

'Have you told Sofia?' Jade asked.

'I rang Mamma. She is eager to see you if she can though she won't be back from Milan for a while.'

Caterina stirred the sauce. 'We would like to learn more from you about Roberto. We can meet up again soon perhaps?'

'We're going out with Mum and Dad and some friends

tomorrow,' Jade said. 'We can try and come the day after, on Friday.'

'We'll bring pictures and stuff,' Amber said. 'Then you'll believe us that Nonno cared.'

'I do believe you, cara. It must be a terrible misunderstanding.' Caterina shook her head.

'We'll sort it,' Jade said. Caterina was right, someone had told her lies – the question was, who? And why?

A car horn blared. 'Time to go,' Mrs Baxendall said. 'Teo's going to run you home if you don't mind a short detour – and if you can survive his driving.'

Nico joined Teo in an old 4x4.

'Goodbye, my dears, safe journey.' Mrs Bax waved and the car crept past a small loggia, then gathered speed and shot through a crenelated gateway guarded by two grumpy-looking stone lions crouched on plinths. At that moment, the sky let go of the rain it had been carrying closer all morning. Torrents of water thrashed at the windows and hail clashed on the roof like handfuls of broken glass. At the end of the road Teo swerved abruptly left and drove fast under trees bending in the wind as if they were trying to grab the car and hurl it over the top of the woods. He drove with macho panache though the road was barely visible except when lightning momentarily lit the way and showed Nico how close they were to the drop down the hillside. He closed his eyes. He didn't care how

143

Teo got him to Florence; he just wanted to get there in one piece.

The storm reached its climax: rain veiled the windows and the sounds of wind and thunder filled the house. Jade listened to Caterina begin the grace. She sneaked a glance at Amber. She was frowning again. Nonno always used to say grace. Now no one bothered any more.

Suddenly the door flew open and threw in a slop of rain and a small explosion of wind that swept in two figures holding waxed jackets over their heads. The taller one shook off his coat and a glitter of raindrops flew from his dark hair. He beamed at Caterina. 'I came as soon as I could.'

'That's got to be the little brother, Matteo,' Amber whispered.

Jade nodded. With those looks it couldn't be anyone else. 'Who's the other?' she whispered back.

Jade began to say, 'No idea,' then stopped, eyes wide in amazement as the figure shucked off its coat and ran a hand through its spiky wet hair.

'Nico!' she said, 'what are you doing here?'

Gaetano knew from the look on Roberto's face that his hopes had been shattered and the rejoicing in the farmhouse was almost more than he could bear.

'The war will soon be over,' Tecla sang, twirling round with her little daughter laughing in her arms while her husband beat out a drum roll of victory on the table. Even Babbo was smiling as he chewed on his half-smoked cigarette and twiddled with the dial on the radio repeating the astonishing news: the Duce had been overthrown.

Mamma put her hand gently on Roberto's shoulder. 'You should be glad. Did you want me to lose both my sons in a senseless war?'

'No.' Roberto shook his head. 'I'll go for a walk and think for a while.'

Mamma nodded. 'That's a good idea. Go into town and see if you can find any rice for sale.' She gave Roberto money. He smiled faintly and left. Gaetano noticed him pause at the door and glance back into the room, his face dark with anger.

Gaetano snatched up his jacket and followed his foster

brother. 'Wait!' Roberto was running down the track. Gaetano caught up with him.

'Leave me alone!'

'Not when you're in this mood.'

'How do you expect me to be? I'm sickened by how happy you all are. The father of our nation has been betrayed by the king and that puppet Badoglio and none of you care!' Roberto turned his back on Gaetano and refused to talk all the way into town. It was even worse for him there: red flags were flying everywhere, people danced in the streets and the local band was busy playing in celebration. Gaetano tried to distract him. 'Let's look for that rice.'

'You'll be lucky.'

Roberto was right; celebrating townspeople or not, there was still no rice for sale. Food was getting increasingly scarce.

The boys trudged back home. Without discussing it they avoided the Villa dei Fiori where Elena lived. Her family would be happy that the king had deposed the Duce. They headed for the pool in the woods. Elena was there, sitting under a tree. The boys sat, one on either side of her.

'I know you're sad,' she said to Roberto. 'But think how wonderful it is that there won't be any more killing.'

'General Badoglio . . .' Roberto almost choked on the name of the Duce's usurper. 'General Badoglio said that we're still going to be fighting with the Germans.'

'No one believes that. Try to be glad. I'd hate to lose you. And Gaetano too, of course.'

Gaetano didn't miss Elena's hurried addition, or the fact that thinking of Roberto first didn't ease his foster brother's despair.

The situation grew worse a few weeks later when the Allies landed in the south and Italy signed an Armistice with them. It wasn't only Roberto who was dismayed: the German reaction was swift and the army immediately requisitioned the Villa dei Fiori. The soldiers were friendly enough but Gaetano and Roberto were forbidden to go there even to see Elena.

Then fortune swung round again: the Germans rescued the Duce and he set up a new government, far away in the north.

'I don't know why you're happy about it,' Gaetano said to Roberto. 'The Black Brigades are sweeping through the country on a raking. You don't really want them to force you into the army do you?'

'No, of course I don't. I'm going to hide in the hills with you like Babbo said.'

'We'd better make sure we're not seen – you know the penalty for running away.'

'Execution,' Roberto said. 'I don't intend to get caught any more than you do.'

Still, Gaetano didn't quite trust his foster brother and didn't let him know when he joined the resistance. If Roberto suspected anything when Gaetano slipped away each evening to train with the partisans he made no comment. He continued to work hard on the farm and run for cover when there was danger of being caught by the Black Brigade.

Ilaria also had plans: she went to work for the Fascist mayor of Borgo Sant'Angelo and acted as a staffetta or courier, passing useful information on his activities to the resistance movement.

Elena stayed at the Villa dei Fiori, meekly carrying out her day-to-day chores and duties. Gaetano knew that because, despite Babbo's orders, he and Roberto went there to see her.

Nothing changed until one day Roberto went to visit Elena during a Black Brigade raking and didn't return. His foster mother was inconsolable. Gaetano couldn't help feeling relief; it meant that he would be freer to carry on with his partisan training.

That was the situation I entered when I parachuted into the hills one gloomy winter's dawn in late 1943. I was met by a group of partisans who escorted me to the farmhouse. There Gaetano's family hid me until the fateful day when we were betrayed.

CHAPTER XII

MURDER IN THE Fifteenth Tower, set in the medi-aeval hill town of San Gimignano, was Nico's second favourite E. J. Holm novel. Alessandro was staying there with his friend Bruno whose daughter Tania was Alessandro's goddaughter. During the visit, a wealthy jeweller was murdered and Alessandro was ordered to investigate immediately.

Nico, Mum and Luisa went to the church of Sant'Agostino to see where Alessandro had begun his enquiries. A fresco near the doorway had made a big impression on the detective and he returned to it several times in the book. Remembering Mum's jibes about the painting in the Uffizi, Nico let her and Luisa monopolise the picture while he sat on a pew and read a passage from *Murder in the Fifteenth Tower*:

> *A small group of officials stood round a shrouded body lying beside the door.*
>
> *'It's a strange one,' the Carabinieri chief said as*

he pulled back the sheet covering old Franco Zilli's body.

Alessandro examined the thick gold chain digging deeply into Zilli's scrawny neck. 'Strangulation. What's so strange about it?'

'Not that. Look here.' The officer jerked the sheet further back to reveal the jeweller's right hand. A paper knife was thrust through the palm. Alessandro leaned closer. The knife was incised with a simple 'Z', the Zilli trademark. That was curious but Alessandro was more interested in the design of laurels etched along the gold handle.

Had Mum finished? No, she was talking in respectful whispers to Luisa who had lit a candle. Nico supposed it was to remember her father. He flipped to another passage in the book, towards the end where Alessandro, spiritless and bereft, stood for a long time in front of the painting.

When Nico next looked up, Mum and Luisa were gone. He went to the fresco and saw immediately what had mesmerised Alessandro. Although the painting was a crucifixion it wasn't *The Man of Sorrows* who had held Alessandro's attention, or the mysterious floating hands and disembodied heads; it was the face of St John, transfixed by silent grief. It mirrored Alessandro's feelings about his beloved Semiramide exactly.

Nico stayed with the painting, thinking about grief.

His life had been mercifully short of it; no one he knew well had died or suffered. What would it feel like, he wondered? He hoped he wouldn't find out for a long, long time.

Outside the city gates Jade and Amber sat on a parapet, swinging their feet from side to side. It was hard to be angry when you were perched on a wall overlooking miles and miles of peaceful countryside dotted with cypress trees and vineyards and with the sun softly stroking your skin. Jade sighed and blew her fringe away from her forehead. 'Don't be mad, Amb.'

Amber stared straight ahead. 'Oh, I haven't got anything to be mad about, have I? Only that my sister thinks our nonno was a fascist and a liar.'

'I don't think either – I told you that last night.'

They'd argued about it for hours. Because Jade said they should ask more questions about Nonno and what he was supposed to have done, Amber had lost her temper, big time. She was still angry.

'I'm just saying, Caterina might've been told the wrong story and we ought to ask her for more details, so we can get it sorted.'

Amber shrugged. Jade knew the subject was closed. 'You want to go for a walk or something?' she asked.

Amber shrugged again and carried on glaring into space.

There was only one thing to do with her sister in this mood – leave her alone. Jade jumped off the wall and went through the gates into the town. She switched off her mobile. If Amber was in such a strop, Jade didn't even want to speak to her.

All E. J. Holm's books had maps of the places Alessandro visited and Nico used the one in *Murder in the Fifteenth Tower* to find his way round the twisting streets of San Gimignano. The one thing he couldn't do was go to the fifteenth tower: E. J. Holm had made that up. Only fourteen out of the original seventy-two straight-sided towers that had once swaggered against the skyline were still standing. Nico thought it must have looked like a scaled-down medieval version of Manhattan. When he got to where the fifteenth tower should have been he found a shop selling traditional ceramics. He went inside to get a present for Mrs Baxendall and chose a blue bowl. She could put some of her flowers in it – if she ever cut them. He'd doodled pictures of her strange garden while he was writing about the viperina. He was sure he'd seen it before and it was driving him mad trying to think where.

After he'd paid for the bowl he wandered round the town still thinking about Mrs Baxendall, and Teo. It was strange that he'd turned out to be related to the twins. Had Mrs Baxendall somehow recognised the girls' names, made the connection and then sent Teo to check them out? Nico didn't see how it was possible. Anyway, just why were so many people interested in the Thompsons? The Signora had obviously set up the dinner at Il Nido so that all those ancient people could inspect Luisa, and now Teo had been dragged in as well. And Nico was certain that the angry old man at the restaurant hadn't been part of Signora Minardi's plan; she'd been as startled as everyone else when he turned up and started ranting. Who was he and where did he fit in?

Jade turned up a steep alleyway with wide steps at the top leading to an even steeper street where she bumped into Nico who was coming down the other way.

'Hi,' he said. 'Are you lost?'

'No, I'm looking for a gelateria. I fancied an ice cream.'

'Follow me!' Nico led the way to a busy ice cream parlour with *Pluripremiata Gelateria* painted over the door.

'That's an unusual name,' Nico said.

Jade laughed. 'It's not a name – it means multi-award-winning.'

'Oh. That's another minus for my Italian teacher.'

They bought their ice creams and wandered away from the milling tourists.

'Does it bother you, not telling your mum what you're really doing in Florence?' Jade asked.

'In principle, yes,' Nico said, 'but it makes life a lot

easier so, no it doesn't, not really. What about you? Are you going to tell your mum about Caterina and the rest of the family?'

'Amber says we ought to stick to our original plan and not let Mum know anything. I'm not sure.'

'Why?'

'Meeting Caterina and the others turned out all different from what we expected.'

'Why? What did you expect?'

'We thought they'd be mad at us just turning up without warning, or not interested. And we only planned how to get to the Villa dei Fiori, not what was going to happen after that or what to do if things went wrong. It's all got so, so . . .' Jade waved her ice cream cone around in frustration.

'Intense?' Nico suggested.

'Yeah, that's it, intense. Now we don't know what to do. All me and Amber have done since yesterday is argue. I don't even know what to *think* any more.'

'There's a place where we can talk privately if you want to,' Nico said. 'La Rocca – it's where Alessandro went for peace and quiet in one of the books.'

'Alessandro! I might've known.'

They walked in friendly silence, finishing off their ice creams as they made their way to a hollowed-out fortress with fig and olive trees growing inside.

'You know good places,' Jade said.

'It's not me, it's Alessandro – and E. J. Holm who puts him in them.'

They perched on a tomb-shaped stone bench set in a large alcove in the wall and basked in the sun.

'Have you started *The Shattered Mirror* yet?' Nico asked.

'Give me a chance – you only gave it me last night!'

'I didn't mean to pressure you, it was just you said you wanted to read about the partisan stuff.'

Jade relented and touched his arm to show she was joking. 'I was going to read it, honest.' She pulled a face. 'I didn't get a chance – I got into an argument with Amber and then I was too tired. I'll read it tonight.'

'No hurry, you've got other things on your mind.'

Jade decided to go straight in with her problem before she lost her nerve. 'You know we told you *why* we didn't want Mum to know we're seeing Nonno's relatives?'

'Yes, because she gets upset if anyone mentions his Italian family, right?'

'Right. But things have got even more complicated.' Jade told Nico everything she'd kept quiet about after he'd turned up at the Villa dei Fiori with Teo, including the fact that Caterina thought Nonno had been a fascist and that somebody *had* threatened to kill him.

'Is that what you and Amber were rowing about?'

'That and the fact I think Caterina's nice. Amber doesn't trust her.' Jade sighed. 'She's right about one thing: I can't really see Mum believing the family want to be friends with us now. And she's never going to have it that Nonno was a fascist.'

'Even if it's the truth?'

Jade winced. She didn't want to admit to herself that it might be true, let alone to Nico. How could she? Nonno had helped bring her up and he loved her. 'It can't be true. He loved me and Amber. *Really* loved us. He was so proud of us. He used to call us his little treasures and take us down to the Italian Club in town to show us off. We used to dance and sing . . .'

Jade's eyes blurred with tears and two small and slender saplings in front of her seemed to sway in a dance as she and Amber had danced for the lonely exiles in the smoky club far away from their homeland. Grief sprang at her from out of nowhere, clutching with a grip as strong as fear. 'I miss him,' she whispered. 'I miss him so much – I miss his smile, I miss his voice. I just miss him.'

Jade felt Nico's arm round her shoulders. She leaned gratefully against his chest and wept.

Nico's phone rang.

'Sorry,' he said and Jade sat up.

'Yes?' he snapped. 'Yes, Mum, Jade's here . . . But I haven't had time to *draw* even! All right – we're coming.' He flipped the phone shut. 'I'm sorry; we've got to go. They've rounded up Amber and they're mad because they can't find us.'

'It's OK, I feel better now.' Jade sniffed and swiped at her eyes with a tissue. 'Does it show I've been crying?'

'Your eyes are a bit puffy, and your nose's pink. I'd do your make-up if I were you.'

'What about your mum?'

'She can wait,' Nico said firmly.

Jade thought Nico was doing a good job of standing up to Hattie.

As the hot and stifling bus lurched its way back to Florence, Mum went on justifying dragging Nico away from San Gimignano. 'There wasn't much point in staying – we'd seen the sites to do with Alessandro. Going back to Florence now means we can go across the river and find the places in *The Shattered Mirror*.'

Nico could hardly say he'd found them already. 'I wanted to stay longer, to see the medieval chemist's and the Etruscan horses.'

'We did those while you were busy sunbathing in La Rocca,' James said.

Nico wasn't going to let him get away with that. 'It doesn't matter. I saw the most important thing, in Sant'Agostino.'

Once the words were out of his mouth he realised they were true: the fresco in Sant'Agostino was at the heart of *Murder in the Fifteenth Tower*. And spending time with Jade instead of being a sad tourist like

James meant he and Jade had . . . had what? Holding Jade when she was upset didn't necessarily mean anything. She hadn't sat next to him on the bus – she was next to Amber at the back talking quietly. That was good, they were friends again and he didn't want to butt in.

He thought about his conversation with Jade, about how she missed her grandfather. He wasn't close to his grandparents – literally: Mum's parents had retired to rural France and were a remote if kindly presence and his father's parents had died before Nico was even born.

*Nobody means that much to m*e, *except Mum and Dad and that's only in the holidays*, Nico thought. He had friends at school and the house masters were OK but they were temporary family; Nico would never grieve for any of them the way Jade was mourning her lost nonno.

Nico found the page in *Murder in the Fifteenth Tower* where Alessandro organised a search for Bruno and Tania who had disappeared. Their bodies were found early next morning on a riverbank.

Tania lay sweetly in her father's embrace at the water's edge, a faint breeze teasing a strand of her dark hair. Alessandro stooped and pulled out the paper clutched in his goddaughter's small hand. On it was an exquisite painting of a forget-me-not. Alessandro crushed it in his fist, hurled it into the river and walked away.

The Signora was having a party. Jade leaned over the balcony, listening to the old lady's guests having a good time. She felt a bit resentful; Amber was fast asleep despite the noise while she was stuck listening to these wrinklies laughing and joking and clinking their glasses. She'd had a difficult day thinking about Nonno and she was angry that the world in general wasn't as sad as she was.

One of the guests came out into the garden. He walked in the careful way of the old and frail to the table and chairs at the end of the tiny garden. He sat, lit by bright moonlight, and sipped at a glass of wine.

He's got a nice face, Jade thought, examining his serene profile, *a bit like Nonno's*. She felt a tad stalkerish, observing the man while he had no idea she was there. She moved to go back inside and jolted the washing line. The rattle of the pulleys caught the old man's attention and he turned and saw Jade. Half his face broke into a gentle smile. He lifted his glass. 'Buona sera, Signorina.'

Jade returned his salute with a wave. 'Buona sera, Signor,' she said and went back inside.

She sat on her bed, stomach churning. The old man only had half a proper face; the other half was ravaged, distorted, the eye a blank socket, the left side of the mouth twisted into a grimace. Gradually her shock drained away and she began to feel ashamed of her reaction to what she'd seen and for shrinking into self-pity over

Nonno. Whatever pain she experienced was insignificant compared with the physical pain the old man must've gone through to end up being that disfigured. She shivered; she needed a distraction from disturbing thoughts. Nico's book would do it. She picked it up from her bedside table and got into bed. She'd only read a couple of pages when her eyelids drooped and the book slid out of her hand onto the floor. *I'll get it in a minute,* she thought as her eyes closed. Within a minute she fell into a deep, mercifully dreamless, sleep.

CHAPTER XIII

MUM AND JAMES were looking for the guidebook in their room. That was good – Mrs Bax wasn't due to pick Nico up for another half hour and Mum was bound to have found the book before then. Nico opened his journal and re-read the last entry.

James's voice rose and fell in irritated bursts like the heart trace of someone with palpitations. Mum's soothed over it like a patient nurse.

Nico flipped to his drawing of Mrs Bax's garden, its tiny strokes of hatching and cross-hatching building up to darken the shadows in the grove. The feeling of recognition he'd felt when he walked in the glade with Mrs Bax crept over him again. He held the book out at arm's length and squinted at the drawing, willing himself to understand. All at once he did. It was so obvious!

He left the journal on the table and went to his room to check through his stack of pamphlets. There it was – a picture of Mrs Baxendall's garden. The painter was Alessandro Filipepi, always known by his nickname of Botticelli, or 'Little Barrel'. Now Nico understood why Mrs Bax was collecting flowers and weeds and planting them in her garden. Nico grinned and imagined himself confronting Mrs Bax with the evidence like Alessandro Lupo confronting the murderer in one of E. J. Holm's novels. He stopped grinning when he got back to the living room and saw Mum reading his journal.

'What are you doing?' He tried to grab it back.

Mum clutched it to her chest. 'Just who are these people you've been meeting behind my back?'

Nico clenched his fists to stop himself from ripping the book out of Mum's hands. 'You read my journal – my *private* journal.'

'Never mind that, you've been lying to me – swanning off by yourself – accepting lifts from total strangers – going to their houses in the middle of nowhere!' Mum's voice rose in stages of pitch and intensity as though she were practising arpeggios. James appeared looking startled.

'Anything could've happened!' Mum shrieked in a perfect top C.

'You read my journal!' Nico stepped forward, his face grim.

Mum clutched the book closer. 'You got lost in a forest!'

'What?' James said.

'Shut up!' Hattie and Nico yelled together.

'Don't tell me to shut up,' James said. 'Calm down, Hattie.'

'Don't tell me to calm down, you patronising fool.' Mum burst into tears and sank into a chair. Nico took the opportunity to wrestle the book from her.

'I can't believe you did that – read my *private* journal.' He glared at his mother. She was going to spoil everything.

'Have you got it safe?' Amber asked Jade.

'Yep, it's in my bag, stop stressing.'

'I'm not – I'm just checking.'

Dad stuck his head round the bedroom door. 'Come on, girls, we're going to be late.' He picked up Jade's bag. 'This's heavy – what you got inside?'

'Project stuff.' Jade took the bag from Dad, slung it over her shoulder and led the way downstairs to the Collier-Croziers. They were going to wait with Nico while the adults started out for Torre del Lago.

Even through the heavy apartment door they could hear shouting.

'Knock and they'll stop,' Mum said.

Dad thumped on the door and there was an abrupt silence. Then the door opened and James beckoned them in. Hattie was wiping her eyes with a tissue and Nico was looking daggers at her. James locked the French windows casually, as though the atmosphere wasn't zinging with tension. Jade tried to catch Nico's eye but he carried on staring at Hattie, lips tight with fury, his skull earring trembling menacingly.

Dad coughed. 'Are you ready?'

'No,' Hattie said. 'We're not going.'

'I am,' James said. Jade admired his calmness.

'Then I'll stay on my own, with Nico,' Hattie said.

'If you stay with Nico you won't be on your own,' James pointed out.

'I'm not staying,' Nico said.

'Oh yes you are!' Hattie shrilled.

'No, I'm not.'

Jade stared from Nico to Hattie and back again. This was the kind of argument that could go on forever if someone didn't break it up.

Amber came to the rescue. 'What's up? Is Nico in trouble?' she asked.

'Yes, he's in trouble,' Hattie said tearfully. 'He wasn't in Florence on Wednesday – he was gallivanting in the mountains with total strangers.'

How did Hattie know? Jade stared in horror at Nico. Had he said anything about her and Amber and what *they'd* been doing?

'She read my journal,' Nico said. 'About how I got on the wrong bus and met an Englishwoman called Mrs Baxendall.' Nico glared pointedly at Hattie. 'A nice *old* English woman who saved me from getting gored by wild boars.'

James perked up. 'You were threatened by wild boars?'

'No, I'm exaggerating, like you do.'

Jade wondered if she could relax a bit. Nico obviously hadn't said anything about meeting her family at the Villa dei Fiori or what she'd discussed with him in La Rocca.

'Wait a minute.' Hattie stared at Jade and Amber. 'You were supposed to be with Nico. Did you know about this?'

There was no point in lying. 'Yes,' Jade said.

'Where were you then?' Dad asked.

Jade patted her bag. 'Doing the project like we said. Nico wanted to see the frescoes properly in San Giovanni so he told us where to go in Florence and he went to Borgo Sant'Angelo. He got on the wrong bus and got lost.'

'Mrs Baxendall wanted me to ring you from her landline,' Nico said to Hattie, 'I didn't because I knew you'd just go off on one. I was quite safe, Mother.'

'Safe! Safe! This Mrs Baxendale . . .'

'Baxendall,' Nico snapped.

'Mrs whatever-her-name-is – she's a madwoman!' Hattie appealed to James. 'You didn't read about her in that journal.'

'You shouldn't have either, Hattie.'

'What?'

'You shouldn't have read Nico's diary.'

'What?' Hattie couldn't seem to believe what James

had said. Jade couldn't wait to hear what was coming next.

'He seems to have managed quite well to me. You do over-react, Hattie . . .'

Hattie gathered breath. James ignored her.

'. . . it's only natural he didn't tell you. If he'd phoned you'd have had hysterics, got a taxi from Lucca and gone to pick him up when he was managing fine by himself.'

Hattie blew. 'Hysterics! I'm a mother concerned for her child. You know nothing of how a mother feels.'

'Since I'm a man I don't see how you can expect me to.'

Dad coughed. 'We've got to go.' Jade knew her father didn't like scenes and wanted to escape.

'Right,' James said. 'Come on, Hattie.'

'I'm not going, I told you.'

'Please yourself.'

It was a total stand-off.

There was a knock at the door. Everyone swung round and stared as James opened it. 'Yes?'

'Good morning,' a very English voice said. 'May I speak to Mrs Collier?'

'And you are?'

'Mrs Baxendall!' Nico ran to the door.

'I know I'm early, m'dear,' Mrs Baxendall said, beaming, 'I wanted to meet your mother. Make sure she knows I'm *bona fide* and not some mad child abductor.'

Nico ushered her up to Hattie. 'Mother, this is Mrs Baxendall, the lady who rescued me in the forest.'

Emily Baxendall pumped Hattie's hand up and down. 'Glad to meet you – and "rescued" is rather an exaggeration.'

Nico introduced her to everyone else before sitting her down next to Mum.

'I can see you're ready for the off,' Mrs Baxendall said. 'I won't keep you – just wanted to give you my contact details.' She passed a sheet of paper to Hattie. 'Here you are – phone me anytime.'

Hattie took the paper. The room, bright with the sun hammering impatiently on the glass, was silent. Everyone waited to see if Hattie was going to give in. Jade didn't think so: only a miracle was going to get Hattie to back down from the noisy stand she'd made.

'By the by,' Mrs Baxendall said, 'I've got something for you. Nico told me you enjoy the Alessandro Lupo novels and I thought the latest E. J. Holm might be just the ticket.' She gave Hattie a book.

Hattie held it reverently. 'But it's not out till next month!' She opened it with exaggerated care. 'It's signed! How did you manage that?' she said in awe. 'E. J. Holm never does book signings.'

'I've written histories and travel books about Italy,' Mrs Baxendall said, 'and Holm and I have the same agent. She always sends me an advance copy of his novels and she keeps a stack of signed book plates for the favoured few.'

'But it's yours.'

Jade almost laughed out loud. Hattie was clinging to the book tighter than she'd clung to Nico's journal. She wasn't going to give it up without a struggle.

Mrs Baxendall smiled. 'I can get another. Please, do accept it.'

Yes, Hattie, take it, Jade urged silently. *Then we can get going.*

'It's very kind of you,' Hattie said quietly, her cheeks pink.

'Don't mention it. Nico told me you're off to Torre del Lago today. Isn't that the setting for *The Coloratura Assassin*?'

'Yes.'

Luisa coughed for attention. 'We ought to go now, Hattie. You can read the book on the train.'

Hattie caved in. 'What were your plans for today, Nico?' she asked primly.

'I'm going to Mrs Baxendall's.'

In the silence that followed Mrs Baxendall glanced from Hattie to Nico. 'I see you didn't tell your mother,' she said and shook her head. 'You can't come with me unless she agrees.'

'Mum?' Nico said.

Hattie looked sternly at him. 'Make sure you behave yourself for Mrs Baxendall,' she said.

Jade smirked as Nico grunted, 'OK.' He'd won the argument and got his way even though his mother had really embarrassed him.

'And what about you two?' Dad asked Jade and Amber. 'What were your plans?'

'We were going to do research on our own,' Jade said. It was true: they *were* doing research, just not on Michelangelo and not in Florence.

Mrs Baxendall slapped her knees. 'Would you like a lift to the railway station?' she asked Hattie.

'That would be very kind.'

Jade had a hard time not snorting at Hattie's meekness.

'I'll be back for you directly, Nico,' Mrs Baxendall said. 'I take it the young ladies will be staying in Florence all day?'

Before Jade had a chance to perjure herself Nico leaped to the door and yanked it open and Mrs Baxendall swept all the adults out.

The room was very quiet without Hattie's shrieking and the old lady's cheerfully loud voice.

'Did you write about us in that diary thing?' Amber demanded.

'No. I never mention you. It isn't any of my business.'

'Too right.'

Jade shook her head at her sister – there was such a thing as being too critical. 'Thanks, Nico,' she said.

'No bother. I suppose you're going back to your relatives in Borgo Sant'Angelo?'

The girls exchanged a quick look. 'Yes, we are,' Amber said grudgingly. 'We're going to prove they're wrong about Nonno.'

Jade didn't want to start that all over again. 'Come on or we'll miss the bus.' She smiled at Nico. 'See you later. We can compare notes.'

Amber grunted a 'bye' and the twins left Nico to himself.

Mrs Baxendall was gone a long time. Nico wondered if she'd got caught in traffic. He decided to wait for her outside. As he opened the flat door he was surprised to hear Mrs Baxendall's loud voice coming up from the lobby. She was talking to someone with a softer voice and Nico couldn't identify the speaker. He closed the apartment door and went down the stairs to find Mrs Baxendall deep in conversation with the Signora. They were so engrossed they didn't notice Nico. He drew back against the wall, his mind racing. From the easy and familiar way the women spoke to each other Nico could tell they were old friends. It explained quite a bit: if the Signora, who was interested in the Thompsons for some reason, had told Mrs Baxendall all about them, she would have recognised the girls' names when Nico told her about them and their mock project. She might even have sent

Teo to the Villa dei Fiori on purpose. What were these two old ladies up to?

Nico listened carefully, cursing his poor Italian, which wasn't nearly good enough to help him understand more than a few words here and there: '. . . serata . . . spaghettata . . . Volpe . . . Alec . . .'

He was getting nowhere. He pushed away from the wall and carried on down the stairs. The conversation stopped and the Signora smiled politely before going into her flat without speaking to him.

Mrs Baxendall wasn't put out. 'Come along, m'dear,' she said, ushering Nico out to her old car. 'Tell me what you wrote about discovering the viperina.'

Clearly Mrs Baxendall's conversation with the Signora wasn't up for discussion. 'I've brought it with me.'

'Good man.'

He read his report out to Mrs Baxendall as she negotiated the chaotic traffic on the outskirts of Florence. 'Just what I wanted,' she said when he'd finished.

'I found out more.'

'Oh?'

'The glade where you planted the viperina – it's exactly like the one in the *Primavera*. I can't believe I didn't see it straight away.'

'We often don't see what's right under our noses.'

'But I know that painting really well.'

'My garden isn't a painting.'

No, Nico thought, though it was a brilliantly mad idea, bringing a fantasy to life. 'It's never going to grow exactly like Botticelli's meadow, is it?'

'Hardly, since he made up quite a few of his plants. Besides, it wasn't my intention, at least not at first. It started after I'd had an argument with my father one spring morning – I had a fearsome temper as a girl – and stormed off into the hills. I flung myself down, full of self-pity, and found myself nose to nose with a wild iris, a tiny perfect thing exactly like the one in the *Primavera*. I dug it up, showed Father. He suggested I make a garden. It kept me out of his hair until I went away to school in England.'

'Did your mother want you to go?' Nico asked, thinking of Mum.

'No, dear.' Mrs Baxendall navigated a slot between two lorries and they were out in the open countryside. As they sped along, Nico learned that Mrs Baxendall's mother had been killed in an air raid while her father was recovering from war injuries. 'There was nothing left for Father in England and he returned to Italy to bring me up alone. It wasn't easy, which was why he packed me off to boarding school when I was fourteen and then insisted I went to university in the UK to study Art History.'

'You came back to Italy after that?'

'Not straight away. I married very young, to dashing Captain Henry Baxendall.' Mrs Baxendall chuckled and blithely navigated her way round a series of hairpin bends. 'I met Henry at the university Leavers' Ball. He was my friend Fiona's brother – she introduced us. We were wed far too young.' Mrs Baxendall laughed again. 'It was the dress uniform that did it for me – I was still naive enough to have romantic notions about the military. Henry was killed soon after, in the war in Malaysia.'

Nico had never even heard of that one. 'I'm sorry.'

'It was a long time ago. Henry's death finally taught me that war is only ever squalid and brutal – which was Father's opinion too after fighting in Italy. Afterwards, I came here to make a life, as my father had done and for much the same reasons.'

The car lurched through the lion gates and stopped in front of the house.

'Come, Nico, and I'll show you just what an obsession Botticelli's garden has become.'

CHAPTER XIV

WHEN JADE AND Amber reached the Villa dei Fiori they saw a bright yellow scooter parked underneath a chestnut tree. Amber immediately got on it.

'Get off!' Jade said.

'Don't be so boring.'

'I said, get off!' Jade pulled at her arm.

'Lighten up – I was only having a laugh.' Amber dismounted.

'Not funny,' Jade mumbled. Why had she panicked like that? They'd both done similar things before and it had never bothered either of them. She decided it was because she wanted to make a good impression on Caterina; after all, how could she insist Nonno had been a good man if she and Amber behaved like idiots?

'You can be so sad.' Amber left the bike and went to the door, Jade close behind to make sure she didn't make a run for it and jump back on the scooter. Caterina answered Amber's knock, her face as smiley as when they'd last seen her.

'Come in, come in,' she said, kissing the girls in welcome. She ushered them through to the sunny kitchen where a tall dark boy stood talking to Teo. 'This is your cousin, Dario,' Caterina beamed. 'He has returned early from his trip so that he can meet you.'

'I'm very pleased you are here,' Dario said in English and shook hands with them.

'Let's talk Italian,' Amber said. 'It reminds me of talking to Nonno.'

Jade groaned inside. *Why does she have to wind everybody up?*

Dario grinned. 'That's good,' he said in Italian, 'my English isn't great.'

Teo threw an arm round his shoulders and shook him. 'You should practise every day like I have to for my work.'

Dario shrugged him off and Teo cuffed him affectionately.

'Why aren't you at Mrs Bax's?' Amber demanded.

Jade began to wonder if she'd ever be able to relax around her sister.

If Teo had noticed Amber's hostile tone it didn't show when he answered: 'I told her I have family business and that I'll be back later after lunch to take your friend Nico back to his mamma.'

Caterina brought refreshments and the atmosphere eased. Dario was funny and Jade relaxed as his jokes coaxed Amber into a better mood, his hazel eyes glinting

175

at each sharp remark she made. *Talk about instant attraction*, Jade thought and hoped Dario's magic would still work when they started to talk about Nonno.

Nico looked at the huge, half-scale reproduction of Botticelli's *Primavera* propped against the wall in an annexe next to Mrs Bax's study. It had sticky notes all over it; blue ones on the bushes and trees, and green on the flowers. Each one was dated and had the name of the plant in Latin, English and Italian written on it.

'How many plants are there?'

'Six trees, two-hundred-and-forty non-flowering pl- ants, forty-two identifiable flowers, several about which one might argue and nineteen absolute fantasies,' Mrs Baxendall said promptly.

Remembering what the old lady had said when she first spotted the viperina at the chapel, Nico looked closer. Nestling under a nymph's foot was a blue flower shaped like a snake's jaws open wide, the hairy stem sprouting leaves growing up it in steps and ending in a collar just underneath the bloom. 'There's the viperina.'

'Well done, m'dear.' Mrs Baxendall thrust a green note at Nico. It read: *E. Vulgaris*, Viper's Bugloss, Viperina – April 2005. 'You can stick this on now, since you found it.'

Nico pressed the note into place. 'How many more plants do you need?'

'I've completed the identifiable ones and all save one of the disputed ones – an *elleboro*, a hellebore or Christmas rose in English. I do have an *elleboro puzzolente* as a stopgap.'

Nico knew the word 'puzzolente'. 'A s*tinking* Christmas rose?'

'An unorthodox but accurate translation.'

'Where is it in the picture?'

Mrs Bax pointed out a strange, greenish plant. It looked like a child's pinwheel.

'Is it anything like the real thing?' Nico asked.

'I'll show you and you can decide for yourself.'

In the study Mrs Bax got up a computer image of Botticelli's hellebore side by side with a photo of a faintly sinister green flower. They didn't look particularly alike to Nico. 'It's gross,' he said.

Mrs Bax laughed. 'I'm inclined to agree with you but I have to have one nevertheless. Besides, it's reputed to rejuvenate the elderly which means I need to find it fairly soon.'

'You don't need it, you're not old.' Nico wasn't good at guessing ages; he supposed Mrs Baxendall was sixty something which was old, but not ancient. Her father must be pretty elderly though since he'd fought in the Second World War.

'Dear boy.' Mrs Bax regarded Nico fondly. 'I've tramped kilometres to find the blessed *elleboro* but never a sign.'

'Where do they grow?'

'Generally, in the woods or woody sheltered areas.'

Outside flowed the endless, tree-covered hills. That was a lot of woodland and Nico only had a week of his holiday left.

Jade put the book on the table. 'From when we were very little Nonno told us stories about his life in Italy. How he was an orphan and how his friends looked out for him. He always wanted to come back to Italy but he couldn't. Then he had a stroke and was too ill even to try. He got worse after a second stroke and we decided that one day we'd come instead and tell you about him. Then we had this idea – to make a book for you, about his life. It took ages.'

Though it had been Jade's idea, Amber had done most of the work. She was good at the practical things: scanning photos, assembling the book and decorating it. Jade was glad Amber had made the book look classy, covering it in the colours of the Italian flag and attaching a small golden frame with a smiling photo of Nonno in it. Now she wished she hadn't sniped at her sister for the hours and hours she'd spent on it.

Amber opened the book. The title page read, *The Book of Memories*. It was the story of Nonno's life. Jade turned to the first page with one black and white photograph on it.

'Nonna Elena!' Caterina touched the tiny photo with gentle fingertips.

'He told us he carried this picture everywhere, even during the war,' Amber said.

'That's why it got so creased and crumpled,' Jade added. She turned the page to a picture of Nonno just after he arrived in Derby.

'He looks so young, just a boy,' Caterina said.

'He looks like Zio Teo,' Dario said. 'Look at the way he's standing.'

Roberto had made a shape, one foot nonchalantly behind the other, cap swinging from the hand on his hip, cigarette held casually in his other hand.

Jade turned the page to a double spread with photos of Nonno's wedding to Granny Grace. Nonno had written the details on the picture.

'They look happy, Roberto and Grace,' Caterina said.

'Yes, they were.' Jade turned to the next spread with its pictures of Nonno, Grace and baby Luisa, then the next pages showing Luisa's wedding to Kevin.

'Mamma! You and Zia Luisa are so alike!' Dario's eyes were wide. 'You could almost be twins like Valentina and Lia.'

'You have to meet Luisa,' Teo said to Caterina.

Jade quickly turned the page to a picture of Nonno and Grace outside their house.

'That's a beautiful house.' Teo whistled admiringly at

the stately Georgian building with ivy climbing to the second floor. 'Not bad for a peasant orphan – becoming so rich?'

'Matteo!' Caterina said.

It *was* insensitive, as though he were saying, how could an immigrant peasant afford a big house like this?

Jade ignored the fist of anger gathering inside her and said coldly, 'Nonno worked in Granny Grace's family company. She inherited a shoe factory from her parents. It's gone now but when Granny and Nonno were young it made money.'

'Nonno earned it,' Amber said. 'He started in the factory and worked hard and learned all about the business. He didn't just walk in and take over.'

'I understand, cara,' Caterina said gently and Amber turned back to the book. But Jade caught a glance passing between Caterina and Teo; a glance that said nothing was going to convince them that Roberto wasn't anything more than a grasping opportunist.

A little green lizard watched Nico from one jewelled eye as it basked on the warm steps of the terrace. He stopped writing and drew the tiny creature swiftly.

'That's rather good.' Mrs Baxendall sat next to him on the step and passed over the orange juice she'd brought out. 'Do you enjoy art?'

Nico nodded. 'I like writing but I prefer art.'

Mrs Baxendall sipped at her coffee and the two of them sat in companionable silence while Nico turned over questions in his mind; which to ask first and how should he frame it? Tentatively he tried: 'Mrs Baxendall, you said you've written books about Italy; what sort of books?'

'Well, there's this book about the *Primavera*. The botany's an excuse to look at history, that's why I'm interested in the stories behind where and how the specimens are found. For instance, the viperina was found at the chapel steps which gives me a reason for writing about the chapel, which is very, very special.'

Special? Nico decided to hold on to that information till later; there was another question he wanted answering first: 'Did Teo really find the cornflower when he saved you from a sheep?'

'I let him think so.'

'What else have you written?'

'Cookery, reminiscences, a history of the partisans who fought against the fascists and the German occupation . . .'

It was so peaceful now; Nico found it hard to imagine war stamping its vile boots over the tranquil land.

Mrs Bax clinked her coffee cup on the step, sending the lizard darting away. 'You've been quite the detective, working out what I'm doing with the garden.'

'Not really,' Nico said. 'When I remembered that

Filipepi was Botticelli's real name it was obvious. I wasn't exactly Commissario Lupo.'

'You still had to put the evidence together – that's detective work.'

Nico thought Mrs Baxendall was being kind and it made him feel patronised. To his fury he felt himself flushing. 'My mother's the one who behaves like a detective, walking round the places in the books to "soak up the atmosphere".'

'Don't you do that as well?'

Only a few days ago Nico had walked in Alessandro's footsteps and grieved with him for his lost Semiramide. He felt vaguely stupid for living someone else's feelings, especially someone fictitious. 'Alessandro's not real – I think Mum's chasing shadows.'

Mrs Baxendall smiled.

'E. J. Holm is real though. I'd like to find him.'

'Why?'

'I'm not sure – I think it's the fact he's secretive. It makes me wonder what he's got to hide.'

'He might be a frightful creature,' Mrs Bax said.

Nico couldn't believe that the creator of Alessandro and Semiramide was any kind of frightful creature. 'Haven't you met him? You told Mum he always gives you copies of his books.'

'It's the agent who gives me copies – I've never even shaken hands with Holm. I think your author's simply a person who values his privacy. Die-hard fans of crime fiction are as interested in the writer as they are in the detective and they view both in a completely unrealistic light. Have you seen the websites?'

Nico had. He'd posted storylines on the most popular fanfic one. 'You can't blame the fans completely,' he said. 'I mean, when Alessandro's solved a case he slips away and lets his colleagues take the credit and E. J. Holm's the same. He writes all these amazing books, gets everyone excited, and then disappears. He's deliberately making himself a mystery – that's why fans get obsessive and go running off to places in the books in case he's there.'

'You might be right,' Mrs Baxendall agreed. 'Or not.'

Nico thought the topic of the elusive writer was exhausted. He went back to his reserve question: 'What makes your chapel "very special".'

'Let's have lunch first and then I'll show you.' Mrs Baxendall smiled mischievously. 'I'll have to swear you to the utmost secrecy first.'

'Why?'

'Wait and see. I promise you'll be more than delighted.'

Nico couldn't imagine what she meant.

CHAPTER XV

BECAUSE IT WAS a fine day and Dario wanted to see the old farmhouse again before it was sold, the family drove out there for lunch. Caterina took Jade and Amber. Dario, who turned out to be the owner of the yellow scooter, bumped along behind and Teo followed in Mrs Baxendall's old 4x4.

After they'd eaten Teo drove back to Mrs Baxendall's house while the rest of them sat round the table with *The Book of Memories*, leafing through pictures of Jade and Amber with Nonno – on holiday, at the club in town, working on the allotment.

'There's a pocket at the back.' Jade opened it. 'Look, there's loads of Nonno's thoughts – his memories and stories written down . . .'

'What's happening?' A harsh voice from the doorway made them swing round. An old man was leaning on a stick, his crooked shape dark against the sunlight behind him.

'Nonno!' Caterina jumped up and hurried over to him.

Nonno? Caterina's nonno? *It's Gaetano,* Jade thought, *Elena's husband, Sofia's stepfather.*

The old man stumped out of the shadows.

Jade stared in disbelief. 'Oh my God!' she whispered.

'It's that man who shouted at Mum in the restaurant,' Amber hissed.

Caterina ushered him forward. 'What are you doing here, Nonno?'

He slumped onto a bench. 'Till it's sold it's still my house. I don't need permission to come here.'

'Of course not, Nonno, we didn't expect to see you, that's all.'

The old man waved his stick at Jade and Amber. 'Who are these girls?' He looked at them with mild hostility but no more. Jade was certain he didn't recognise them from the restaurant in Borgo Sant'Angelo; he'd been too intent on staring at Luisa.

'Jade and Amber are visitors from England,' Caterina said.

Gaetano grunted and thumped *The Book of Memories* with his gnarled brown hand. 'What is this?'

'It's about our nonno,' Jade said.

'Why have you brought it here?'

'The girls are Roberto Volpe's grandchildren,' Caterina said. 'They came to find us and bring us news.'

Veins in the old man's neck bulged and his face turned an ugly, dark red. 'You bring the traitor's spawn here – to defile my house!' He almost choked on his venomous outburst. 'I told you after I saw the woman in Il Nido that they were all to be kept away – yet you defy me!'

He snatched up the book. 'You dare to come here with news of the fascist – the traitor – the coward.' He hurled the book to the floor.

'No!' Amber dived for the book and held it tightly in front of her like a shield. Jade rushed to her, put a protective arm around her shoulders.

'Nonno, let me explain,' Caterina said.

Gaetano made a grunt of such contempt Jade felt like punching him.

'Dario,' Caterina said to her son, 'your cousins didn't have time to see the stables the last time they were here. Please show them now. I want to talk to Nonno on my own. First,' she appealed to Amber, 'please trust me with the book.' She held out her arms.

Amber looked at Jade. She nodded. 'Go on.'

Amber clung to it for a moment before she handed it over. 'You'd better look after it.'

'I will.'

Dario led the way to a door at the far end of the room.

Nico swore to keep Mrs Baxendall's mysterious secret to himself and, after lunch, she unlocked the door to the chapel. Inside it was more or less as E. J. Holm had described his chapel – a box shape with whitewashed walls and seating down either side. At the end, an altar held a crucifix and two golden candlesticks. Behind it, light filtered through narrow windows set high up and lingered over a gilded panel painting. The only difference was that E. J. Holm's candles had been lit and his windows were red stained glass with ruby light that played over the altar like splashes of blood. And his chapel had the body on the scaffolding.

Nico nearly jumped out of his skin when Mrs Bax boomed, 'Look behind you!'

For a wild moment Nico thought the book had come to life. Just as in *The Shattered Mirror*, a wooden platform supported by scaffolding ran the width of the wall. A man was sitting on it, slumped forward. Nico's heart hammered until he realised the man wasn't dead, only leaning forward to work on a fresco partly hidden under an old layer of dingy plaster. He twisted round.

'Let me introduce you,' Mrs Bax said to Nico. 'This is Edoardo Rossi, who's busy restoring the old frescoes.'

'Hi,' Nico said, trying to be polite. It was hard when all he wanted to do was focus on the astonishing paintings in front of him.

A narrow stone staircase draped with a thick grey bunting of spiders' webs led down to a stable lit by hazy sunlight filtering through cracked windows. Amber leaned against one of the empty stalls, her arms crossed, her face closed tight as a safe door.

Jade shivered. 'It's ghostly in here, and sort of sad. It shouldn't be so empty.'

She meant the whole house not just the stable.

Dario seized the chance to talk about a neutral topic. 'The house will be sold soon – these places are very popular with the English and Germans – and the stables will probably be turned into a big kitchen and dining room.'

Jade thought of the bullet holes across the front of the farmhouse. 'Won't it feel kind of weird if you sell to a German? I mean, with the war and everything?'

'Not for me, or for my parents – it was a long time ago and we are all Europeans now. It's true it's still hard for the old people.'

Jade thought about the bullet holes again. She couldn't imagine what it would be like to have her father butchered in front of her and the rest of the family dragged away to die in another country.

Amber pushed off from the stall. 'If the *Germans* were the enemy, what's your nonno got against our nonno?'

'You don't know?'

'I wouldn't have asked if I did.'

Dario stumbled for the right words. 'It's hard for me . . . Mamma told me only yesterday the truth about Roberto being my Nonna Sofia's father and . . . you have to understand this was a big shock for me . . . before she told me, I only knew Roberto as . . . as . . .'

'As a fascist – yes, we know.' Amber glared and Dario took a step back.

Even though Jade agreed with Amber she couldn't help feeling sorry for Dario. 'Lots of people were fascists early on in the war,' she said. 'Some of them, when they knew the truth, they changed. Nonno might've been a fascist to start with . . .' She ignored Amber's angry gasp '. . . but he fought with the partisans later. He wouldn't have done that if he stayed a fascist, would he?' She swept her arm wide. 'He even helped save the English spy who hid here.'

'What?'

'He told us he warned the partisans that someone had betrayed them and the enemy were sending soldiers to capture his foster brother and the spy.'

'No, no!' Dario shook his head. 'That's not right!'

'What isn't right?'

'Roberto Volpe didn't *warn* the partisans; he betrayed them. He was the one responsible for Gaetano's family being killed.'

Mrs Baxendall pointed her stick at the fresco. 'This gem's been covered up for almost five hundred years. It takes technical expertise of the highest order to uncover it safely and restore it to its former glory.'

'It's in Botticelli's style,' Nico said.

'Well done, Nico!' Mrs Bax beamed. 'Better still, it's by Botticelli himself.'

'No!' Now Nico understood why Mrs Baxendall wanted it kept a secret: it was going to cause a sensation when news of the unknown frescoes got out.

Mrs Bax plumped down on a pew and patted the one next to her. Nico sat.

'I was rummaging around in the house archives a few years ago and came across a contract for this cycle of paintings. By the time Botticelli was commissioned to paint them his skill had become an expensive commodity. It meant he could choose his own subject rather than have his client tell him what to do.'

Mrs Bax waved her stick at the fresco. 'And this is the result: a fresco, in a chapel, of the only Bible story that makes no mention of God. A story of sex and violence and the power of beauty.' Mrs Bax beamed. 'It must've offended the authorities terribly. D'you know the story of Queen Esther?'

Nico shook his head.

Jade's brain didn't seem able to work properly. 'Our nonno? Betrayed Gaetano?'

Amber laughed. 'Are you crazy or what?' Shock had made her switch to English.

'I'm sorry, I don't understand these words,' Dario said.

'Our nonno was a hero,' Jade insisted in Italian.

Dario shook his head. 'The whole town knows that Roberto Volpe was a traitor. The old people, they still talk about it.'

Suddenly Jade knew who the elderly people at the restaurant were – the ones who'd inspected Luisa so carefully; Luisa, who strongly resembled her father, who was Caterina's double and who spoke Italian with the accent of the region.

Jade spoke to Amber in rapid English so Dario wouldn't grasp what she was saying. 'Those old people at the restaurant? The Signora set us up! They were ex-partisans. That's why they were staring at Mum – they were checking her out!'

'What? You saying you believe all this traitor crap?'

Jade hesitated. She wasn't sure any more.

Amber grabbed Jade and shook her violently. 'Tell me! Tell me you don't believe it!' she yelled.

'Get off me!' Jade pushed Amber away and she staggered against a stall and knocked over an old beam propped against it. It crashed against the stairs sending a papery lump suspended over the stairwell swinging. It started to vibrate and hum.

'Calabrone!' Dario yelled as a huge black and yellow hornet dropped from the lump and circled angrily. More followed in a heaving vortex.

'This way!' Dario grabbed the twins and shoved them

to the outside door. He shook it as hard as he could. 'It's stuck!'

The three of them battered at the door. It burst open, showering them with dust and crumbling mortar as they stumbled into the courtyard. A small, hard object hit Jade on the head and clattered to the floor. She stooped and picked it up. It was a tin.

Dario spun round and slammed the door shut. 'Quick, come on!'

Jade pushed the tin into her jeans pocket and ran after Dario, across the courtyard and up the steps to the farmhouse door.

'Here,' Mrs Bax said, 'is Xerxes, King of the Persians, receiving Esther. She's come to plead for the lives of her people who've been betrayed by her uncle, Haman.'

Xerxes was dressed like a Renaissance prince and Esther, in a filmy gown, looked as if she'd strayed in from the *Primavera*.

'How do you know for sure this is Xerxes and Esther?' Nico asked.

'Because it follows the story exactly: "The King held out to Esther the golden sceptre that was in his hand. So Esther drew near."'

There was a chuckle from the scaffolding and Edoardo Rossi said, 'Also, the contract you found promised

Botticelli eighty-four florins for frescoes depicting the story of Esther.'

Mrs Bax was unfazed. 'With thirty-five florins to be paid if he – and I quote – ". . . will paint all the faces and all the said parts of the figures from the waist upwards and that the mixing of the colours will be done by the said master himself." The contract's very specific.'

Edoardo rested his forearms on the scaffolding and leaned over. 'To the left will be scenes of Xerxes at a great banquet, summoning Vashti, his queen. She refuse to come and he banish her for disobedience. Then Xerxes, he chooses Esther for his new queen. After that comes the painting I am working on now.'

'I don't get why it was plastered over,' Nico said.

'Church authorities probably though it unseemly,' Mrs Bax said. 'My guess is the fresco shows Esther and all the other beautiful young virgins, with the eunuchs teaching them how to make themselves appealing for Xerxes.'

Edoardo continued the story: 'Then there will be a painting of Esther tricking Haman and making him lead Esther's father, mounted on the king's horse, through the city of Shushan. And last all,' Edoardo thrust his brush at a high point over the door, 'there will be the hanging of Haman and the great celebrating of Esther's people.'

Nico stared at the place on the wall where Haman's

hanging was hidden under centuries of grey plaster. It was exactly the spot where Alessandro Lupo had found the dangling corpse in *The Shattered Mirror*.

My role, from late 1943, was to cause as much disruption to the enemy as possible and to help organise attacks on specified road and rail targets. To do this successfully I was ordered to liaise with the partisans and provide tactical support. It was hoped that our actions would divert their forces away from the Allies' highly secret planned area of attack in the south. It worked.

I settled into my new home. Gaetano's family shared all they had with me and made me comfortable in the stable where I – and my radio equipment – shared sleeping quarters with the oxen and a mule. I soon got used to the animals' smell, which inevitably transferred itself to me. Gaetano sniffed me with approval one day as we sat among the snowy hills watching for enemy movements. 'You whiff of hay and dung. At last you smell like a real peasant, Englishman.' The boy was an excellent companion whose dry wit often made me laugh. We quickly became friends.

The winter and spring of 43–4 was bitter and there was little to eat. Without the chestnuts that provided flour for *the ubiquitous polenta we might well have starved. Many were close to it. Everyone shared what he could and when, occasionally, the Allies' ammunition drops included food – especially chocolate and cigarettes – the rejoicing was profound. One drop even included a photograph of my wife, Rebekah, and baby daughter, Emily, affectionately known as "Millie". The picture was wrapped in a map of the area. I didn't need a map by this time; I knew the terrain well thanks to the partisans. I passed the photograph round the dinner table one evening and it was received with cries of admiration from the women and grunts of approval from the men. We each of us knew that that was what we were fighting and dying for: our children.*

We used the arms provided by the Allies, as well as those stolen from the Germans and the Italian army, to carry out increasingly successful acts of sabotage. The more successful we became the more savagely we were hunted by the Black Brigades. Still, we stayed safe and undisturbed.

In March, we planned our most ambitious project: blowing up a railway bridge and the train that crossed it loaded with arms and carrying troops. It was dangerous, not only because of the act itself but because there was a strong possibility of reprisals. One night, our group – the Uccelli Squad – were sitting round the table as usual, maps and diagrams spread all over it, planning the attack when young Gaetano came in, his face drawn and white.

His father stood. 'What's wrong?'

'It's Roberto.'

'He's dead?' Though the stoical farmer was impassive I knew he was fearful for his foster son.

'No! It would be better if he were.'

'He's at the Villa Triste?'

It was no wonder the old man had paled; the Villa Triste was a place of horror where Partisans were routinely tortured.

'No, you don't understand, it's worse.' Gaetano flung himself onto the bench.

Worse than death or the Villa Triste?

'Explain yourself,' the farmer demanded.

Every eye was on the boy. 'He's been seen in Florence. He's joined the Black Brigade.'

CHAPTER XVI

THE SOUND OF a scooter engine starting up made Jade and Dario turn at the top of the steps.

'My *motorino*!' Dario stared in disbelief at Amber riding out of the courtyard.

Jade ran down the steps shrieking, 'Amber, don't be so stupid!' It was no good, her sister was already out of earshot, disappearing fast down the track through the chestnut trees.

'What is she doing?' Dario yelled. 'Where is she going?'

'No idea.' Jade ran back up the steps two at a time and burst into the room where Caterina and Gaetano sat at the table, *The Book of Memories* between them.

'It's Amber, she's run off!' Jade said.

'On my *motorino*,' Dario said.

Caterina leaped to her feet. 'Does she know how to ride one?'

'We ride trail bikes – it's not that different,' Jade said.

'Different enough,' Dario said. He glared at Jade. 'Has she got a licence?'

Jade shook her head.

Caterina flapped Jade and Dario out and helped Gaetano hobble down the steps to a battered three-wheeled truck. By the time Jade and Dario were belted into Caterina's car and she had started up the engine, Gaetano's little blue Api was already bouncing along the track. It slowed Caterina down and Jade seethed with impatience. There was no sign of Amber or Dario's yellow scooter.

Mrs Baxendall sent Teo to drive Nico back to Florence and as soon as the car hit the main road into the city, Teo began driving competitively. A black Yamaha swooped past. Teo's jaw tightened, he stamped his foot down and the rust bucket of a car surged forward. It swerved violently round a Dutch lorry. The lorry hooted, loudly and melodiously. Teo took no notice, doggedly following the flash scooter swinging smoothly in and out of the traffic. Nico braced himself as the old car jerked wildly between lorries, buses, cars. *It's not a contest*, Nico thought. *Being macho isn't going to impress anyone if you get us killed.*

A fresh spurt of speed had them racing a Norbert Dentressangle lorry, overtaking it, diving in front, getting trapped behind yet another lorry. Teo kept swinging violently out to the left to try and catch sight of the black Yamaha. Nico clung on grimly.

*

Jade strained to see Amber. 'There!'

'I see her.' Jade was jerked from side to side as Caterina drove recklessly round the curve bending into the outskirts of Florence. The traffic was speeding up, getting impatient with smaller vehicles, hooting and blaring at scooters. The stop-go of traffic made it easy for Amber to weave in and out and Gaetano's Api was small enough to catch up and follow closely. Caterina dodged here and there while the other drivers honked and swore. She closed in on the yellow scooter.

A black Yamaha swept by with a jeering blare and a decrepit old car rumbled after it with a furious roar, swooping across traffic streaming round the wide arc in the road. Both vehicles headed straight for Amber. 'No!' Jade screamed.

With a growl, Gaetano's Api popped out like a cork from a fizzed-up bottle and pushed its way between Amber and the Yamaha and its pursuing car.

A bus appeared, filtering in recklessly. It swerved, missed Gaetano and swerved again to avoid Amber. Brakes and gears shrieked, tyres screamed, horns blasted.

The old car lurched to a halt, stopping just short of the low garage wall. Amber and Gaetano shot into the forecourt. The Api squealed to a stop, spinning wildly and crashed sideways against the wall. Amber was thrown from the yellow scooter and it toppled on to her. Jade screamed again as Caterina, white-faced, screeched into the forecourt and slammed on the brakes. Jade threw herself out of the car and ran to her sister. She dragged the scooter away.

Amber's eyes were closed and she lay motionless, her right leg sickeningly twisted.

Jade took her sister's limp hand. 'Please be all right, Amber. Please say something. Please, please.' She looked round wildly for help.

Miraculously Mum and Dad were running towards her with Hattie and James close behind.

'She's hurt!' Jade clung to Amber's hand.

Mum knelt down and stroked Amber's tumbled hair away from her forehead. Dad crouched next to Jade and put his arm round her. 'She'll be all right, love. She will.'

Jade felt safer in her father's arms and her mind began to clear. 'Where did you come from?' she asked, though she kept looking at Amber the whole time. She was so still. Really, really still.

'The bus from Torre del Lago, the one that nearly . . .' Kevin couldn't finish.

A wail of sirens made them swing round to see a police car screaming up to Gaetano's truck pressed against the back wall of the forecourt. A little crowd, with Caterina and Dario at the front, was standing by the open door and Jade could see Gaetano slumped back in his seat, his face bloody, his eyes closed. *He's dead*, Jade thought, her stomach lurching sickly. Then she saw his hand move in a sharp gesture that meant, Leave me alone.

The old car that had almost hit the front wall had its doors open too. For some reason, Nico was sitting on the low wall next to it.

'What's Nico doing here?'

'Nico?!' Hattie looked from Mum to Nico and back again.

'Go,' Mum said.

Hattie sprang up and ran to Nico.

'You go as well, mate,' Dad said and James sprinted away to join Hattie just as two ambulances bawled into the forecourt.

It's strange, Nico thought dreamily, *the way all cities and towns are ugly on the fringes*. Oddly, he was drawing, his pencil outlining concrete apartment blocks, power lines strung across the road, the weedy grass growing round the garage wall . . . Someone embraced him. 'Nico!' Mum was hugging him.

He hugged her back. 'What's happening?'

'Amber's hurt, the paramedics are sorting her out,' James said. 'And that old man in the van. We'll get them to give you the once-over as well.'

'No need. I'm fine.'

'Are you sure you're not hurt?' Mum asked.

'Yes, honest.' He looked round, wondering where Teo was and saw him with the group surrounding Amber.

'How is she?' Teo asked.

In her dazed state, it didn't seem odd to Jade that he was there too.

'Not very good but it could be worse,' Dad said. 'Her leg looks badly broken and she's unconscious but she's breathing fine and doesn't seem to have any other injuries.'

Jade had no idea how her father knew this; the paramedics had spoken in Italian and no one had translated for Dad.

A hand touched Jade's shoulder. It was Dario. Jade jumped up and pulled him to one side.

'How's your sister?' he asked.

Jade told him. 'How's Gaetano?'

'He's not so bad – he has to go to the hospital though, because he's old.'

'Will you tell him, thank you – for saving Amber?'

Dario nodded. 'I have to go – Mamma and I are driving to the hospital.' He kissed Jade formally, mechanically, and went back to Caterina.

After treating Amber, the paramedics lifted her into the ambulance and Mum climbed in beside her. Dad hugged Jade briefly, saying, 'We're going with Amber.' He nodded towards Teo. 'That man, he works for Mrs Baxendall, he's agreed to follow with you, OK?'

Jade was still too dazed to say more than 'yes'; explanations about already knowing Teo would come later. Jade shivered as the ambulance made its raucous way out of the courtyard and Teo gently led her away. Despite its rough ride, the old car started up with no problem and a very subdued Teo drove cautiously through the throng of bystanders who'd come to gawp. Jade glimpsed Nico sitting on the wall, Hattie to one side, James to the other.

That was all right then. All she had to worry about now was Amber.

Nico drew steadily. It was soothing. Mum went to the loo and James bought Nico a bottle of water from a shop next to the garage. He drank it in hasty gulps.

'Hey, hey, take it easy, Son, you'll make yourself heave!' James pulled the bottle away and water slopped onto Nico's drawing book. He began to laugh.

'What's up?' James asked.

'Nothing. I don't get it, that's all.'

'What?'

'Mum. She goes ape about what might happen and when something does, she's calm.'

'She's got too much imagination, like you, but she's a good woman, and brave.'

Nico didn't know what to say to that. He wasn't used to the muppet James being a normal human being.

'Here's the taxi.' James waved.

'What taxi?'

'The one I ordered to take us back to the apartment. What's the Italian for, *you took your time?*'

'No idea.' It was reassuring, having James back to his supercilious self.

Jade sat in the sombre waiting room. Outside Mum and Dad talked intently to the medics. The hospital was quiet and the conversation hushed. Not like the confusion and chaos when they'd first arrived with ambulances and police sirens blaring. Gaetano and his family had been sent to another part of the hospital and soon after Jade was almost sure she'd glimpsed Mrs Baxendall with Signora Minardi. Then there'd been the police, definitely the police, with their questions about why Amber was riding a scooter illegally and without a licence or insurance.

Jade thumped her head back against the wall. She was in big trouble yet all she'd wanted was to meet their Italian family and bring them news of Nonno. So had Amber.

Mum and Dad came into the waiting room, holding hands like children. Jade sprang to her feet. 'How is she?'

'She's awake and the head injury's not serious,' Dad said.

'What about her leg?'

There was a rasp of stubble as Dad rubbed a tired hand over his face. 'It's ugly. She's going to need emergency surgery as soon as possible and then maybe more afterwards.'

Mum sank onto a chair as if her legs couldn't support her any more.

'Mum?' Jade's voice wavered. 'Are you all right?'

Luisa ignored the question and looked at Jade, her eyes still darkened with fear and dread. 'What was she doing on a scooter? Why didn't you try and stop her?'

As Mum's accusing questions tumbled out Jade saw the simple, beautiful plan for Nonno exposed as what it really was – a self-indulgent daydream covered in lies and deceit. She burst into tears.

The church bell rang loudly, four times. Nico had heard it at twelve, one, two and three. He gave up trying to sleep and went into the kitchen to get a drink. He thought about sneaking into his mother's room and lifting the new E. J. Holm book but when he peered in he saw it lying on the bed between her and James. She must've gone to sleep reading it. He sloped back, picked up his drawing book, threw himself onto the sofa in the sitting room and worked on his drawings. Strange that he'd sat on the garage wall in a sort of trace and drawn, ignoring all the drama going on around him. The drawings weren't bad either.

He shot upright, not believing what he saw on the page. Why hadn't he realised while he was drawing? He began to laugh. The laughter grew into loud, dry hiccups that made his eyes water.

'What's up?' It was James, bleary-eyed. 'Are you crying?'

'Of course not,' Nico said. 'I need to go out. Will you get me a taxi?'

'Now? In the middle of the night?'

Nico stood up. 'Yes, now – it might be too late if I leave it.'

'You're not making sense. It's delayed shock.'

Nico thought for a moment. Was he in shock? He looked at the drawing again. 'No, I'm all right. I just *have* to go.'

'I'm coming with you. No need to disturb your mother – I'll leave her a note in case she wakes up.'

'OK.' After he'd pulled on his clothes Nico picked up the blue bowl he'd forgotten to give Mrs Baxendall after all the drama of Mum's encounter with the old lady. It would be more useful than he'd imagined when he bought it. Then he rummaged around in the kitchen cupboards, searching as quietly as he could. By the time James was ready Nico had collected a set of cutlery and a torch in addition to the blue bowl. James eyed them.

'Where are we going?'

'Back to the garage where the accident happened.'

'Are you absolutely certain you're not in shock?'

'Yep.'

James's mobile buzzed. 'Taxi. Let's go.'

They crept out stealthily to the surprise of a cat who was sleeping on the lobby mat and objected loudly to being moved.

Jade was all cried out. She tossed and turned, her eyes constantly drawn to the empty bed next to her. She'd never been parted from her twin at night, ever, and it was horrible. She needed so badly to talk to Amber about telling Mum and Dad everything – almost everything: their scheme, Caterina and Dario and Gaetano. She'd left out the discovery that Nonno had been a fascist and that the story he'd told them about rescuing an English spy was a complete lie. Mum had had enough shocks for one day without having to take in the fact that her father had deliberately caused the deaths of freedom fighters and children.

Jade threw her covers aside and got out of bed. What could she do to take her mind off the horrible thoughts running endlessly through her head? Music didn't help. She switched the light on and saw *The Shattered Mirror*, the book Nico had brought her, lying on a chair. She picked it up and began to read from the beginning.

Nico shivered in the cold night air as he crouched at the base of the garage wall. The spoon was flimsy and it soon bent. The knife was better and sliced easily into the asphalt. 'Move the torch a bit,' he told James.

James pointed it at a patch of weeds soaked in sump oil. A police car swished by. James crouched lower. 'Hurry up! We're going to get arrested in a minute.'

Nico grunted and gouged with the fork. 'I'm done. Give me the bowl.'

James passed it over and Nico scraped furiously at the soil under the asphalt.

'Can we go now?' James said.

'Yep.' Nico tucked the bowl under one arm and swung back over the wall, James following closely. They ran for the taxi waiting round the corner.

'Go!' James ordered and the taxi shot off.

'God, I feel like the bloody Mafia.' James slumped back and eyed the bowl. 'I hope it's worth it. This taxi fare's going to be astronomical.'

'It is.'

Nico hugged the bowl in silence till they got back to the apartment and found the Signora waiting for them with the cat in her arms. 'Is all well?' she asked.

'Yes, thank you,' James said. 'We couldn't sleep and went out for a walk to take our minds off things.'

'I see.'

She sees too much, Nico thought.

'Goodnight.' James grasped Nico's free arm and propelled him towards the apartment door.

'I think we just about got away with that,' he muttered.

CHAPTER XVII

NICO KEPT THE blue bowl and its contents in his room; he had no intention of telling Mum about it; she'd only want to butt in and take over and he wasn't going to let that happen. James didn't mention it either, Nico supposed for much the same reason. Mum went to the hospital to support Luisa and Kevin, insisting that James stay at the flat and supervise Nico. He couldn't even talk to Jade; she was at the hospital with Amber where, according to Mum, Luisa and Kevin were keeping her on a tight rein as well.

Nico felt too restless for drawing or reading. He decided to go the Bargello museum. It was only a few streets away and Nico had noticed there was a special exhibition on. First he'd have to persuade James. When Nico went to check he found James sprawled on his bed snoring, his guidebook gently rising and falling with his noisy breathing.

Nico left him to it, slipped quietly out of the flat and walked to the Bargello. Suspended down one wall was a vast banner advertising an exhibition of work by Vincenzo Danti. Nico had never heard of him. He bought a ticket and went into the exhibition. He stopped dead and stared.

In a dimly lit tableau were three huge bronze figures stained with blue-green verdigris. A woman stood on the left, her body twisted away from the man kneeling before her but looking at him over her shoulder. To the other side of the man, an executioner pivoted on his toes, sword raised, caught at the exact moment before he slashed his sword downwards and beheaded the kneeling man.

Nico sat on a bench and drew the faces: the woman riveted, appalled; the condemned man serene; the executioner concentrating, open-mouthed, gathering his strength for the final stroke. Nico started on the hands, the long and shapely limbs. The humanity of the figures made Nico feel as though they might move. He could almost hear the shriek and clang of metal as bronze muscles flexed. His mobile rang and he dropped his pencil. The attendant scowled as Nico scrabbled for it and tried to answer his phone at the same time. It was James.

'Where the hell are you?'

Nico told him.

'Stay there. I'll be with you in a few minutes. Don't move!'

Nico sank back onto the bench and doggedly carried on drawing.

*

Amber slept in the recovery room with Mum and Dad on either side of her bed. Jade sat near the door. Her parents had hardly spoken to her and she didn't know if it was because they were still angry or because they were exhausted.

A movement in the glass panel of the door caught her eye. Dario!

She got up as casually as she could manage and said, 'I'm going to the cafeteria. I'll get you coffee.'

She closed the door behind her and pushed Dario away from it. 'What's the matter?'

'I wanted to see how Amber is,' he said.

Jade pulled him further down the corridor. 'She's fine. Let's go and talk in the cafe.'

Over drinks Jade told Dario that Amber was sleeping off the anaesthetic after a successful operation to pin the complicated break in her leg.

'And the head injury?'

'Not serious. She'll be in hospital for a bit though.' That had caused problems for Dad: sorting out work and insurance and changing travel plans. The Signora had said they could stay in the apartment for as long as they needed to. Fortunately, she didn't have any more bookings for another month. She helped with the arrangements at the hospital too, cutting through red tape and ensuring that everything ran smoothly. She'd been very efficient: officials unhesitatingly did everything she asked.

'You're *sure* she's all right?' Dario asked.

With a jolt Jade realised just how much Dario felt for Amber – and he'd only met her for about five minutes. She thought Amber felt the same about him – or was beginning to. 'Yes, she'll be fine. How's Gaetano?'

'Oh, he's good. He'll be going home later today. Mamma will fetch him.'

'He was brave, pushing in between the car and the motorino like that.'

'He's a good man.'

'So was my nonno.' Oh, why did she have to say that?

'I suppose he was, to you . . .'

Jade put her hand on Dario's arm to stop him talking. 'My dad's coming.' He was approaching them, looking quizzically at Dario.

'Where are those coffees?' Dad asked.

'I got delayed.'

'Oh?' Dad looked pointedly at Dario.

Jade took a deep breath – this was a moment she'd been dreading. 'Dad, meet Dario. He's Mum's nephew – great-nephew – something like that. His mum is Caterina, who I told you about yesterday.'

Dario offered his hand.

Dad shook it. 'Is your mother at the hospital?'

'Sì. I tell her to come here, no?'

Dad nodded and Dario left. The intense silence between Jade and Dad felt as though it went on for hours though it could only have been a few minutes before Dario came back with his mother.

'Bloody Norah!' Dad said. In spite of everything Jade couldn't help grinning at her father's reaction to Caterina's dramatic resemblance to Mum.

Dad stared, right up to the moment Caterina joined them. 'Can we talk?' he said, getting straight to the point. 'There's a lot I'd like to know before I speak to my wife.'

'Of course,' Caterina said eagerly, her bewitching smile lighting up her face.

Dad asked Jade to take a coffee to Mum while he talked to Caterina.

'I can see Amber also?' Dario asked Dad.

He agreed and Jade went back to the recovery room with Dario almost running to get there as quickly as possible. He looked longingly at Amber's still, pale face and Mum gently told him to take a chair by the bed. He practically jumped into it.

'Who is this boy? And where's your dad?' Mum asked.

Jade answered both questions. Mum smiled briefly at Dario and then turned back to Amber. Jade couldn't bear her mother's reproachful silence another moment. Let Mum and Dario sit holding Amber's hands; they didn't want her, no one did.

'Mum? Can I go back to the apartment?'

She didn't even look at Jade as she spoke. 'Yes, be careful.'

'OK.' Jade wasn't sure what she was supposed to be careful of but at least the comment showed Mum was still bothered about her. Up to that moment Jade had felt Mum had written her off as though she'd done something terrible. But she hadn't, she really hadn't. All she'd done was try to find out the truth about Nonno. She'd been the cautious one, not Amber. It wasn't fair.

James arrived at the Bargello with a grim expression on his face. He sat by Nico. 'What do you think you're up to?'

'I wanted to see these.' Nico tipped his head towards the mighty bronze statues. 'They're big because they come from high up over the front of the Baptistery and you have to be able to see the details from the ground. It's the beheading of John the Baptist. That's Salome on the left, then John, kneeling, and that's the executioner.'

James lost the sour look and whistled softly. 'They're quite something.'

Nico closed his book.

'Have you finished drawing?' James asked.

'For now. I'll need to come back.'

'Yes, you're not going to get it in one sitting, are you? If ever.'

What did that mean? Did James actually understand how difficult it was to capture the sculptures' power and beauty, or was he saying Nico was an incompetent artist?

'D'you want to look round while we're here?' James asked.

Was he kidding?

'You can explain the art to me.'

That was a first too. 'All right.' Nico guided James round, telling him about the sculptures and the men who made them; about what they were trying to do and how they looked with the eyes of the Renaissance, not the twenty-first century. They stood and watched restorers working on Donatello's small bronze David, a lithe and graceful boy nothing like Michelangelo's majestic marble creation that the whole world knew and marvelled at.

When they got back to the flat James disappeared into his room with a pile of books and pamphlets he'd bought from the Bargello. Nico took *The Shattered Mirror* and his leather-bound notebook out into the garden. He sat under the umbrella and copied out E. J. Holm's descriptions of the chapel. Next to the writing he drew the inside and outside of Mrs Baxendall's chapel. The only real difference Nico could see between the fictional one and the real one was that the fresco cycle wasn't named in the novel. What did that mean? What was Mrs Bax's connection with E. J. Holm – apart from the fact they had the same agent? Had she invited E. J. Holm to her house and shown him the chapel? If so, why did she say she'd never even shaken hands with the man?

'The man.' Mrs Baxendall had definitely referred to

E. J. Holm as 'he'. At least that settled the question of whether the writer was a man or a woman. If Mrs Bax had been telling the truth.

'Hiya!' Jade was leaning over the balcony pegging out washing on the line. She waved.

'Want to come down?' Nico called.

She joined him in seconds.

He asked after Amber and Jade explained that her sister was with Luisa and Dario and Kevin was talking to Caterina.

'Amazing! How about you?'

'I've been doing useful stuff.' She pointed up at the washing. 'Mum and Dad won't have to do it when they get back now.' She put an object on the table. 'When I emptied my jeans for the wash I found this in my pocket.'

Nico picked up a blue, red and gold tin a bit bigger than his palm.

'I found it at Gaetano's old farmhouse yesterday,' Jade said, 'I forgot all about it with the crash and everything.'

Nico examined the tin while Jade told him how she'd found it in the stables. 'Wild Woodbine Tobacco,' he read from the lettering across blue diagonal stripes. 'It's pretty old.'

He shook it.

'I did that,' Jade said. 'You can't hear anything. You can't open it either, the lid's all rusted up.'

James shuffled out into the garden. 'What's up?'

Jade explained about the tin. 'I know what you need,' James said, went back inside and returned with a Swiss army knife. He scraped at the lid, blew away the rust and passed the tin to Jade. She opened it.

'Well?' Nico asked.

'It's a bit of manky old cloth.' Jade pulled out a yellowing piece of folded silky material. 'It feels like there's something inside it.' She looked closer.

'It stinks!' she dropped it on the table. 'You look,' she said to Nico.

'Thanks!'

'Oh, for God's sake, you pair of prima donnas.' James unfolded the silk. Inside lay an old black and white photograph of a plump, fair woman, smiling shyly. There was nothing shy about the toddler in her arms: she was beaming straight at the camera from under a mop of blonde curls.

'I wonder who they are?' Jade gingerly turned the old photo over. On the back in neat, precise writing was:

Rebekah and Millie – 1944.

'That's not much help,' Nico said.

'The child looks about a year old, which means she'd be in her sixties now,' James said. 'They were probably a soldier's family and he carried the photo to remind him of home.'

'If it was that precious why did he leave it in the

stable?' Nico said. 'And what was he doing there in the first place?'

'Perhaps he was hiding from the enemy and had to get out in a hurry,' James said.

'That's it!' Jade blurted out. 'According to Caterina, her grandfather's family were sheltering an English spy and the Germans heard about it. When they came to get him, he escaped to the hills.'

'Who's Caterina?' James asked.

Jade hurriedly ran through the bones of the events, missing out Nonno's part in the story of the spy.

'Quite a tale.' James picked up the photo. 'I wonder if there's any way of finding out who the spy was and returning this to him – or his family if he's dead. You could ask your Caterina.'

'I can't, not with the mess over the accident – Caterina's got enough to worry about.'

'Of course.' James smiled at Jade and put the photo down.

Since when did he turn into Mr Sensitive? Nico thought.

James held the silk square up to the light. 'I've read about these. They were used by the Special Operations Executive – a secret network of spies. This is a map disguised as a handkerchief – it's printed in invisible ink.' He squinted at the fabric. 'You can just about see faint traces after all this time.'

Nico and Jade took a corner each to steady the cloth

and leaned forward for a better look. James was right – there were the merest hints of lines.

'The only way you can make it properly visible is by peeing on it.'

'Eww!' Jade let go of the handkerchief. 'That's disgusting!'

'Oh, don't worry; I'm pretty sure it hasn't been used. Nico could always go and test it out though.'

'I don't think so!' Nico drawled and let go of his corner of the cloth.

James grinned. 'Just kidding.' He stood up. 'I'm going to get lunch. You two . . .' he pointed a finger at them, 'are going to stay here. Your mothers hear that you've run off and I'm dead.' He stabbed the air for emphasis. 'And I'll take you with me.'

Nico watched him go, still surprised he was behaving like a regular human being.

'There's something else in here.' Jade was pulling out what looked like paper from the tin.

'What is it?'

The paper came free. 'It's an envelope.' Jade turned it over. She stared at it in astonishment.

'What?' Nico said.

Jade held out the envelope. 'It's addressed to Roberto Volpe. That's my nonno's name.'

'Open it.'

Jade turned it over again. 'It's been opened already.'

'If the tin belonged to the English spy he must've read it for some reason.'

'Why would he have a letter addressed to my nonno?'

'You might find out if you read it.'

Jade scanned the letter. Then she read it again, carefully. 'It's so sad – but . . .' She looked puzzled. 'I don't understand it.'

'Why? What does it say? Who's it from?'

'It's from Elena – the woman my nonno was in love with when he was young.' Jade chewed at her lip.

Nico reached out and squeezed her hand. 'Don't tell me any more if you don't want to.'

'I've got to tell somebody and I can't tell Amber, Mum's not speaking to me and Dad's got too much to worry about already.'

Nico listened as Jade took a deep breath and then told him all about her relatives and Elena, Gaetano, Roberto and the betrayal.

'Do you believe it, about your nonno?' Nico asked.

Jade pulled a face. 'I don't want to but Caterina and Gaetano are so sure. And now there's this letter.' She pushed it towards Nico.

'I can't get much past, "My dearest Roberto".' He grinned. 'My school doesn't equip us for the language of real life – you'll have to tell me what it says.'

He was rewarded with a brief smile that lit up Jade's face and made his heart give a peculiar jump. 'It's quite hard to translate literally – I'll do my best to give the main meaning of it.

"My Dearest Roberto," Jade read out, *"I don't think you received my previous letter – if you had, I know you would have answered me. I asked you to come and rescue me from my parents. Roberto, we are having a baby and my parents are so angry and ashamed of what I . . ."* Jade faltered.

Nico squeezed her hand again. 'Go on, you're doing fine.'

'Thanks.' Jade cleared her throat, *" . . . ashamed of what I have done and even more ashamed that it was with a fascist boy when the family is loyal to the King."*

'How could Elena's parents be loyal to the king? Italy hasn't got a royal family, has it?' Nico asked.

'It did have. After the war, the Italians voted to have a republic instead.'

'How do you know this stuff?'

'From Nonno's Italian Club – they were always talking politics.' Jade nodded at the letter. 'Elena says, *I'm sick and I can't leave the house and my parents are watching me all the time. I cry and I cry. If you don't come for me now I'll have to marry Gaetano. I don't love him but he will save me from shame and care for me and the baby.*'

Jade lowered the letter. 'She says she knows it will be difficult for Roberto to leave the Black Brigade but lots of boys have run away from them and joined the other side.'

'Who were the Black Brigade?' Nico asked.

'A sort of militia dedicated to fighting partisans and punishing them.' Jade looked stricken. 'They were really, really brutal. Everyone hated them.'

'Does Elena say anything else?' Nico asked gently.

'A bit; it's sad. She writes, *I'll find someone I trust to post this letter. I love you with all my heart, and I know you love me too, and I truly believe that you will come to me as soon as you read these words.*'

'You're right, it is sad.' Nico thought about this girl from long ago, only a teenager like Jade, sick and frightened, alienated from her parents, without the boy she loved who was fighting on the wrong side in a bitter, ferocious war that had raged for years.

Jade put the letter back in its envelope. 'I wonder who she gave it to and why it never got posted. And how come it ended up in the spy's tin?'

'I think the only way you're going to find out is to do what James said: ask someone. Maybe Gaetano would be the best bet – the tin was on his property.'

Jade snapped the tin shut but kept hold of the letter. 'I can't ask him about this.' She waved the letter. 'I just can't. He'll say something bad about Nonno. I have to know more first. I can ask him about the tin, see what his reaction is and then think again.' She put the letter in her pocket.

Nico squeezed Jade's hand a third time. She didn't seem to mind. 'Good idea.'

'I can't do it on my own, he's scary. Will you come with me?'

'Course I will.' Nico decided it was the right time to hug Jade. He was about to lift his arms when James appeared.

'Lunch,' James announced. 'D'you want it out here?'

Nico squashed the thought of a thousand savage and excruciatingly painful evils he could inflict on James. 'We'll go after lunch if you like,' he said to Jade.

'Go where?' James asked.

'On an errand of mercy.' Nico smiled at James though he wanted to smack him with the umbrella pole. 'You can take us if you like.'

Despite our concerns about what Roberto might do there was no sign of him in the local town and he made no attempt to contact his foster family. I asked Gaetano bluntly, 'Will he turn us in?'

Gaetano shook his head. 'No. He likes swaggering around in the uniform and he likes the Duce and the promises he made to the peasants and the workers. He believes all the lies. But he doesn't want to hurt us.'

'What about me? I'm the enemy. I'm a spy.'

'He doesn't know you're here.' The boy grinned. 'Let's keep it that way, eh?'

And we did, making sure we were doubly careful to cover any trace of a link to our activities. The Germans and the Fascists became ever more frustrated as we stole arms, slashed tyres and cut telephone and railway lines. The partisans' successes only increased the violence of the enemy's retaliation. We had to decide before each attack if the consequences were worth it. Generally, the answer was yes, but not always as the inhabitants of the farm and the small town of Borgo Sant'Angelo were to discover later.

We were kept informed of enemy plans by Ilaria. As the daughter of a lawyer she'd had no difficulty finding work in the offices of the local mayor, a puffed-up, preening Fascist. Ilaria was a clever girl: level-headed and shrewd, and knew when to appear naïve and when coquettish, whereas by nature she was neither. She had no problem in deceiving the mayor and his Fascist friends both Italian and German. So when she arrived at the stable one day, looking for me, I assumed it was with intelligence information. It turned out to be more personal: a problem to do with a letter to Roberto. It was from her friend, Elena. Although the Germans had requisitioned the Villa dei Fiori after the Armistice and used it as a communications and coordination centre, I knew that Gaetano and Ilaria went there clandestinely. Ilaria flirted with the soldiers in order to glean information from them and Gaetano visited Elena; he was sweet on her.

'I don't know what to do with this,' Ilaria said and thrust the letter at me. 'What do you think?'

It was a pitiful thing. The poor girl was pregnant by Roberto, whom she'd last seen just before Christmas. She was now three months gone and desperate to get in touch with him. She'd written to him once before and received no reply. Now she was pleading with Ilaria to deliver this letter direct to the Black Brigade HQ in Florence. I folded it up. 'It would be dangerous to go to the heart of the Brigade. And if you did manage to get the letter to Roberto and he did do his duty and came for Elena, he might well discover I'm here, and the Uccelli Squad, and that would be the end of us.'

'Yes, all that's true. But Roberto really does love Elena, you know.'

'Not enough to respond to her first letter. And look, she says here that Gaetano loves her too and if Roberto doesn't come for her Gaetano's willing to marry her. Your friend will be safe and well cared for.'

'I suppose so.' The girl's face was troubled. 'We were all friends when we were children.'

I couldn't help smiling. Ilaria was still only seventeen; her childhood was not far behind her though the war had made all these youngsters grow up faster than they should have.

'Elena was the best thing for Roberto. We thought she could talk him round, make him give up his belief in Fascism.' Her voice trailed off hopelessly.

I folded the letter up and put it in my tobacco tin. 'Let's think about it for a day or two and decide later.' I covered it with the silk map. I had no intention of the letter getting to the Black Brigade HQ; it was far too risky. I hoped that by delaying Ilaria, who was a sensible girl, she would have time to realise that too. She did and I forgot about the letter.

I might have advised differently if I had known the tragedy that was about to befall us.

CHAPTER XVIII

JADE RANG DAD to say she and Nico were on their way to the hospital. Dad told her Amber was doing well enough to be moved to her own room. Once Jade knew her sister was improving she felt able to ask about Mum. 'Did Mum talk to Caterina?'

'Yes, she did.'

'And?'

'And what?'

'Dad! Did they get on? Are they going to see each other again?'

'Give me time to breathe, girl!'

Jade hopped from foot to foot in impatience – she had to know before she and Nico went to see Gaetano.

'Your mum was fine with Caterina,' Dad went on. 'They talked for a long time. I don't know what her plans are – she's got a lot to think about. I'll tell you one thing though, she went to see the old man, Gaetano, to thank him for helping Amber.'

Jade hadn't expected that. 'How did it go?'

'OK. He just grunted that he couldn't let a child get hurt and wouldn't say any more.'

Jade was surprised Gaetano hadn't ranted at her mother. Maybe he was still feeling exhausted and hadn't the energy to get worked up. She didn't tell Dad that she was going to see Gaetano too.

After a quick detour to buy chocolates, Jade and Nico went to Gaetano's room. He was reading. 'What do you want?'

Jade ignored his surly face. 'I found something, in your stables. I thought you might want to see it.' She held out the tin.

'*Dio mio!*' Gaetano dropped his book and took the battered old tin in trembling hands.

'It was hidden over the top of the stable door,' Jade said. 'We thought you might know who it belonged to.'

'Yes, I know.'

Jade turned to Nico, 'He knows who owned the tin!' she said in English.

'I can speak English,' Gaetano said, switching languages. 'The man who owned this tin, he taught me.'

Jade leaned against the end of Gaetano's bed. 'Who was he?'

'My friend,' Gaetano said in a tone of voice that meant, *and that's all you're getting out of me.* He opened the tin, lifted out the silk map, unwrapped it and took out the photograph.

'Do you know who they are?' Jade asked.

'The child, I know her. She is the daughter of my English friend.' He returned the photo and the map to the tin, and put it on top of his bedside cabinet. Then he picked up his book and began to read again.

Jade frowned. That was it? He wasn't going to tell them any more?

Nico tugged at her arm and gestured for them to leave. Outside Jade glared at him. 'He didn't even say thanks!'

'The tin was on his property and he knows who to give it to – I suppose he can do what he wants.'

'He might've told us who the spy was – or his daughter. We'll never know otherwise.'

'Doesn't it give you a nice warm feeling knowing you've done the right thing?'

'You're not serious.'

Nico laughed and Jade couldn't help half-smiling back. 'Yeah, I'm kidding,' Nico said. 'It was still the right thing though, wasn't it?'

Jade shrugged. 'I guess. I'm still glad I kept the letter. Elena wrote it for my Nonno, she didn't ever want Gaetano to see it.'

'What are you going to do with it?'

'I don't know yet – I'll show it to Amber some time, when she's well enough.'

'Jade!' a voice exclaimed. Caterina was hurrying towards them, with Signora Minardi close behind.

Caterina said eagerly in English, 'You have been to see Gaetano?'

Jade nodded. 'We found something at the farmhouse, an old tin, and we took it to him.'

'A tin?'

'I found it in the stables – it fell on me when we got chased by hornets and had to bash the door to get out. The shaking must've dislodged it.'

'What was it like, this tin?' the Signora asked.

Jade told her.

'Was there anything in it?'

What did it matter to the Signora? Jade wondered. 'There was an old map disguised as a handkerchief and a photo of a woman and a baby. It had "Rebekah and Millie – 1944" written on the back.'

Without a word the Signora went into Gaetano's room and shut the door firmly behind her. The three of them stared at the closed door. 'I don't think she wants us in there, do you?' Nico said.

'They are old friends,' Caterina said. 'They were partisans together; perhaps Signora Minardi knows something of this mysterious tin.'

Jade gaped. The frail old lady a partisan!

'I have your book.' Caterina gave *The Book of Memories* to Jade. 'I showed the pictures to Nonno Gaetano. It helped him to realise that you knew nothing of Roberto's true past. He had deceived you also.' She patted Jade's hand. 'Now, you will forgive me, I have to go. I need to finish quickly the business arrangements Signora Minardi and I were discussing.'

'You do business together?' Jade said. How many more surprises were there to the Signora?

'Yes, I supply her restaurant.' Caterina swiftly kissed Jade a formal goodbye and hurried away.

'Restaurant? The Signora has a restaurant?' Jade said.

The light dawned on her and Nico at the same time: 'Il Nido!'

'She set us up,' Jade said. 'I bet those weird old people who kept staring at Mum were ex-partisans as well.

'Why the set-up though?'

'I'll ask her.' Jade turned to rush into Gaetano's room and confront the Signora.

'Wait!' Nico said.

'What?'

'You need to cool down a bit otherwise the olds will start getting suspicious about us. We haven't visited Amber yet and if we take too long they'll be grounding us again.'

'Amber!' Jade's hand flew to her mouth. 'I've hardly even thought about her.'

'You've had a lot on your mind.'

What kind of sister am I? Jade thought, her stomach turning. She ran to Amber's room. It was pretty full when they got there: Amber lay propped up on a bank of pillows, looking pale and hollow-eyed, with Mum and Dad to one side, Hattie and James to the other.

'You took your time,' Amber said.

'Sorry . . .'

'We stopped to get you these,' Nico said. He passed the box of *Baci* chocolates to Amber.

'You look like the queen with her court,' Jade said. 'How're you feeling?'

'Apart from my screaming headache and wanting to chop my leg off it hurts so much, not bad.' She gave the box of chocolates a tired pat. 'Thanks for these.'

Dad stood up. 'There's too many of us in here. Let's give the girls a chance to catch up in the quiet.' He ushered everyone out. 'You've got an hour,' he said to Jade.

It was the first time the twins had been alone since the accident. Jade climbed onto the bed and lay down next to her sister. They hugged, carefully so as not to jolt Amber's leg, and everything was all right.

Jade still wasn't going to tell her sister about the letter. There'd be plenty of time for that later.

Inevitably Kevin's group ended up at the hospital cafeteria and just as inevitably Kevin and James argued over whose turn it was to pay. While they haggled at the till Nico sat with Mum and Luisa. 'Mum, have you finished that E. J. Holm Mrs Bax gave you?'

'Yes I have. I was going to pass it on to Luisa.'

Luisa waved the idea away. 'That's OK, I'm a slow reader compared to you two – I haven't finished *The Prince Without a Country* yet.'

Nico was startled to receive a warm smile from Luisa. He'd never seen her look this relaxed. Yet, according to Jade, she'd spoken to both Caterina and Gaetano, who were part of the family she'd tried very hard to avoid.

Mum gave him the book and in seconds he was engrossed. By the time the hour was up he was a fair way into it. He was still reading as he went back to Amber's room and only came out of the story when he walked into the door. Nico didn't know whether to tell Jade what was in the book or not. In the end, he decided to wait until he'd read the whole thing in case there was more to tell her – not that what he'd read already wasn't startling enough.

As the goodbyes began, Dario came in and it was clear from Amber's face she didn't mind the others leaving. The minute Jade stepped back from hugging her Amber held out her hand to Dario.

'That was quick,' Nico said in a low voice as he and Jade left the room.

'That's her all over – she doesn't mess around once she's made her mind up.'

'What about you?'

'I like to take my time.'

That was ambiguous and Nico wasn't sure what it

meant; he ignored the hopeful feeling glowing inside him. 'I think we ought to go and see the Signora.'

'To ask her about Il Nido and the partisans?'

Nico nodded. 'And the tin.'

Jade knocked on the door.

'Could we speak to the Signora?' she asked when Ornella answered.

Ornella opened the door wide. 'She's expecting you.'

The old lady was sitting by the door to the garden, a book on her lap. She waved them to a seat. 'You wish to ask me some questions, I think. What would you like to know?'

Jade came straight to the point: 'Why are you so interested in my family, especially my mother?'

The Signora squared her shoulders and took a deep breath. 'I realised as soon as I saw your mother that she was related to a man called Roberto Volpe. She resembles him strongly – and, even more so, she resembles his granddaughter, Caterina Biagi, whom I know very well. Now I know for certain that your mother, she is Roberto Volpe's daughter.'

'Why are you so bothered about my nonno?' Jade asked.

'Roberto was a man who did a terrible thing that led to the death of a family who had loved him and cared for him. He did it out of jealousy and for spite and to betray the partisan group of which I was a member.'

Jade felt her stomach twist as though she were teetering on the edge of a high cliff: to hear what Nonno had done described in such plain, cold language made it feel real and terrible. She didn't want to accept it; couldn't accept it.

'My nonno wasn't like that, not jealous and spiteful. I don't understand.'

The Signora's knowing eyes were bright. 'It is easy for people to behave well towards those whom they love, like you, especially when nothing is demanded in return.'

Jade tilted her chin defiantly. 'I think you ought to say exactly what Nonno was supposed to have done and what proof you've got.'

The Signora nodded. 'Yes, you are right. I will tell you.' She closed her book and put it on a side table.

'We were friends, the four of us, Roberto, Gaetano, Elena and I.'

'You were friends with my nonno?'

'Yes.' The Signora folded her hands on her lap. 'Elena and I were from, how do you say it, comfortably off families? Gaetano's family were peasant farmers who owned their own house and land. Roberto was an abandoned child who lived with his grandmother. She did her best, though she was resentful and somewhat harsh. When she became too sick to care for Roberto, Gaetano's parents took him in. He came to think of them almost as the mamma and babbo he never had. He spent a lot of time with them and his dear foster brother, Gaetano.'

Jade found it hard to match old Gaetano with the boy Signora Minardi was talking about – the boy Nonno had told her about too, though without ever mentioning his name.

'Elena was always a beauty and in time both Roberto and Gaetano came to love her. She fell in love with Roberto. She became pregnant but her parents would not let her marry Roberto – he was a Fascist supporter, something they despised.'

That matched what Elena had written. Jade felt sick with what she knew was coming next.

'As I said, Gaetano loved Elena also and he offered to marry her and bring up Roberto's child as his own. Elena's parents accepted. They did not want her to suffer the stigma of an illegitimate child – especially by a Black Brigade boy.'

'Are you sure he was a Fascist?' Nico asked. 'Maybe he started out one and then changed sides.'

'There was no changing of the sides,' the Signora said. 'Because we believed Roberto had been misled, and because he had been our dear friend, we were careless; we never thought he would betray us. We were wrong. When he was told that Elena and Gaetano had married, he immediately informed the Black Brigade of rumours

237

that a spy was hiding at the farmhouse. He even led the Brigade there. It was Easter Sunday and the spy, two escaped prisoners of war and several partisans were sharing in the celebration Easter dinner with Gaetano's family. There was a terrible fight; the English spy was dreadfully wounded but some partisans and one of the prisoners of war managed to get him away, and Gaetano with Elena also.

'The other prisoner of war was killed and the Black Brigade – they rounded up Gaetano's family. They shot his father dead, then they took away his mother, his sister and her husband and their little daughter. They were deported to a labour camp and never heard of again. Gaetano searched for many years. He did not discover even a trace of them.'

There was a profound silence in the room. Jade found her face was wet. She hadn't known she was crying and even now she didn't know whom she was weeping for – herself, the grandfather she seemed never to have truly known, or Gaetano and his lost family.

Nico broke the silence. 'Signora Minardi, are you absolutely sure Roberto organised the raid?'

'I saw him running to the Black Brigade headquarters. I was at the farmhouse when the Black Brigade, it arrived with Roberto at the forefront. There was no mistake.' The Signora cleared her throat, as though speaking was difficult. 'Though I had gone to the farm as soon as I realised what Roberto Volpe was going to do, my warning came too late; there wasn't enough time for everyone to make their escape.'

'I'm sorry,' Jade whispered. 'I know it doesn't mean anything but I am.'

'My dear, you have done nothing wrong and neither has your mother. You do not deserve to be upset. That was why I wanted to keep Gaetano from seeing you and your family.' The Signora smiled wryly. 'My plans didn't work. I needed to be absolutely certain that you were Roberto Volpe's family and I arranged for other members of our old partisan brigade to come and make sure that I was not imagining your mother's likeness to Roberto and to Caterina. Someone told Gaetano there was to be a brigade reunion and he came along to see why he had been left out. He caught sight of your mother and the rest . . .' she shrugged eloquently '. . . you know!'

'Nonno told us he could never come back to Italy because his enemies said he would be killed. Is that true?'

'Yes,' the Signora said. 'Gaetano shouted that as he escaped with Elena.'

'He must really hate us too. No wonder he was angry when we were at the farmhouse.'

'He doesn't hate you. If he hated you he wouldn't have helped your sister when she was in danger.'

'That's true,' Nico said to Jade. 'I guess he was angry at the farmhouse – and the restaurant, come to that –

because it was such a shock to see people from Roberto's family.'

Jade nodded. 'I suppose.'

The Signora stood up. 'You will forgive me if I end our conversation; I am very tired and should like to rest.' She smiled to show she wasn't just dismissing them, and showed them to the door.

In the lobby Nico said, 'We need ice cream.'

Jade agreed and they went to Bar Vivoli. They sat among the polished wood and glittering glass and went over and over what the Signora had said.

'We didn't ask about the tin,' Nico said.

'No – and the Signora never mentioned it, or the letter.'

'Gaetano didn't talk about the letter either. D'you think they really didn't know it was there?'

'I don't know what to believe any more. My lovely grandfather turns out to have been a vindictive traitor and the Signora was a girl freedom fighter.'

'Did you notice the Signora was reading a copy of E. J. Holm's latest book?'

E. J. Holm? Again? Jade shook her head irritably.

'I think that's a bit weird. Where's she got an advance copy from? Mrs Baxendall? If so, how come Mrs Bax has got access to all these advance copies? Why give one to the Signora?'

And why do you always have to work everything round to books? Jade thought. *Even when I'm really upset.* She squashed a sigh. 'Didn't Mrs Bax say she had the same agent or something?'

'She also told Mum the advance copy she gave her was a one-off. I still think it's odd if it turns out she had two.'

'Does it matter?' Jade snapped. She had more important things to think about than stupid crime books.

'It might.'

'Why?'

'Yesterday, when Mrs Bax picked me up to go to hers, I saw her speaking to the Signora. They seemed very cosy together – like old friends.'

'What were they talking about?'

'I don't know, it was all in Italian. I caught *serata* and *spaghettata* – I think that was it.'

Jade laughed. 'It's a sort of spaghetti party. That makes sense 'cause on Thursday night, when I couldn't sleep, I heard the party and went out on the balcony. A really old guy came out. It was strange; at first he looked normal then he turned and faced me . . .' Jade hesitated; perhaps moonlight and shadows had distorted the old man's face.

'What?'

'He was disfigured, really badly.' Jade traced a finger down her left cheek. 'His face was sort of crumpled in on this side. His eye was just blank and when he saw me he smiled at me and only half his mouth moved.'

Nico whistled softly. 'He must've had an accident.'

'I guess.'

'Poor guy.'

'He had a nice voice. He said, "Buona sera" really politely.' *He had the same in-built politeness as you*, Jade thought. 'Anyway, this conversation – did the Signora and Mrs Baxendall say anything else you recognised?'

'Not really, though I think I heard them mention a couple of animal names: Lupo and Volpe.'

'Volpe? That's Nonno's name. They were talking about my nonno!'

'Maybe not – isn't "lupo" wolf? And "volpe" fox?'

'Yes, so?'

'Mrs Baxendall told me there were wolves on her land – they might've been talking about problems with predators.'

'Really?' Jade looked at Nico as though he should've understood more of the conversation between the two old ladies though she knew it wasn't his fault. To her annoyance he brought the conversation round to the books, yet again.

'Have you finished *The Shattered Mirror* yet?'

Jade rolled her eyes. 'No.'

'You know I told you it's got a lot in it about the partisans.'

'Is there a point to this?' she said.

'Towards the end there's a thread about two boys, one a fascist and one a communist, who fall in love with the same girl.'

Jade's eyes widened. 'What happens next?'

'E. J. Holm doesn't say. The book ends with another murder and Alessandro vowing to find out what happened to the girl and the two boys. He's certain they're linked to the serial killings. They're the subject of the last one in the series. I thought if you read *The Shattered Mirror* tonight and I read the last book we could compare notes in the morning.'

Jade thought Nico would be lucky to read a fat book in one evening. She wasn't sure she'd manage to finish hers even though she'd already started it. She agreed anyway. 'All right, I'll give it a try.'

'Great. There might be things you notice that I didn't.'

Nico leaned back and licked the last of his ice cream. 'I need to pay Mrs Bax another visit. I'm certain she knows a lot more than she's let on so far.'

A suspicion was growing in Jade's mind. 'You think she's E. J. Holm, don't you?'

'Yes, I do. When she talked about him as "he" I think that was to put me off. I asked her if she'd ever met him and she said she'd never even shaken hands with him. She was being evasive – she wouldn't shake hands with herself, would she?'

'If she's kept it a secret this long why do you think she's going to confess now?'

Nico did his sly smile. 'Because I've got something that she really, really wants.'

Jade had no idea what it could be and she could see that Nico wasn't telling.

Jade had no difficulty in finishing *The Shattered Mirror* that night. She was gripped by the story and could see why Nico had pressed her to finish it. At the end, she dropped the book by her bed and lay thinking of where the story would go next and how it would end. Nico had better keep his part of the bargain and finish the last book, *Revenge unto the Fourth Generation*.

Nico finished the novel at around three in the morning. He put the book carefully on his bedside table. Mum would never, ever, forgive him if he damaged it.

Nico relaxed, going over what he'd just read. His mind chased possibilities round and round. He got up and drew the last flower in the chart he'd begun before he ever arrived in Florence. The set complete, he lay down in bed and fell instantly and satisfyingly asleep.

In April, Elena and Gaetano married in the church in Borgo Sant'Angelo. It was very quiet, almost secretive, with only the two sets of parents, the witnesses – I was honoured to be one – and the priest present. No one outside that select group knew that the child was not Gaetano's. Nevertheless, though Elena's parents were distressed they were resigned to the situation while Gaetano's were accepting and welcomed the girl into their home. She soon settled into the household routine and, as Easter approached, looked forward happily to helping her new mother-in-law and sister-in-law prepare the Pasqua feast.

CHAPTER XIX

THE WAITER AT the Bar Vivoli grinned at Nico and Jade. 'One pistachio and one strawberry?'

Nico didn't like to think of himself as predictable and toyed with the idea of changing his mind. He decided he liked pistachio too much to bother and nodded at the waiter. As he and Jade went to their favourite table at the back of the room Nico asked, 'What did you think of *The Shattered Mirror* then?'

'Strange. Some of it seemed very close to our story; I mean the story of Nonno and the partisans, but most of the book's about Alessandro solving the main murder and then it just ends like you said, with Alessandro vowing to find out the truth about the partisan thread.'

Nico slid his notebook across the table to Jade. It was open at the chart of flowers.

'You showed me this before,' she said.

'I know. I finished it last night and now I understand what the flower business is all about.' He spooned a dollop of pistachio out of the tub and Jade smacked his hand.

'Don't you dare eat till you've told me what it's about.'

That was so unfair; Jade had started on her tub already. 'In the early Alessandro books there were sub-plots about deaths that turned out later to be murders staged to look like accidents. The only link is that all these victims had flowers on their bodies somewhere.' Nico shovelled a spoonful of ice cream into his mouth before Jade could stop him. He swallowed quickly. 'I need to lubricate my throat, with all this talking,' he said.

'Now,' he tapped at the flowers at the end of his chart, 'when you get to these – ranunculus, laurel, rose and fern – Alessandro knows there's a serial killer on the loose and that the flowers are his signature. By this time, the killer's leaving drawings of the flowers on the victim's body. He's got arrogant and over-confident and he's flaunting what he's doing in Alessandro's face. When we get to *Murder in the Fifteenth Tower*, it's got personal for Alessandro because the killer drowns his best friend, Bruno, and little goddaughter, Tania. The murderer puts a drawing of a forget-me-not in Tania's hand.'

'That's horrible!'

'It gets worse.' Nico considered another spoonful of ice cream – it was starting to melt. He decided Jade wouldn't stand for it. 'Alessandro realises that all the flowers are from the *Primavera* painting by Botticelli and they're the code names of a partisan brigade who're killing off old fascists who never got punished after the war. In real life, lots of them did really well post-war; they even sometimes stayed in the same jobs, police chiefs, medics and so on. In the books, the flower brigade decides that isn't right and over the years they pick off their old enemies. That means there isn't one serial killer, there's a whole group. Each partisan kills the person they hate the most and leaves their own flower signature on the victim's body.'

'But why was Semiramide murdered?'

Nico shoved his tub to one side. 'You know partisans are all really old by now?'

'Well, they would be – it is 2005.'

'Yep, sixty years since the war ended and obviously quite a few partisans have died. So, in the Alessandro novels, their descendants are carrying on the "executions" as the flower brigade call them. One of the killers is Semiramide's older brother, Marco, acting for their father who died before he could carry out his execution.'

'No!'

'Yes. Because she's Alessandro's girlfriend, Semiramide knows a lot about the killer and works out some of what's been happening. She goes to Marco who admits he was the one who killed Alessandro's friend, Bruno. The partisans figure that a traitor's guilt passes down the generations and Marco was originally going to kill Bruno's father, who was on the enemy side, but since he's no longer around, Marco decides to kill Bruno instead even though he didn't have the same views as his father.'

'Why Tania? She was only a little girl.'

'She just happened to be with Bruno when Marco attacked him and he had to kill her to prevent her from identifying him.'

'That's horrible, killing a child!'

'She was in the wrong place at the wrong time.'

Nico knew he and Jade were thinking the same thing: Gaetano's niece had been at the farmhouse at the wrong time. He hurried on with the story: 'Marco's so full of deranged hatred that he's blind to everything except vengeance. He expects Semiramide to agree with him but she flies at him screaming, "How could you kill a child and an innocent man?" She says she's going to tell Alessandro . . .'

'No!'

'That's right – Marco kills Semiramide.'

'Does Alessandro find out? Well, course he does, I mean how does he find out?'

This was the difficult part, Nico thought, the part where the story turned from Semiramide to the final victim in the series.

'After Semiramide's murder Alessandro deduces who the latest victim is going to be: a Black Brigade boy who'd betrayed his best friend because the girl they both loved had rejected him and was going to marry the best friend.'

Nico ran through the rest of the plot. It mirrored Roberto's story almost exactly.

Jade huddled in her seat. Nico reached over and took her hand. 'Are you OK?'

'Yes.' She squeezed his hand briefly and pulled hers away. 'What happened to the Black Brigade boy?'

'Nothing.'

'What? Don't the partisans take revenge?'

That had puzzled Nico too, at first. 'Alessandro prevents the killing of the old ex-Black Brigader, and rounds up Marco and the other murderers. The book ends where Alessandro thinks about vengeance and how it turns in on itself until innocent people like Tania become victims. It's the end of the murders and the end of the Alessandro books altogether. I think E. J. Holm is saying there's a time for payback to stop.'

Jade chewed at her lip. 'I don't understand . . .'

'What?'

'How did E. J. Holm – how did Mrs Baxendall, if she is E. J. Holm – get to know so much about the story? And why write it?'

'I suppose she wrote it because it's a good story; on the other hand, how she got to know about it . . .' Nico spread his hands wide. 'We know she's friendly with the Signora who's friendly with Gaetano – perhaps he told Mrs Bax.

That's the sort of thing I want to ask when I go and see her.'

Nico's phone weebled. 'It's from Mum. She wants us to come back ASAP.'

'Why?'

'She doesn't say.' Nico put out his hand again and this time Jade took it and held onto it. He pulled her to her feet and slipped his arm round her. Outside they walked along quietly. 'What are you thinking?' Nico asked.

'The letter from Elena – I was wondering, is it in the book too?'

'No, it isn't.'

'It's not exactly the same story as my nonno's then?'

'No, and don't forget, we're talking about a novel we know is different from the facts – for a start the fictional Roberto is still alive and in Tuscany. Besides that, maybe E. J. Holm – Mrs Bax – didn't know about the letter and is guessing what happened to the real Roberto – who knows?'

Nico's phone weebled again. 'Apparently the Signora wants to see us.'

'Why?'

'Mum doesn't say that either. Let's get back or she'll keep harassing us.'

Jade agreed and they walked the rest of the way lost in their own thoughts.

*

When Jade knocked on the Signora's door she came out immediately, elegantly dressed in black set off with a colourful scarf in green, red and white. 'I have hired a taxi for the afternoon. We will go first to a cafe in the Piazza della Repubblica.'

OK, Jade thought, *apparently we don't have any choice.*

The taxi dropped them off close to a grand, glossy cafe where a waiter hurried over. 'You would like a seat?' he asked the Signora in a deferential manner.

'We will sit outside,' she said in English.

'Of course.' The waiter was fascinated by the Signora's scarf. Jade didn't think there was anything particularly special about it apart from a central motif of an eagle, which seemed a bit out of character for an elderly lady.

'I find you the good table.'

The waiter wafted them to a seat bathed in sunshine and shaded by a white umbrella. He took their order and they made small talk until the drinks arrived.

'Why are we here?' Jade asked bluntly. 'Are you going to tell us more about Nonno?'

The Signora put her cup down delicately. 'In a way.' She did one of her abrupt changes and smiled at Jade. 'You are from Derby, no?'

'Yes.' *And what's that got to do with anything?* Jade wondered.

'I did some investigations and discovered that during the five years of the Second World War, seventy-four people were killed in Derby and over three hundred wounded. During the four weeks of the battle to liberate Florence, two hundred and five partisans were killed and four hundred wounded. That is to say, one hundred and thirty-one more people died here in those few weeks than died in Derby during the whole of the war.'

Jade didn't know what the Signora expected her to say; there was no point in saying 'sorry' because this time the tragedy had nothing to do with her.

'During the German occupation of Florence the resistance movement here in the north harassed the enemy constantly. There were consequences. A special police force was set up, the Banda Carità. It was named after the chief of Police, Mario Carità. He had begun his life's work in Milan when he was just fifteen years old, assassinating those who did not share his political beliefs.'

Fifteen! *My age*, Jade thought, *and a year younger than Nico.*

'Carità's methods of torture were feared even more than those of the German secret police. The partisans decided something had to be done to stop him.' The Signora paused to sip at her coffee. She put the cup down without even the suggestion of a tremor and carried on with her story in a matter-of-fact, emotionless voice.

'This cafe was popular with German officers and high-ranking Italian fascists including Mario Carità. It was decided to assassinate him here at eight o'clock, the cocktail hour, on 8th February 1944. A young couple was selected to carry out the killing – Antonio Ignesti and a young woman of eighteen . . .'

Was this young woman the Signora? Jade wouldn't have been surprised by anything that the steely old lady had done.

'Her name was Tosca Buccarelli, Toschina to her friends. For several weeks Toschina and Antonio came here, pretending to be an engaged couple. They noted Carità's movements and where his favourite table was. A partisan, who worked as a waiter here, fixed a hook under the table next to Carità's usual seat.

'The date arrived. Although the cafe was crowded, Toschina and Antonio managed to sit next to Carità's group. Toschina took a small parcel wrapped in tissue paper from her handbag. It was a bomb. Antonio lit a cigarette and used the match to light the fuse. Toschina fumbled for the hook under the table and dropped the bomb. She picked it up, pinched out the fuse and put it back in her bag.'

Jade couldn't even begin to imagine putting a half-lit bomb in her bag. 'Was it safe?'

'Yes, but a German officer had seen what happened and raised the alarm. Though Toschina managed to slip away Antonio was detained. He was in poor health – she knew he would never survive interrogation and she turned

254

back. In the following confusion Antonio escaped. This time, Toschina did not.'

The Signora finished the last sip of her coffee, her grip still steady.

'What happened next?' Jade asked. 'To Toschina.'

'She was taken to the House of Sorrow.' The Signora stood. 'That is where we are going next.'

I learned later that during the massacre at the farmhouse, Gaetano's father was dragged into the courtyard and shot dead in front of his family. They were loaded onto a truck and never seen again. Henryk and a partisan were also killed, as was a Black Brigade member. Two partisans and three escaped prisoners of war who'd joined our band of resistance fighters were taken prisoner and executed later.

In the time it took for the Black Brigade to achieve their 'victory', Gaetano, Ilaria and others in our band had got Elena to safety and me into hiding. A local doctor did his best to patch me up temporarily, and partisans supported me along the Freedom Trail to the Allies who then took over my care.

I know this part of the story from talking to survivors of the massacre long after the war had ended. I was also told that the boy who shot me was Roberto, the friend turned traitor. He had decided to sever the ties of childhood loyalties at last; his political beliefs overrode his personal affection for his foster family and he chose to alert the Black Brigade. It was bad luck that we were all gathered together – such an easy target – on that fateful Easter Sunday.

I asked Ilaria if she remembered what Roberto had said immediately before he shot me. She told me that in the noise and confusion of the fighting she couldn't make out the words.

Now I'm writing this memoir of my time with the partisans and my small part in their victory. I hope that in writing it, I may even recover the last, fugitive memory that has eluded me for so many years.

CHAPTER XX

THE TAXI STOPPED in a side street of affluent-looking houses and flats. They got out on a corner facing an elegant apartment block in shades of grey.

'What do you think of it?' the Signora asked, waving at the tall building.

Jade didn't really have an opinion. She'd never thought about architecture at all until she came to Florence – it was just an ordinary block of flats to her.

Nico was looking at it thoughtfully, his eyes narrowed. 'It's strange. At first sight it looks imposing – those two wings jutting out from the central column, and the proportions are really well thought out but . . .'

'What?' Jade said.

'There's something a bit . . . brutal about it. The wings are aggressive, in-your-face, and they suck you into the entrance.'

Jade saw what he meant. 'It's not very welcoming.'

The Signora made a strange sound between a snort of derision and a laugh. 'It is called "Villa Triste" – "the

House of Sorrow". Come with me.' She ushered them across the road to the entrance of the apartment block. After what the Signora had called it Jade saw the building differently and, despite its stylish proportions, she felt uneasy in its shadow.

'This was always the fashionable place to live,' the Signora said. 'It has wonderful views over the city. During the war, the German secret police liked it so much they took it over and allowed Mario Carità to have the basement and the first floor. It was here they brought Toschina.'

Signora Minardi pointed to a stone plaque set into the wall. 'Can you understand this?'

Jade knew Nico couldn't. She scanned it quickly, meaning to read it out to him. Despite being written in a complicated poetic way she realised what it meant and knew there was no way she could read it aloud without choking up. 'Not really,' she said to the Signora.

The old lady placed her hand gently on the hard grey wall. 'I have thought many times of how to put this into English and I think you will understand if I translate it thus:

"This is no longer a place of sorrow if you
recognise that within its walls dwells a
fraternity of innocent souls who, when they
lived, faced their torturers armed only with

their consciences and a determination not to
betray their compatriots. To this end they
were willing to languish, suffer and die.'"

'I don't know what to say,' Jade whispered.

'My dear, I am bringing you and Nico here only so
that you might begin to understand what it was like for
us when we were the age you are now.' The Signora
glanced up at the plaque. 'I can give you the numbers, I
know them by heart: of 224,000 partisans 62,000 were
killed and 33,000 were badly wounded. Of the ordinary
people trying only to survive, 15,000 were murdered
and 5,000 wounded. Fifty-seven priests in the Florence
area were tortured and killed. There were 35,000 women
fighters. 5,000 were imprisoned, six hundred and fifty
were executed or died in combat, and 3,000 were deported
to Germany. Seventeen were awarded the gold medal for
valour.'

The Signora paused. 'But these are numbers – they
are cold. You understand more in your hearts if I tell
you about a single person; that is why I am showing you
the story of Toschina. She was brought to the House of
Sorrow and interrogated. Bright lights were shone into
her eyes so that she became blind. Days, weeks of torture
followed – sometimes Carità and his mistress watched
and sometimes a priest played the piano and sang songs
to drown out Toschina's screams.'

Jade went white. Nico hugged her protectively. 'We get the message – I think that's enough for now,' he said to the Signora.

'I think so also. It is time to drive far away from here, to the hills to sit in a pleasant cafe and forget the war for a while.'

Eating was the last thing Jade wanted to do but the Signora was already walking briskly back to the taxi. 'You OK?' Nico asked.

'No.'

'D'you want to go back to the apartment?'

'No.'

Jade was grateful that Nico accepted what she said and didn't ask further questions. She wanted to know more – about Toschina, about the Signora, about Nonno. Eventually she'd get herself together and be able to ask for answers.

The Signora instructed the taxi driver to take them to Fiesole and he drove into the countryside to a small town perched in the hills. They got out in a piazza with a wide view over the flowing countryside.

'We will do the little tour like proper tourists,' the Signora said with a smile and Jade cracked a grin as Nico pretended to look horrified.

Signora Minardi took them to the Roman amphi-theatre with lizards basking on its stone terraces. They sat on the warm steps and the Signora talked about the little town's long history. Jade let it all wash over her, taking in a bit here and there and gradually finding her frozen soul warming. With a jolt she realised that Nico and the Signora were looking at her expectantly.

'What?'

'We're hungry, how about you?' Nico said.

As if in answer Jade's stomach rumbled. She patted it apologetically. Nico pulled her to her feet and then offered his arm to the Signora. They walked to where the taxi driver was waiting patiently. He dropped them off at a restaurant and promised to be back in two hours. The waiters made a fuss of the Signora, ushered her to a terrace with astonishing views down to Florence and wafted her to a table in a secluded corner.

'They know her, don't they?' Jade whispered to Nico.

'Yep – everybody seems to in these places. And have you noticed how they seem a bit scared of her?'

Jade saw what Nico meant. Within minutes of placing their order the manager appeared and greeted the Signora effusively, his eyes darting to her scarf. The Signora responded like a queen and serenely waved him away. He left as quickly as he'd appeared, red-faced and sweating.

'I'm ravenous,' Jade said.

'Me too, I could eat a horse,' Nico agreed.

'And I,' the Signora added. 'Fortunately, the food here is very good, there is no need to eat the horses. While we are waiting we can admire the views.'

To Jade's surprise Nico came out with, 'È incantevole.'

'Indeed.' The Signora patted her hands together in polite applause. 'If you look over this "enchanting" view to the horizon, to the mountain peak on the left, and imagine the place behind it, that is where the Carrara marble quarries are.'

'Where Michelangelo got his stone from,' Jade said, pleased to be able to join in a conversation about art. In the end, the fake project had turned out to be interesting.

The food arrived swiftly and was replenished unobtrusively as they chatted about the art and history of the area. 'Signora Minardi,' Jade asked, 'what happened to all the art during the war?'

'Many treasures were hidden in villas throughout Tuscany. Still the enemy found them and sent truckloads of priceless art away. Much has been found again and restored to Florence.' The Signora sighed. 'The architecture suffered too. Most of what was reduced to rubble has been rebuilt and the damage to the Duomo has been repaired.'

'They bombed the Duomo!'

Jade could understand Nico's rage; she'd never forget the effect their first sight of the cathedral had had on her family.

The Signora waved her arm over the panorama far below. 'The Germans bombarded Florence from here in Fiesole. The ancient bridges over the Arno had been blown up before this time, except for the Ponte Vecchio and that was blocked with rubble to prevent the Allies from using it to cross into the city. The enemy had even weakened the wooden beams of a secret passageway above the bridge and mined each end. There were also the sharpshooters – snipers, I think you call them now.

'Despite this, the partisans and British agents ran a telephone line along it to communicate with the Allies on the south side of the Arno.' The Signora smiled. 'They lowered the line down a rope to an American vehicle with a transmitter.'

'Neat,' Nico said, his voice full of admiration.

'People still died,' Jade said. 'It wasn't a game.'

'No, cara, it wasn't,' the Signora agreed. 'They were great adventures all the same.'

The Signora's eyes shone. Were they lit by pride, Jade wondered? Or something else that Jade would never be able to understand. Jade took a deep breath; if the Signora, as a girl, had been brave enough to fight a powerful and vicious enemy then Jade surely had enough courage to ask a few questions? After all, it was only her feelings that were bruised.

'Signora Minardi, what happened to Toschina? Did she die?'

'No, my dear, she didn't. Would you like me to tell you the rest of her story?'

'Yes, please.'

'After months of suffering at the Villa Triste, Toschina could no longer speak or even move very much. She was of no use to Carità and she was sent to a women's prison run by nuns. The Mother Superior, Ermelinda, was ordered to nurse Toschina back to health and then tell Carità so that he could begin her torture again.

'For some reason, Carità seemed to lose interest in her, even to forget her. And then, months later, a group of uniformed Nazis arrived with documents authorizing Toschina's release. The guard at the prison picked up the telephone to check that this was correct. One of the "Nazis" pulled out a pistol and told the guard to drop the phone.

'Mother Ermelinda heard the noise and came to see what was happening. When she realised the soldiers were partisans in disguise she made them release all the other political prisoners as well.'

The Signora smiled at Jade. 'So you see, cara, Toschina's mission, though it failed in its objective of killing Carità, saved many lives in the end – including mine.'

'Yours? You were a prisoner there?' Jade's stomach twisted.

'That's right. I was a *staffetta* – a sort of messenger. We acted as couriers for the resistance because it wasn't safe to use the telephone or the postal service. We carried ammunition in our bags or in cushions pushed into our skirts to make us look pregnant. Sometimes mothers took their babies out for a walk in prams lined with bombs.'

'Didn't the enemy suspect anything?'

The Signora laughed. 'In those days women were thought to be passive, weak creatures without enough intelligence to deceive the military.'

'Why were you in the prison?' Jade asked.

'I grew careless, too bold after the massacre at the farmhouse and eventually I was captured. They took me first to Villa Triste. I was not there for very long before I was sent to the prison. Later, as I said, I escaped with the others who were freed by Toschina's rescuers.'

What did 'not there for very long' mean, Jade wondered. The Signora might've been there for days, weeks even. Jade wouldn't have survived for more than a few moments, she was sure of it. 'No wonder you hate my nonno,' she said.

'It is true that I hated Roberto – perhaps I always will – but as I said last night, never you or your sister or your mother. I am not a believer in the saying that the sins of the father shall be passed down to the third and fourth generation.'

'Isn't that the title of E. J. Holm's latest book?' Nico said, '*Vengeance unto the Fourth Generation.*'

Not again, Jade thought. Why did Nico have to bring everything, every time, back to E. J. Holm?

The Signora wasn't fazed, and she didn't pretend not to know what Nico was talking about. 'Yes. It is called that because the book is about what happens when revenge is taken beyond what is reasonable and enjoyed for its own sake.'

'That's one interpretation,' Nico said.

'It is not an interpretation, caro, it is what I know to be true.'

Jade didn't see how the Signora could possibly know that for sure unless she also knew who E. J. Holm was and he – or more likely, she – had told her. *Nico can hardly challenge her on that*, she thought; Signora Minardi was an elderly lady who deserved respect. She was wrong: Nico came straight out with, 'I think Mrs Baxendall could be E. J. Holm – what do you think?'

'It is not for me to say, caro.'

That was interesting. She hadn't said, 'I don't know,' which anyone who *really* didn't know would've said.

'I think perhaps you should ask her yourself,' the Signora added.

'D'you think she'd tell me if I did?' Nico asked.

'You will not know unless you try.'

'That's true,' Nico said, his eyes very bright. Jade knew that now the Signora had practically given him permission, Nico was going to be visiting Mrs Baxendall as soon as possible.

*

Nico waited for Jade in the apartment garden while she visited the hospital to talk to Amber about what she'd learned from the Signora. She didn't look all that happy when she got back.

'How did she take it?' Nico asked as Jade flopped into a chair.

'My sister,' Jade said grimly, 'is not the same since Dario.'

Nico thought that was a bit cryptic. 'What?'

'I mean before, any suggestion Nonno was even a little bit guilty and she blew like a volcano and now . . .' Jade shook her head. 'It's as if she's accepted it because Dario says it's all true and whatever Dario says is bound to be right.' She wrinkled up her nose in disgust. 'It's like he's God or something!'

'Isn't that a bit unfair . . .'

Jade glared at him.

Nico hurried to repair the damage. 'I only meant she's had time to think about it and it's hard for her to keep denying the facts.'

'Nothing's convinced her before.'

'What about you? How do you feel?'

'Blank mostly. But I keep coming back to Elena's letter – why it was in that tin and why it never got delivered.'

'I think you'll have to show it to Gaetano.'

'I guess. Will you come with me? I don't want to face him on my own, he's such a, such a . . .'

Nico used the very worst Italian expression Jade and Amber had taught him.

'That's the one. Will you come with me?'

'Only if you come with me to Mrs Bax's tomorrow.'

'I'm really sorry, I can't; I promised to spend the day with the family.'

'It's OK,' Nico said as casually as he could, hoping his disappointment didn't show.

'Are you really going to ask her straight out if she's E. J. Holm?'

'Yep.'

'D'you think she'll admit it?'

'Yes.' Nico's quirky smile crept back. 'I'm certain because . . .'

'What?'

'I'll tell you afterwards when I've got my answers.'

'That's not fair!'

Good, he'd piqued Jade's interest and provoked a reaction. 'In the meantime,' he said, 'you've got to read this.' He pushed *Revenge unto the Fourth Generation* towards her.

Jade picked the book up. 'It's even fatter than *The Shattered Mirror*!'

'Get reading,' Nico said. She opened the book un-enthusiastically. Nico took out his drawing book and doodled idly for a while. When Jade was hooked into the story he began to draw her, confident that she was no longer aware of him or what he was doing.

England – a room with white walls, a large window – people coming and going – strangers – silence

The memories come again. Noises: screaming, commands shouted in Italian, Polish, English – gunfire – the smell of cordite – the ping and smack of bullets against stone

A girl slamming a door, turning, what's her name? Ilaria. The boy's face, laughing – the shotgun – why can't I remember?

A cool wind and the susurration of leaves – the sound of hooves on a dirt track, on shale and scree, on rock – jolting along – rock and more rock

Thirst and pain

A girl slamming a door – turning – Ilaria. The boy's face, still laughing – the shotgun – why can't I remember? Why? Why?

'What are you trying to remember?'

I turned my head and it hurt. I found myself looking at a nurse, an English nurse in a blue uniform with a white cap and apron. She was young and had large, round eyes. 'I don't know,' I mumbled. Thinking was too hard, my face hurt and something was wrong with my eyes. I closed them and went to sleep.

When I woke again I was fully conscious and aware of my surroundings: a room in what was obviously a hospital, the walls white, the curtains green, the bed metal-framed, the linen crisp and clean and the mattress far more comfortable than the hay I had grown used to sleeping on. The smell was largely of disinfectant. There was a vase of tulips on the table near the window. It was all very British.

I called out, or rather I tried to call out. Pain lanced down my face as I opened my mouth and at the same time I realised that it was bound with dressings. I felt tentatively at the bandages and found they extended over my left eye.

The memories intruded again: a girl – Ilaria – slamming a door, turning – a boy's mocking face – the shotgun – he said something and then fired. Why couldn't I remember what he said?

The other memories began to make more sense: a mule carrying me through the chestnut woods, sure-footed on the scree of the higher slopes of the hills and then I was struggling on foot, sometimes being carried, over the Marble Mountains. Finally, blessed relief in reaching the Allies who airlifted me – where? My thoughts continued, strained and jumbled, until I fell asleep again.

This was the state of affairs I found myself in for some time: sleeping, waking, struggling to remember; remembering too much. In time, I learned most of what had happened.

The boy had used a shotgun – one of the miscellany of arms commandeered by the Black Brigades during a rastrellamento *or raking – and shot me in the face. Fortunately for me, even at close range, his aim was hasty and went wide. Most of the discharge whistled past my ear but the spread of pellets ripped into the side of my face, stripping much of the skin, damaging parts of the underlying muscle and inflicting some nerve damage also. My left eye was irreparably damaged.*

Somehow – I couldn't remember how – I was got out of the farmhouse and through the woods behind it. I was treated, as far as was possible under the circumstances, by the local doctor (thankfully a partisan supporter) before being helped to safety and an Allied field hospital on the other side of the mountains. After patching me up, they flew me out to a military medical centre set up by the British in Naples. After that, I was flown back to England and cared for in a specialist plastic surgery unit.

The left side of my face remained badly damaged. I was scarred and unable to move some of the muscle properly meaning that my mouth was left permanently twisted. Though my left eye was saved I was never going to recover its use.

As I went through the surgery, the skin grafts and the periods of recovery, I brooded on my confused memories, always tormented by that question: what was it that the boy said before he shot me?

CHAPTER XXI

JADE LOOKED UP as Dario came into Amber's room. Now she was going to feel a real gooseberry while they sat and held hands. It was a shame Mum and Dad had gone to discuss Amber's discharge date with the doctors.

'Gaetano would like you to go and see him,' Dario said to Jade.

'Why?'

'There's someone he wants you to meet.'

'Who?'

'You'll see.' Dario slipped into the seat next to the bed as Jade left it. *Bet you wouldn't jump into my grave as quick*, she thought, then felt mean. It was hardly Amber and Dario's fault if they had feelings for each other.

She knocked on Gaetano's door and a woman's voice called, 'Avanti!' Jade went in and stared in surprise at the two people sitting either side of Gaetano's bed: one was Signora Minardi, the other the scarred man Jade had seen in the garden. By daylight the extent of his horrible disfigurement was clear: the left side of his face was distorted: scarred and twisted, the eyelid almost closed over a blank, bluish mass. Even his carefully cut, thick white hair couldn't disguise the furrows running from his eye socket and along the side of his skull. He stood, the mobile half of his mouth smiling at Jade. 'How do you do.'

'Pleased to meet you properly,' Jade said wondering who the man was and what he had to do with the Signora.

The old man chuckled. 'I'm Alec, Emily Baxendall's father,' he said.

'Oh.' Jade was more confused than ever. She couldn't think of any reason why she should be introduced to him or even why he was here with the Signora.

'Come, come.' Gaetano beckoned impatiently to her.

Too bemused to protest, she went.

'I have this for you.' He thrust the battered tobacco tin at Jade.

She took it. 'I don't understand.'

'I told you I would give it to the person who owned it but now you are here while he is visiting me I decided that you can give it to him yourself.'

'I still don't understand – who do I give it to?'

'Him.' Gaetano pointed to Alec. 'He left it behind when we took him to the hills.'

Mrs Baxendall's father was the English spy? Jade gave the tin to Alec. 'I found it hidden in a gap over the stable door.'

Alec prised up the lid and took out the silk map and the photograph. As he read the inscription on the back of the picture a smile tugged at the undamaged side of his face and Jade saw a shadow of the young soldier in his features. 'I carried this with me through the war. It never occurred to me that it might come to light after so many years. I thought it had gone for good.'

The Signora spoke: 'I'm glad it's been found again, Alec. I know it was precious to you.'

Alec turned the photo towards the Signora. She waved it away. 'Gaetano showed me yesterday.'

Alec put the photo back in the tin and snapped it shut. 'I'm glad to have it,' he said in a soft voice.

That's all peachy, Jade thought, *but it still doesn't explain why Nonno never got the letter*. She plucked it out of her bag. 'What about this?' she said, her voice coming out louder and more challenging than she'd meant it to.

'What is it?' Signora Minardi said.

'It's a letter from Elena to my nonno.' Jade said. She was gratified to see the effect that had: Alec puzzled, Gaetano taken aback, the Signora – what? Angry, from the set of her mouth. Well, Jade was angry too, so angry she was surprised her hands didn't shake as she read the letter out. When she got to the part where Elena talked about marriage to Gaetano she folded the paper over and used her own words. 'Elena says if Roberto doesn't come for her she'll marry Gaetano instead because she loves and respects him.' Though it was hard for her to say that when she knew how Elena really felt, she couldn't hurt the old man, not after all this time and especially not after what he'd done for Amber. 'She says she's going to ask someone she trusts to post the letter.'

She put it away. It was addressed to Nonno and no one was going to read it except his family. 'What I want to know is, who was the person who was supposed to deliver the letter and why did it end up in the tin?'

'I would like to know these things also,' Gaetano said.

'I can tell you,' the Signora said.

'You?' Jade frowned.

'Elena gave the letter to me,' Signora Minardi said calmly. 'I worked in the town and could post it for her, and she trusted me. I took it first to show Alec.'

'Why?' Gaetano said.

'I didn't trust Roberto and wasn't sure if I should send it to him. I hoped Alec would know what to do.' The Signora smiled at Alec. 'Do you remember? You had no more idea than me; you put the letter in the tin and said, "We'll talk about it another time and decide what to do then."'

'I do remember that,' Alec said slowly, his eye focussed on somewhere far away as if trying to envisage that moment. 'I hoped that you'd realise for yourself that it was far too dangerous to take the letter direct to Volpe in Florence. In the end, there was no "other time" to talk and then it was too late.' He gripped Gaetano's shoulder. 'You married your Elena and I forgot about the letter till now.'

'That's convenient,' Jade said. Alec might seem a cuddly old man with a nice smile, but he'd been a soldier and a spy. He'd held onto that letter and stopped Nonno from having the chance to go to Elena. She didn't believe he was absent-minded. He agreed with her.

'Age hasn't made me forget,' he said. 'Some of my memories of that time are hazy because Roberto Volpe shot me in the head.'

The ravaged face in front of Jade was like a reproach and she felt sick. Nonno had done that to Alec? No, no! He couldn't have; she wouldn't believe it.

'I've recovered most of my memories now,' Alec said gently, 'though I still have no recollection of anything in the moments before it happened.'

Signora Minardi spoke coldly. 'Whether the letter was delivered or not makes no difference – Roberto Volpe chose to betray us and everything changed: the partisans fought to get Alec away to the hills and over the mountains to the Allies. That put an end to operations for some time while the partisans regrouped and more agents were parachuted in. Who knows how many innocent people the Black Brigades killed as a result of that? And there were reprisals: a tenth of the local people were executed as an example of what happened to those who defied the fascists. And I – I was eventually taken to the Villa Triste. After what happened at the farmhouse, Elena had no more love for Roberto Volpe than we did.'

'You don't know what Nonno would've done!' Jade protested. 'You didn't give him a chance. If only you'd told him straight away he might've come for Elena and that might've changed him.'

Gaetano snorted in contempt.

'You think you know all about him,' Jade shouted. 'You don't. He loved his wife – my grandmother Grace – and my mother, and he loved Amber and me. Who are you to say he wouldn't have loved Elena and the baby just the same?'

The door flew open and a nurse came in. 'You're distressing the patient,' she said to Jade. 'I think you should leave now.'

'I'm going,' Jade blurted out and ran from the room.

Nico and Mrs Baxendall sat on the sofa in front of her spectacular view. Nico lowered the plastic bag he'd been carrying carefully and it hit the floor with a loud thunk. Mrs Bax stared at it. 'I assume that's the surprise you rang me about? I despatched Teo immediately you said that you needed to see me urgently.'

'I exaggerated a bit. I wanted you to have it sooner rather than later. You'll know how to look after it properly.'

Mrs Baxendall craned forward as Nico lifted out the

blue bowl he'd bought in San Gimignano. There was a plant in it. Though it was only a collection of faintly sickly, yellowish-green leaves Mrs Bax's reaction was startling. She flung herself on the bowl, grasped it to her ample bosom and gazed at the plant as though it were the crown jewels. 'My dear, where did you find it?' she demanded.

'Up against the wall of the garage where the accident happened. The ground was soaked in sump oil. Funny sort of fertiliser but it seemed to like it. It's the elleboro isn't it? The last plant you needed to finish your set?'

'Indeed it is!' Mrs Baxendall was rapt.

Nico felt smug. 'Here . . .' he took handwritten pages out of the bag, '. . . is my report, in detail, of how I found it.'

Mrs Baxendall beamed at him. 'How will I ever repay you?'

Although Nico knew she didn't mean it literally, she'd unwittingly given him the chance to challenge her with the question he was burning to ask. 'Actually, you can do something for me.'

'Hm?' she said absently, all her attention on the ugly plant.

'It's about E. J. Holm.'

Teo poked his head round the door. 'Signora Bax?'

Go away, Nico thought. *Please, go away!*

'You have visitors,' Teo said and ushered in Signora Minardi and an elderly man. For a moment Nico's guts clenched as he took in the man's heavily scarred face and blank eye. He had to be the man Jade had seen in the garden; there couldn't be two people with an identical disfigurement.

'Nico,' Mrs Baxendall said, 'let me introduce you. This is my father, Alec – Father, this is Nico who has brought me the most magnificent gift.'

'Whatever can it be,' the old man said. He held out his hand to Nico. 'How d'you do?'

Nico saw past the hideous facial distortion to the striking man standing in front of him with a dignified, uncompromising bearing. 'How d'you do, sir.'

'Call me Alec.'

The four of them sat down, Alec eyeing the ugly plant. 'I presume that's your incomparable gift to my daughter?'

Mrs Baxendall explained, heaping praise on Nico till he wanted to squirm with embarrassment. Desperate to change the subject he asked the Signora, 'Is there any news of Gaetano?'

'He is doing very well and will return home tomorrow. Alec and I have just been visiting him. He wishes to pass on some news to Emily and since it involves your friend Jade, we will share it with you also.'

'Oh?'

Alec put the familiar tobacco tin on the table. 'Jade found this, as I'm sure you know already.'

'Yes, I was there when she gave it to Gaetano.' Nico

had no idea what was coming next. Whatever it was, he didn't think he was going to like it.

'Since Gaetano knew that it was mine he asked Jade to return it to me herself. He thought that was fitting.'

'That means you were the spy!' Nico blurted out as Mrs Bax reached for the tin.

'I was in the SOE – the Special Operations Executive – set up to work with the partisans throughout Europe. I joined the Uccelli Squad in the winter of '43. I was lucky enough to be billeted on Gaetano's family.'

Lucky? That was an odd thing to say when you ended up being shot in the head, Nico thought.

Mrs Baxendall found the picture. 'A photo of Mother and me,' she said softly.

'There was more than a handkerchief and a photograph inside,' the Signora said. 'Jade also found a letter.'

To Nico's mounting horror, Signora Minardi recounted the story of how the letter came to be hidden and what the consequences were. It was hard to take in; it must've been harder still for Jade, especially when she was confronted with Alec bearing the indisputable marks of her grandfather's brutality.

Alec's soft voice broke into Nico's roiling thoughts. 'Your friend, Jade, might need company. She was very distressed at what she learned.'

'I'll go now,' Nico said. He gave polite if perfunctory goodbyes and Teo drove him back to Florence. Jade wasn't answering her phone, which probably meant she wanted space. He sent a text saying he knew about Alec and asking her to contact him when she was ready, then he asked Teo to drop him off Oltr'Arno. Jade wasn't the only one who needed time and a place to think.

Jade didn't tell her family about what Nonno had done; it was too horrific. She'd talk to Nico about it later. Instead she told them about the letter and how it had been lost until now and then she gave it to Mum. She read it out loud.

'When I told them about the letter,' Jade said, 'I left out the bit about Elena not loving Gaetano. I thought that might upset him.'

'Good girl,' Dad said.

'What do you want to do with it, Mum?' Amber asked.

Mum held it for a moment then ripped it up.

'Mum!' Jade and Amber shouted.

'What's the point of keeping it? The story's over and done with, your nonno's gone, Elena's gone. Gaetano mustn't know what Elena really said; it would be too cruel after all this time. We're making friends with our family over here – we don't need an old letter stirring things up again.'

It's a bit late for that, Jade thought. How were those traumatised old people ever going to get over what Nonno had done to them? Especially Alec.

Mum threw the pieces in the bin. Her face was glowing. 'It's a relief to get to the truth, even if it's not the truth I wanted. And tomorrow we've got a real treat, at least I have.'

'What?' Jade said.

'I'm going to meet Sofia. She's coming back from Milan especially. We're going to the Villa dei Fiori tomorrow to meet my sister.'

Nico walked and pondered. He wondered what Jade would tell her family, especially Amber who, until Dario, wouldn't hear a word spoken against Roberto. Nico was certain the shock of seeing Alec must've hurt Jade more than the Signora's lecture tour; he was a living example of what Roberto had done and it couldn't be explained away no matter how much the twins wanted it.

Nico headed for Alessandro's trattoria near Via Drago D'Oro. Mum and James were sitting at a table outside. They looked happy. Nico didn't mind any more. He decided not to disturb them and found a small square with a restaurant serving pizzas.

He made himself stop thinking about Jade and Roberto and concentrated on his search for E. J. Holm. Mrs Baxendall definitely had strong connections to the Alessandro Lupo books: there were the locations in the novels while the theme based on the Roberto–Gaetano–Elena triangle surely had to mean E. J. Holm was a friend or acquaintance of the people involved? Mrs Baxendall was certainly friends with Gaetano, and they were both friends with Ilaria Minardi.

Nico groaned in frustration and switched to people-watching. Locals went about their business, laughing and smiling; a young woman stopped and washed her feet in a nearby fountain and chatted to an elderly man perched on its rim. The warmth and friendliness and lack of inhibition about things that didn't matter summed up everything he liked about being in Florence.

After his meal, he walked to the Church of Santa Maria del Carmine, which was on his must-see list. He found the fresco he wanted to look at. It showed Adam and Eve walking from Paradise into the real world. It was a simple painting, in muted ochres and washed-out blues and greens, and it felt to Nico as though the two figures embodied the grief of the world. He thought of the partisans, of the Villa Triste, of Roberto, Gaetano, Elena and Alec and lit a candle for them all.

Jade knocked at the Signora's door and Ornella let her in. Signora Minardi was sitting by a window reading *Revenge unto the Fourth Generation*. Jade noticed she'd almost finished it.

'I'm sorry I got angry at the hospital,' Jade said. 'It was a shock.'

'I understand.' The Signora didn't look particularly understanding though Jade didn't blame her.

'The letter, from my nonno, I need to ask you about it.'

'What would you like to know?'

'It's not exactly that I want to know anything. It's that you've read it and even though it was a long time ago you probably still remember it.'

The Signora smiled. '*My* memory is reliable.'

'I thought it would be,' Jade said. 'I expect you noticed, when I talked about what was in the letter, that I changed it a bit? Elena didn't really love Gaetano like I said. I mean, she said she liked him but she loved Roberto. I didn't think Gaetano needed to know that.'

'You are a wise child,' the Signora said. 'And a kind one.' Her stern expression softened.

'You won't tell Gaetano will you? My family won't and Nico said he won't and Mrs Baxendall's father can't remember.'

'I agree that there is no point after all this time. It is a sin of omission that will hurt no one. However, there is still a problem.'

'What?' Jade asked warily.

'The letter itself; your mother will no doubt want to show it to Sofia, perhaps even Caterina, and the truth will one day emerge, as the letter has done.'

Jade shook her head. 'No, Mum ripped the letter up. It's gone, for ever this time. Mum said we've found new friends and family over here. She doesn't want to spoil things by talking about what happened in the past.'

'Ah, at last.'

That's a weird thing to say, Jade thought. And even stranger that the Signora sounded elated. Ilaria Minardi rose from her chair. 'Thank you, Jade, it's good to know that the story has ended. We each of us know the whole truth and can put the past behind us.' She placed her hands on Jade's shoulders. 'Don't you agree?'

'Yes,' Jade said.

She went back to the apartment wondering why the Signora's words, when they were perfectly reasonable, had left her feeling so uneasy.

CHAPTER XXII

NICO'S MOTHER HAD been thrilled with her invitation to visit Mrs Baxendall, awed by the house and overwhelmed at the sight of shelves of E. J. Holm books in the lounge.

'Emily, these are wonderful,' she gushed.

It wasn't that long ago, Nico thought, that his mother had been calling Mrs Bax a dangerous old bat and forbidding him to go near her.

Mum touched one of the books. 'May I?'

'Of course,' Mrs Bax said. 'Help yourself.'

Mum opened a copy of the first in the Alessandro Lupo series, *The Leopard's Kill*. She stroked the ornate bookplate reverently. 'This is signed and there's a dedication in Italian.' Mum had never tried to learn Italian; her excuse was that she was rubbish at languages. 'What does it say?'

'Something along the lines of, "To a fellow Italophile,"' Mrs Bax said airily.

'How wonderful.' Mum slotted the book back, sighed

noisily and sank into the sofa. 'I wonder if we'll ever know who E. J. Holm is.'

'I would imagine the truth will come to light sooner or later,' Mrs Bax said. 'Not much stays hidden these days.'

Nico wondered if that was a covert message for him.

'Now, I know that young Nico here has told you all about my *Primavera* project. Would you like to come and see it?'

Mum, dragging James with her, followed Mrs Baxendall to the study where the hellebore was flourishing in its blue bowl next to the computer.

Mrs Baxendall stroked a petal of the greeny-yellow hellebore as though it were the dewiest of roses. 'It's difficult to believe that I have all the plants at last.'

'What will you find to do next?' Nico asked with a grin.

'Plenty – first I have to finish the book on Botticelli's garden. Which means, Nico my dear, you have to perform your last task.' She wafted everyone into the annex and gave Nico a sticker and a marker pen. 'You know what to do.'

Nico wrote, *Hellborus Viridis – elleboro – hellebore* and stuck the note on the pom-pom flower under the grace's foot.

James leaned forward and peered at it. 'Is that in the right place? It doesn't look like the real plant.'

'It's correct,' Mrs Bax said, 'and I shall be eternally

288

grateful that Nico found such a beautiful specimen for me.'

James straightened up. *Please*, Nico thought, *please don't say you were the one who took me to the garage where I found it and I couldn't have done it without you.*

'Brilliant stuff,' James said. 'I'd never have noticed it if I'd gone round looking with a plant guide in my hand.'

'Nico has flair for seeing things the rest of us miss,' Mrs Bax said. 'Now, would you like to see Botticelli's garden itself?'

When Mum and James said they would Mrs Bax gave them directions and sent them off while she kept Nico with her. She sat on a tall stool, brogues planted at ten to three, and studied the picture. 'D'you see that modest yellow flower near the middle grace's foot?'

'Yes.'

'It's a euphorbia, a sunspurge. Medicinally it's said to be good for the eyes; symbolically it means, "Look carefully".'

Nico remembered a passage from *The Shattered Mirror* where Alessandro Lupo was researching the *Primavera*. 'Isn't the middle grace supposed to be the historical Semiramide and Mercury is Lorenzo di Pierfrancesco de' Medici? And Cupid's aiming his arrow straight between the grace's shoulders.'

'*I* believe the message is indeed *Look carefully at Mercury – he's Lorenzo, your intended bridegroom*, while the

289

message to the observer is *Look carefully at this painting, it contains many messages.*'

Mrs Baxendall pointed to a white flower. 'That unobtrusive little plant is an antirrino, what we call bachelor's buttons in English. In Latin it's *Lychnis alba*, which means "white lantern" and symbolically it's saying, "See the light". Put those two flowers together and what message do you get?'

'Look carefully and see the light?'

'Exactly.' Mrs Bax sighed contentedly and closed her eyes.

Nico concentrated on the *Primavera*: what was he supposed to be looking for? Clues to who E. J. Holm really was? Or was Mrs Baxendall simply saying, Open your eyes, the answer's right in front of you, which she was at that very moment. The old lady didn't move, not even to blink or yawn. She looked as though she'd gone to sleep, upright on her stool. Nico waited a bit longer. Nothing happened. He clumped out as quietly as his boots would let him.

Jade was surprised Mum had agreed to let Teo drive them to the Villa dei Fiori. She was quite serene on the journey though Teo's driving was still style over substance and Dad, on the back seat next to Jade, watched every manoeuvre that he made.

Jade giggled.

'What?' Dad asked, taking his eyes off Teo for a moment.

'I was just thinking of your roadie stories, about doing the accounts while you were driving the Xtreme Measures van?'

'That was then – I'm a grown-up now.'

Jade snorted, 'Since when!'

Dad leaned over and whispered, 'Don't tell anyone, I don't ever intend to grow up.' He straightened and said loudly, 'Since I became a dad. It gives you a different way of looking at things once you're responsible for children.'

A red flush crept up the back of Teo's neck. The car slowed down though not much. It had reached the dirt road and jounced along between the stream and the chestnut trees till it reached the Villa dei Fiori.

'Pretty,' Dad said as they got out.

Mum smiled. 'Yes, it is.'

Jade couldn't get used to the way her mother was opening up to the things she'd denied herself for so long. Her face was glowing as she took in the terracotta tiles, the golden stucco and the wisteria blossom.

The door opened. Caterina flew out to kiss Mum and hold her hands. 'You are ready?'

'Yes.'

Mum was calm, which was more than could be said for Jade: her heart was pounding as she and Dad followed the two women and Teo into the kitchen. A short, plump woman sat at the table, her hands resting on a surface so fiercely polished its shine reflected the vase of young irises set in the centre.

'Mamma,' Caterina said, 'this is Luisa and her husband Kevin and one of the twins, Jade.'

Jade had never felt more in need of her sister than right now. She'd have done anything to be able to link arms with Amber for mutual support.

The woman stood up, her chin tilted proudly – or maybe defiantly, Jade couldn't tell.

Caterina drew Mum forward. 'Luisa, this is my mamma – your half-sister Sofia.'

There, it was said. Jade's heart raced even faster.

'I'm very pleased to meet you.' Mum held out her hand.

Sofia took it and leaned forward to give her long-lost sister the customary two kisses. 'Welcome to the Villa dei Fiori.'

'We'll leave you to talk,' Caterina said.

'We can't leave Mum!' Jade said.

'Our mammas, they need to talk on their own.'

'She's right, love,' Dad said.

Jade was hustled outside. She wasn't even given the chance to look back and make sure Mum was all right before she found herself on the way into Borgo Sant'Angelo. 'I wish Amber was here,' she said.

'I know,' Dad said, 'me too, but you can tell her all about it on your next visit to the hospital.'

It wasn't the same and Dario would probably be with her, which would definitely mean Amber wouldn't be paying attention to anyone but him.

Caterina parked in the piazza and they went into the bar-cafe. Jade and Dad sat at the old-fashioned bar while Teo ordered and Caterina chatted to the locals. When Dad's coffee arrived, he sipped it and a big smile spread over his face. 'What's this called?'

'Caffè corretto,' Teo said.

Dad repeated it. 'I approve of that, coffee corrected with booze.' He swirled the coffee round and sniffed at the grappa. 'How'd you say, "I'd like another"?'

'Ancora,' Caterina said.

Dad pronounced it perfectly with no trace of his midlands accent.

'How come you're up for learning Italian properly, Dad? You never would at home,' Jade asked.

'No need. I picked up enough to know what was going on. I didn't need to learn to speak it just 'cause your nonno said I ought to. Now . . .' Dad waved his arm in a sweep taking in the bar, the town, the whole of Tuscany. '. . . I need to ask about the food, the history . . .'

'And *il calcio*,' Teo said.

'Definitely the football.'

They chatted away, filling up the minutes until Caterina got a phone call to say it was time to go back to the Villa dei Fiori. All four of them were on edge as they went into the kitchen. Sofia was tasting a sauce. 'You haven't put in enough oregano.'

'Really?' Mum added half a handful of chopped herbs. 'How's that?'

Sofia tasted again. 'Better. You are a good cook and I will teach you how to become even better.' She waved the spoon towards Caterina, Jade and Dad. 'Make yourselves useful, we have much to prepare for Sunday's Easter feast.'

'Sunday?' Dad said. 'That's not for four days! How big's this feast going to be?'

'Huge,' Mum said with a smile as wide as Caterina's. 'It's at Mrs Baxendall's house and everybody's going including the Colliers. People are coming from miles around.'

That was a big change; Mum didn't like large groups and always made excuses for keeping away from them. Dad was grinning all over his face too. Jade had never seen her parents this openly happy and she realised with a jolt that it wasn't only Mum who'd made big sacrifices for Nonno, Dad had too. That was what he'd been trying to tell her. While Roberto had idolised his adoring granddaughters he'd cast a long dark shadow over many others down the years. Now the shadow was receding and Mum and Dad and Sofia were laughing, working together, at ease with one another.

There was even more laughter when Dario arrived with a man Jade hadn't seen before.

'Who's that?' Dad asked Jade.

'I think it's Carlo, Caterina's husband. He looks like the man in the photos she showed me.'

There was a lot of hugging, kissing and loud talking and within moments Jade and Dad were swept up in introductions while the kitchen rang with the sound of chinking glasses and the gurgle of wine and water being poured. Jade leaned back against the wall trying not to be noticed. It was unreal: Mum chatting animatedly with the half-sister she'd only just met and whom she'd silently resented till now; Dad, who'd always refused to speak Italian on principle, scooping up the language like a five-year-old let loose at a sweetie counter. She'd never seen her parents this happy.

Why don't I feel happy? What's wrong with me? she thought.

She brooded on her restless unhappiness all through the day and late into the evening. She tried reading, listening to music – nothing worked.

There was a knock at her door and Dad poked his head around it. Jade waved him in as the city bells rang midnight. He sat on the end of her bed. 'What's up?'

'I can't get my head round Mum being friends with

295

Sofia – cooking with her like they've been friends since forever. It's freaky.'

'They're finding out they've got things in common, especially that their father hurt them and their mothers. Now he can't hurt anyone so don't you go and spoil it for your mum by making a fuss.'

Was she the only one who still believed something good about Nonno? It felt to Jade as if her whole family had turned their backs on her beloved grandfather. 'It's . . .'

Dad shook Jade gently by the shoulders. 'Don't say it's not fair. Life isn't fair. It wasn't fair there was a war. It wasn't fair I didn't earn enough from doing what I loved to support my family and had to get a dead-end job in a factory. It wasn't fair I had to move into your granddad's house and listen to the miserable old bugger complaining for twenty years but, *Hey! That's life and you just gotta live it the best way you can.*'

'That's Xtreme Measures!'

'Yeah – poetry, isn't it?'

Jade smiled.

'That's better. Lie down now and go to sleep.' Dad tucked the covers round her as though she were still a little girl. 'It's time to forget the past, love, and look to the future. Remember, that's what the partisans fought for – a future for their country. Don't let that sour old man cheat you out of *yours*.'

Dad kissed her goodnight and switched off the light. Though she still wasn't happy exactly, she felt better than before and managed to fall asleep.

Nico didn't sleep well either. He'd got out all his notes on E. J. Holm and pored over them till one in the morning. In the end, he'd pushed the journals and books under his bed and gone to sleep. He dreamed that he went to Mrs Baxendall's chapel. It was dark and lit by guttering candles. Mrs Bax was there and she laughed when she saw Nico. She pointed to the body swinging from the scaffolding. It swayed, slowly beginning to swing round. Before Nico could see the features, Mrs Bax cried, 'This is E. J. Holm – you shall never see his face,' and slashed the rope. The body fell on Nico, crushing him on the stone flags.

He woke in a sweat to the sound of bells chiming six. He staggered into the kitchen and made a cup of instant coffee. 'I'm going to find out who you are if it kills me,' he hissed at the faceless E. J. Holm. Then he remembered the end of the dream and wished he hadn't said it.

There was another question too, one which I didn't dwell on because I was afraid of what the answer might be. When I could no longer avoid thinking about why my wife never visited me I realised that I had known the answer all along: she was afraid to look me in the face. I didn't blame her; I could barely look at myself in the mirror.

Shortly before my discharge from the hospital, my commanding officer paid a visit. I was sitting by the window overlooking a sloping lawn with a single birch tree in the centre. I stood. He gestured for me to sit and drew up the chair opposite.

The time had come to ask the question. 'You've come about my wife, Rebekah?' I said.

He nodded.

'She's refusing to see me, isn't she?'

'It isn't that, Wolfe.'

'Oh?' There was only one other reason I could think of and I knew I was right as soon as the Major began to speak: 'I'm sorry . . .'

'She's dead, isn't she?'

'She was killed in an air raid, just after you arrived here.'

'My daughter too?'

'No, she's completely unharmed. At the moment she's quite safe, evacuated to the country. She's being well looked after by a nice couple.'

'Thank you, sir.'

'Have you any questions?'

'Not now, sir.'

The Major extended his hand. I shook it. 'Good luck,' he said and left.

I sat and looked at the solitary tree until the nurse came in with supper.

CHAPTER XXIII

'NO MAKE-UP?' MUM asked.

'No, not tonight,' Nico said. He'd decided to be himself at Mrs Bax's party.

Mum carried on blow-drying her hair, a small smile of satisfaction curling round her lips. *It won't last*, Nico thought as he sat on the end of her bed, *not when she hears what I've got to tell her.* 'Mum, I've been thinking.'

'Oh dear!' Mum switched off the hairdryer and looked expectantly at Nico.

'You know I've been going to the Bargello a lot the last few days.'

'Yes, doing those marvellous drawings of the Baptistery statues.'

'I wasn't just drawing.'

'I know you've spent a lot of time with Jade while Amber's been in hospital.'

Nico shrugged that off. It was true he and Jade had talked for hours, mostly about how Jade was upset with what she'd discovered about Roberto, and Nico with what he hadn't discovered about E. J. Holm. They'd also discussed the bombshell Nico was about to drop on Mum.

'I meant I've been talking a lot to Edoardo Rossi, the man who's restoring Mrs Baxendall's frescoes. He showed me round the conservation programmes in the museum.'

Mum waited expectantly.

'I asked how you trained for that kind of work.'

'But . . .'

'No "buts", Mum, listen! After school, I've got to do four years' Art History at uni here and be able to pass my exams in Italian.'

'That sounds all right,' Mum said cautiously.

'When I've done that it's another four years at the Liceo Classico.'

'You'll be twenty-six before you're finished,' Mum said faintly.

'It's only the same as if I did a PhD. There's nothing to stop me working as well; people do.'

Mum examined her hairbrush closely.

'According to Edoardo the money's good,' Nico tried. Mum could boast about that to her book club. 'And you can become a professor and head up a university faculty.' She could boast about that to Dad. 'What d'you think?' Nico tensed for his mother's barrage of objections.

'From what you've said about Mr Mowatt I think we'd

better get you a tutor if you're going to get your Italian up to scratch.'

'You don't mind?'

'You needn't sound so incredulous.' Mum reached out and touched Nico's cheek lightly. 'Italy's changed you.' A wistful expression drifted across her face. 'I've tried to ignore it and I can't. It's hard though – we've been together against the world for such a long time, just you and me.'

Her forlorn face brightened, her back straightened. 'To hell with your father – to hell with me – it's your life. Do what makes you happy – it's the only thing that matters.'

James stuck his head round the door. 'It's time to leave – you'll have to get a move on.' He peered at Mum. 'Your hair's sticking up, Hattie, about here.' He patted his head to show her where.

'And to hell with you too!' Mum threw the hairbrush at him. It missed and bounced off the wall. She burst into tears and ran into the bathroom.

James stared at the brush lying on the carpet as if he'd just discovered a small dead thing. 'What was that all about?'

'Mum needs you,' Nico said. It was the first time he'd admitted that and it wasn't lost on James. He went after Mum, punching Nico awkwardly on the shoulder as he passed. Nico went to his own room, shutting the door behind him.

*

302

Although they arrived early Nico was amazed to see how many people were already at Mrs Baxendall's party. Greetings flew from all corners of the dusky garden: 'Ciao! Buona sera! Hello!' There were young people and old and people in between; a sprinkling of professori and dottori; many signore and signori; a bishop and a priest and a lot of children who ran off as soon as the introductions were over and disappeared into the darkening garden. Alec was there too and he waved at Nico. James took it as a cue to join the group. Mum and Nico exchanged wry glances and followed him. Nico made the introductions and the partisans carried on with their reminiscing; out of politeness they spoke in English.

'Do you remember,' Gaetano said, 'how we honoured Potente's dying wish to fly his red shirt over Florence when it was free?'

There were murmurs from the group. 'It was the 7th September, 1944,' Professoressa Mussi said, 'in the courtyard of the Fortezza da Bassa. It was packed with partisans and their families.'

Signora Minardi nodded. 'A fourteen-year-old partisan boy sounded his trumpet to announce the arrival of the Allied commander. Everyone stood to attention and the Italian tricolore flew together with the American flag.'

'And alongside it flew the flag of the Arno Division topped by the red shirt of Potente.' Gaetano's eyes shone with an emotion that Nico knew he'd never be able to understand. He wished that Jade were with him.

Teo brought Jade and her family to Mrs Baxendall's house in the late afternoon while the last of the sun still loitered over the hills.

'Welcome, welcome.' Mrs Bax shepherded them through the house, slowly because Amber was walking with crutches. 'We're lucky to have a warm, late Easter. It means we can be outside till it gets too chilly.'

They joined a group made up of Sofia and Caterina and their family. Dario hurried over to Amber and sat her gently on a chair. Jade saw Nico with James and Hattie and a cluster of the old partisans including Signora Minardi, Gaetano and Alec. The Italians were all wearing red, white and green scarves, knotted to show the eagle motif at their throats. Jade went over to the group.

'Buona sera,' she said shyly. 'I hope you don't mind me asking . . .' She pointed. 'Are those your brigade scarves?'

'Yes indeed, we are the Uccello Band,' the elderly priest said proudly. 'Though we were a small band, we were an effective one.'

Gaetano barked a laugh.

'He is *il Falco*,' the priest said, 'and I am *Il Corvo*.'

The falcon and the crow; they'd grown into their names, Jade thought, what with Gaetano's beaky nose and the priest's black vestments. 'What was your name?' she asked the Signora.

The other old people chuckled. 'Ilaria was so small and thin we called her *Il Passerotto*, the little sparrow,' Gaetano said.

'You're all codenamed after birds then,' James said.

'Apart from *Il Lupo*,' Gaetano said. Murmurs and smiles rippled through the group.

'Who's he?' Jade asked. 'Why did you call him "the wolf" instead of a bird name?'

'You've met him,' Gaetano said with the nearest thing to a smile Jade had seen.

'I have?'

'He means me,' Alec said. 'As I worked with the brigade I had to have a partisan name. Since my surname's Wolfe they called me *Il Lupo*.'

Gaetano drew on his cigarette and breathed the smoke out through his nose. 'After the war, when he came to live here, he wanted to have a real Italian name. We chose Sandro for him. He has been our good friend for many years since then.'

'We are all lucky to have lived so long,' Alec said.

'God watched over us,' the priest added.

'If you say so,' the Signora said and Jade couldn't help thinking she had a point.

'I do say so,' the priest said firmly and poured more wine into Ilaria Minardi's glass. 'Let us drink to that.'

The old partisans shared the toast, some with more enthusiasm than others.

Jade raised her glass to Nico and grinned.

'What?'

She laughed and drew him away.

The dell was dotted with lanterns casting wavering shadows over the stone head making benevolent smiles flicker over its mossy lips. Nico sat on a boulder, his arm around Jade. 'What's up?' he asked, hugging her tightly.

'Weren't you listening to the oldies?'

'Yes, why?'

'Remember what they called Mrs Bax's father.'

'Sandro?'

Jade knocked gently on Nico's forehead. 'No, you dingbat – his code name, *Il Lupo*.'

'The wolf? So?'

'So his last name's Wolfe and his first name's Alec which might be short for Alexander. And his Italian friends called him Sandro, which is definitely short for Alessandro. Now,' Jade said with exaggerated slowness, 'what's Alessandro Lupo mean in English?'

Nico made the connection. 'Oh my God!'

'The lights are on then.'

'Cheeky cow!' Nico kissed Jade. He ought to rush straight off and challenge Mrs Bax but somehow the kiss went on. In the end Jade pushed him away. 'Not to be boring or anything, but shouldn't you go and talk to Mrs Bax?'

Nico thought for a bit then said, 'No,' and leaned forward again.

Jade scooped up freezing water and threw it over Nico. 'Cool off and go and talk to her! It is what you came to Italy for, isn't it – to find out who E. J. Holm is?'

Jade was right. Nico went to find Mrs Bax. She was no longer in the garden and he went into the house. When he still couldn't find her he went into the study. The computer showed several images of a hellebore. Nico went to have a closer look and noticed a small photo fixed to the side of the computer. It was the one Alec Wolfe had carried with him throughout the war. On the other side of the computer was another old black and white photo, of a youngish man in uniform. He was dark and good-looking, as Alec must once have been. Nico unpinned it and turned it over. An inscription on the back said, *Captain Alexander Edward Jacob Wolfe – Daddy* in childlike writing. Nico pinned the photo up again and sat in the swivel chair, spinning idly, looking at the pictures of Mrs Baxendall's family, mother and child on one side of the computer, father on the other. *A bit like my family*, Nico thought, *only I've got the Atlantic Ocean between my parents.*

'Here you are!' Mrs Bax's voice boomed behind him.

Nico pivoted round. 'I hope you don't mind me sitting here?'

'Not at all. Jade said you wanted to see me.' Mrs Bax perched on a corner of the desk and twinkled at Nico.

'Even though you're not E. J. Holm it's got to be someone who knew about the story of Gaetano and Roberto and Elena as well as you do because the plot of the last two books follows their story quite closely. And whoever wrote the book must at least have talked to Gaetano or Elena – there's no chance they could've talked to Roberto.'

'I see.'

Nico chewed his lip. He wanted to get the words right. 'Your father was called Alec Wolfe and the partisans knew him as *Il Lupo* – the Wolf. According to what you wrote on the back of his photo Alec is short for Alexander, which, in Italian, makes him *Alessandro Lupo*. I think that's too big a coincidence to ignore.'

Mrs Baxendall carried on twinkling.

The light blazed brighter. 'And his middle names are Edward Jacob!'

In his excitement Nico swirled round in a full circle of triumph. 'E. J. – Edward Jacob! Your father is definitely E. J. Holm!'

'Then where does the "Holm" come from?'

Nico stopped swinging in the chair. 'I don't know yet, I'll work it out eventually.' He looked Mrs Baxendall straight in the eye. 'I'm right aren't I?'

'All right – I give in. Yes, Father is indeed E. J. Holm.'

'Yes!' Nico leaned forward triumphantly, eagerly. 'Did he talk to you about it, his writing I mean?'

Mrs Baxendall nodded. 'Certainly. And I helped organise his notes and his research. I did the typing – Father doesn't get on with computers – and talked to him about his plots and his characters and what each book meant and what the message of the whole series was. At first it was that revenge is a dish best served cold.' Mrs Baxendall chuckled. 'Father has a measure of vanity – he saw E. J. Holm as his alter ego wreaking vengeance on the villains who'd escaped reprisals and even flourished after the war. That's why he gave Alessandro his own name.'

'Now he's finished the whole series,' Nico said.

'It's ended on a positive note that's taken Father a lifetime to learn; the final message is that revenge is ultimately destructive and that by the third and fourth generation it's absolutely past its sell-by date. He'll be delighted to chat with your friends, the Thompsons, and see that the story he told really does have a positive resolution.'

'It's mixed though, isn't it?'

'Mixed?'

'The end of the real story – that's not your classic happy ending. I mean, Jade and Amber know now that their nonno was a traitor who caused the death of Gaetano's family – that's not a very positive resolution for them.'

'True, though acknowledging what Roberto did, and regretting it, enables them to achieve what Roberto, the orphan boy, longed for and never got – to be truly part of Gaetano's family.' Mrs Baxendall slapped her knees and stood up.

'Now, young man, let's go back to the party and you can have a good long chat to E. J. Holm.'

'He won't mind people knowing?'

'Not any more. Times have changed and he no longer fears his appearance being exposed to the world and ridiculed. He realises if people recoil from him it's not his problem, as you young people say – it's theirs. Besides which, the Alessandro Lupo books are at an end and he thinks the time's right for proper attribution to be made.' Mrs Baxendall's mischievous smile was back. 'We could always start by telling your mother.'

'Jade! Where've you been?' Amber was hopping towards her, swinging far too fast on her crutches.

'Nowhere.'

Amber peered at her. 'You've been snogging Nico again.'

'You can talk – you're always playing tonsil hockey with Dario.'

Amber smirked. 'I know.'

'What do you want?'

'Mum's got news. C'mon.' Amber hopped back

to where Mum and Dad, and Sofia and her family waited. Dario instantly stood by Amber and supported her.

Mum took Dad's hand and said, 'We've made a decision.' Her face was alight with happiness. Jade wondered at the magic Italy had cast over her mother.

'When we went to see the old farmhouse this morning, I fell in love with it.'

'I knew you would,' Amber said.

'Dad and I have talked and decided to use Granny Grace's trust fund to buy the house from Gaetano.'

Jade felt a huge grin spread over her face.

Gaetano grunted, 'It will be good to bring the old place back to life again.'

'The happy memories are the ones we'll choose to remember,' Sofia said.

'We can start by chiselling off that inscription over the door,' Dad said.

Gaetano grunted again in what Jade supposed was agreement.

'And we can make new memories,' Mum said. 'Happy ones.'

'Magic!' Amber let go of Dario and hugged Jade and they staggered in mad circles, whooping with excitement.

'Signora Minardi had already put in an offer but she stood down for us,' Mum said.

'She's still getting a lot of the land,' Caterina said. 'She and I have been in business for some time and we are looking at extending our partnership.'

Jade and Amber stopped twirling. 'Are we going to live at the farmhouse full time?' Jade asked.

'Eventually,' Dad said. 'We've got to restore it first. I'm going to junk the factory job and organise summer music schools there.'

'Good job it's isolated,' Amber said.

'Why don't we just move over here now?' Jade asked.

'Give it time,' Mum said. 'You need to get your exams over first while we're rebuilding and restoring. After that, who knows?'

'Yes!' Jade and Amber said at exactly the same time. They were like speakers in balance once again.

Dusk turned into night and the white moon sailed into the sky for its night shift. In the dining room Mrs Baxendall raised her glass and said, 'Welcome all, to our Pasqua feast.' Glasses chinked and Easter greetings flew around the table.

'Go carefully with that wine,' Mum said to Nico then started on the topic that had obsessed her since Nico had told her about E. J. Holm. 'I still want to know why Alec chose the name Holm as his pen name. He wouldn't tell me when I asked.'

'Give him a break, Mum! He's only just revealed his identity – you can't make him tell you everything at once.'

James leaned over and splashed more wine into Nico's glass. He winked. It had always made Nico want to grind his teeth when James did that; he should tell him some time. 'Nice trees around here,' James said.

'What?'

'The trees – nice trees, don't you think?'

Nico didn't think they were particularly. 'They're OK,' he said cautiously. He didn't want James starting a lecture on arboriculture.

Too late, James talked on: 'They're a particular species, you know.'

'Right.'

'We had them round our house when I was a child. They're called holm oaks. Interesting that, don't you think?' He raised his glass. 'Chin, chin.'

Holm oaks. That's where E. J. got his surname. And James – James! – had worked it out.

Mrs Baxendall stood and began to sing.

'I've heard that song before,' Nico said to Jade. 'It's what Mrs Bax was singing when she found me on the chapel steps.'

'It's a partisan song called *Bella ciao*. The old people at Nonno's Italian Club used to sing it a lot. How could Roberto sing along with them? It was so hypocritical,' Jade said bitterly.

'Forget it; it doesn't matter any more. Tell me what the words mean?'

'It's about waking up one morning and finding your country's been invaded. You join the partisans and hope if you die you'll be buried in the mountains among the wild flowers. Then, when the war's over, people will pass by the flowers and say they're beautiful; they're the flowers of freedom.' Jade jumped to her feet.

'Wait,' Nico said, 'don't run.'

'I'm not going to – *I'm* not a hypocrite.' Jade began to sing along with Mrs Baxendall. Awkwardly Amber stood too, supported by Luisa. They linked hands and joined their voices with Jade's and Mrs Baxendall's, then the Signora joined in, then Ornella and then, one by one, all the other women at the party.

'Bella ciao, bella ciao, bella ciao, ciao, ciao.' Farewell, my beloved.

The men joined in one final, rousing chorus of defiance and hope that echoed round the darkling garden.

'Bella ciao, bella ciao, bella ciao, ciao, ciao.'

Once I was demobbed and discharged I decided to return to Italy for good. I had no ties to England apart from Emily and felt at home amongst my Italian friends whom I visited several times before coming to my decision. We had shared comradeship and privation and fought together. They did not comment on my appearance nor shy away from it. We were at ease with each other.

They told me more of what had happened at the farmhouse that day. Somehow, most probably from an informer in the pay of the Fascists, Roberto had heard that I was there and reported the fact to the head of the local Black Brigade who instantly ordered the attack in the hopes of capturing me. As it was Easter Sunday we were lax and shamefully unprepared for what happened.

In the ensuing fight, Henryk, one of the Polish POWs, was killed, and a partisan. Roberto had burst into the farmhouse, found me in the kitchen and fired the shotgun. The blast threw me back and I hit my head on the corner of a cupboard. It was that blow which impaired my memory. Outside, the others temporarily pinned down the Black Brigade enabling Jerzy and Ilaria to drag me from the farmhouse and into the woods. From there a chain of support saw me taken to a hideout where the local doctor did the best he could to keep me going. Over the next few days I was taken over the Freedom Trail; I rode a mule for most of the way until even that became impossible. I was fairly mobile but had little stamina and once we reached the crest of the mountains a bull of a man carried me over them and down to the Allies.

Gaetano told me about the aftermath of the attack. In retaliation for the death of the Black Brigade member and for harbouring an enemy spy, the town of Borgo Sant'Angelo was decimated. The Fascists didn't discriminate in deciding which tenth of the population were culled: women, children, the elderly, the town's priest were all selected and mown down with machine gun fire. There is a memorial to them in the square, opposite the small fountain with its statue of Arion riding a dolphin.

CHAPTER XXIV

'THERE'S STILL SOMETHING not right,' Jade said over her farewell ice cream at the Bar Vivoli.

'What do you mean?' Nico asked.

'It's the Signora – I went to see her, to tell her Mum destroyed Elena's letter and didn't want to talk about the past because she was worried about upsetting our new family.'

'And?'

Jade went on the defensive. 'You'll think I'm seeing stuff that isn't there.'

'Try me.'

Jade couldn't resist Nico's quirky grin. She puffed out a breath. 'It was the look on the Signora's face. It was kind of . . . like relief and . . . almost like she'd won.'

'Won what?'

Jade shook her head. 'That's the thing, I don't know. The look was gone so quickly I thought for a minute I'd made a mistake but I hadn't, I know I hadn't. She said a weird thing too: she said, "At last".'

'Any idea what she meant?'

'No. And there's something else that doesn't add up.'

'What?'

Jade wrinkled her nose, concentrating on recalling the conversation as accurately as possible. 'You remember the Signora explaining to us what Roberto had done? She said he was angry when he was told about Elena and Gaetano.'

'What's your point?'

'I don't see how she'd know that unless she was actually there when someone spoke to Roberto about it. So, who's this mysterious someone? How did they know about what had happened and why did they tell Roberto? And how come the Signora was there when it kicked off?'

Nico stood up. 'C'mon.'

'You haven't finished your ice cream,' Jade pointed out.

'Doesn't matter – you've got to get this sorted. We're leaving tomorrow and you need to talk to the Signora now, before it's too late and you torment yourself to death.'

Nico was right: Jade felt as if she were tying herself in knots trying to work out her sense of unfinished business. Even if fronting up to the Signora meant she had to face more horrible truths about Nonno it had to be worth it. Maybe not though? The argument raged in her head. By the time Nico was knocking on Signora Minardi's door

Jade had decided to back out. It was too late; the old lady opened the door. 'Yes?'

'Can we come in a minute?' Nico said. 'Jade wants to speak to you.'

Signora Minardi beckoned them in. Jade was surprised to see Alec sitting by the open French windows. That was going to complicate matters. She wasn't sure she could accuse the friend of this brave old man of some kind of deliberate cover-up.

'Hello.' Alec stood politely until Jade sat down then sank back into his chair. 'I don't recommend getting very old,' he said. 'It was almost better fighting in the hills – at least I was capable of running!'

'I prefer the peace,' the Signora said, sitting next to him. She turned to Jade. 'How can I help you?'

After the Signora's comment about peace Jade wished she'd left well alone. Signora Minardi looked at her expectantly.

She felt Nico squeeze her hand in encouragement. 'It's about what happened at the farmhouse. Something's wrong. I know Nonno did bad things . . .'

The Signora snorted contemptuously.

Jade broke eye contact with the old lady and looked at Alec. 'What Nonno did was terrible, unforgivable, but he loved Elena, he did, and he'd never hurt her on purpose.' She was almost pleading with Alec to believe her. 'He'd never have gone along with that massacre without some kind of reason.' The words sounded ridiculous, even to her, and Jade wasn't surprised that Alec's expression was pitying.

'What possible reason could there be? I was there, I saw people die, I saw . . .' He rubbed his hand over his face as if trying to obliterate a vision of corpses, blood, terror.

Jade didn't like upsetting Alec, not even to find out the final truth, if there even was one. She glanced at Nico for support.

'Don't ask him,' he said firmly. He jabbed a finger towards Signora Minardi: 'Ask her!'

Crash! Alec's cup smashed on the floor. He was gripping the sides of the chair, the veins in his hands bulging out. 'I remember!' His good eye was wide, the white showing all round the iris. 'Ask her! He said, *Ask her!*' Alec was staring at Signora Minardi.

I knew there was more, Jade thought. *I knew it.*

'I'll get some water,' Nico said. Jade was glad he'd taken charge; she was as numb and unable to move as Alec and the Signora.

Nico came back into the shocked silence. 'Here.' He gave Alec a glass of water. When he'd drained it Jade knelt in front of him and said gently, 'What did you mean? Who said, *Ask her*? What happened?'

Alec closed his eyes momentarily as though gathering his newly remembered memories into proper order. When he opened them again he said, 'The fighting was still going on in the courtyard. Gaetano was with Elena and Ilaria in the kitchen. We were intending to help them get out of the house from the back. That way they could hide in the woods and once they were safe, Gaetano and I could double back and re-join the fighting in the courtyard. We were about to make a run for it when Volpe broke in. Gaetano and Elena were at the door, with Ilaria and me between them and Volpe. He had a shotgun. It was aimed at Gaetano.

'Ilaria shouted, "Go!", pushed Elena and Gaetano out and slammed the door after them.

'"I want them," Volpe said. "Move or I'll kill you now." I needed to distract him, even if only for a moment, to give us a chance to disarm him, delay him, anything. "How did you know we were here?" I shouted.

'"Ask her!" he said and pointed the shotgun at Ilaria. Then, without warning, he swung it on me and fired.'

Both old people looked stricken, deathly pale, propped up in their chairs like living corpses.

'What did he mean, Ilaria?' Alec said.

'He meant that it was me who told him about Elena. It was me who provoked him into revenge.'

Jade gasped. 'Why?'

'I didn't mean to – you have to believe me!'

A strange calm settled over Jade. *Maybe,* she thought

hazily, *it's because now I'm going to know what really happened.* 'I believe you,' she said.

She sat on the arm of Alec's chair, one hand across the back as though she were protecting him. 'Tell us what happened,' she said to Ilaria Minardi.

The Signora folded her hands in her lap, twining her fingers compulsively. She spoke directly to Alec. 'It began on that Easter Sunday, at my parents' house in Borgo. I was helping them prepare the Pasqua feast with what little food the enemy had left us when he – Roberto Volpe – came knocking at the door.' A faint smile tugged at the old lady's lips. 'A Black Brigade boy at your door was not a thing to be welcomed. I took him into the garden where we could talk unobserved. He said that he'd been to Elena's house and her parents had turned him away telling him that Elena no longer lived there. He came to me to find out what they meant and where she was.

'I told him that, because he hadn't bothered to answer Elena's letter, she'd married Gaetano. He was bewildered; he said, *What letter? What marriage?* I didn't believe him then; I was certain that he'd ignored the letter to avoid his responsibility to Elena and the child. Anger burst from me. I goaded him. He said, *I knew nothing of any letter! You're lying!* I will never forget his expression – contorted with pain. It was then I knew he was telling the truth: for whatever reason, he had never received the first letter.'

322

'And you hid the second one,' Jade said. 'He never had a chance to come for Elena.'

The Signora nodded. 'I knew it but I denied it to myself and provoked him further. I said, *At least Gaetano truly loves her. She's better off with him than you; he's even happy to raise your bastard child.*'

Jade gasped. 'How could you!'

Signora Minardi raised her hands as though protecting herself from Jade's accusation. 'I still thought Elena would be happier with Gaetano than with Roberto. I thought I could drive him away with words. But it was war and words were nothing when guns could speak. He stared at me with contempt for a moment, then left. I knew that he was going to report to the Black Brigade and that they would attack the farmhouse immediately. I also knew there would be more victims than they anticipated because of the Pasqua feast for the partisans and their friends. I didn't even stop to tell my parents what I was doing; I went to the hills as fast as I could. I reached the farmhouse only moments before the Black Brigade; I had a bicycle and my feet, they had vehicles. There was no time for flight, only for fighting. Because of me, good men died – Gaetano's family died. And there were reprisals afterwards – Elena's parents were executed, as were mine, along with dozens of townspeople. The Black Brigade did it as an example to those who supported partisans and sheltered Allied spies.'

Jade felt numb and sick yet there was one more truth that needed to be spoken out loud. 'Signora, like Alec said, nothing – *nothing* – can excuse what Nonno did.'

'Nevertheless, if I hadn't tormented him, scorned him, he might have left us alone. It was I who was responsible for those deaths.' She turned to Alec. 'And you, my friend – Roberto had heard rumours that you were at the farmhouse but he only knew for certain when he came face to face with you in the kitchen.'

Alec gave his twisted smile. 'I think they call that collateral damage these days.'

'How can you joke about such a thing! You were terribly hurt because of me and have spent all these years in torment trying to remember the truth, which I could have told you in a heartbeat. That is unforgivable.'

Alec took her hands. 'We were young and foolish and the war was all around us. Yours wasn't the only mistake we made, and it wasn't the worst. Dear friend, there is nothing to forgive.'

Alec released Ilaria Minardi's hands and smiled again. 'You can tell me though, what I need to know to fill the gaps in my poor brain.'

'Anything.'

'How exactly did I get out of the house and onto the escape route?'

'When Volpe shot you, I snatched up a meat cleaver and attacked him. I severed some of his fingers and he dropped the shotgun. I snatched it up and fired at his legs. He fell, screaming. Jerzy broke through the door and we dragged you out. Jerzy carried you into the forest where we were joined by other partisans. They and the contadini helped us to unite you with the Allies.'

'You returned to fight again.'

'Yes.'

Jade couldn't bear to listen to any more. 'Signora, thank you for telling us the truth. Now I know exactly what to think of my grandfather.'

'You will tell your parents about me?'

Jade shook her head. 'I'm not going to say anything to anybody.' *Not even Amber*, she thought. Her sister, like the rest of the family, had made her peace with what she thought was the truth; there was no point in stirring up more pain.

'And you?' Ilaria Minardi asked Nico.

'No,' he said. 'It's over, really over, finished for ever.'

'We're going now,' Jade said. 'We'll say goodbye before we go home tomorrow.'

'Thank you,' the old lady said. But she wasn't looking at Jade; she was looking at Alec.

Nico took Jade for a meal at the cafe on the other side of the river. They didn't speak much till Jade said, 'At least I know how Nonno really lost his fingers and why he limped. He was such a liar. Just think, we were so keen to find out why Nonno's relatives rejected him and why he thought he'd be killed if came back. Now we know and the truth's horrible.'

'Amber doesn't know everything.'

'She knows enough.' Jade laughed.

Nico hadn't expected that. 'What's funny?'

'We made an album, *The Book of Memories*, for our Italian relatives because we wanted to show them what a lovely person Nonno was by sharing our memories of him. Instead of that, they showed *us* what he was truly like – a murderer. Amber threw the book into the Arno this morning.'

Nico didn't know what he was supposed to make of that. 'Don't you think it was a bit drastic?' he said cautiously. 'Roberto did love you and Amber and from what you told me, he loved Grace and your mum too.'

'Nah, the memories were all false. He didn't love us enough to tell us the truth and say he was sorry for what he'd done. Signora Minardi's sorry – properly sorry – for what she did, you can tell.'

Nico agreed. 'I get that.' He paused. 'Will you be able to live with what you know? You haven't got anyone to share with.'

'There's you! Or are you going to go home and forget about me?'

'No!' Nico grinned. 'Anyway, I haven't got a choice – your mum's already invited my mum to your farmhouse in the summer, even if it's not finished.'

'Charming.'

It was getting dark. 'Let's walk,' Nico said. 'We can watch the lights along the riverbank.'

They went hand in hand towards the Arno. 'What about you?' Jade asked. 'Did you get what you came to Italy for, apart from outing E. J. Holm I mean? You said it was to find out if you and your mum can get on with James long term. Can you?'

Nico hadn't thought of James as the muppet for some time. He shrugged. 'He's not that bad. He likes Mum and she likes him. They're good for each other. I can put up with him for her sake I guess. It does get her off my back.' Italy had made Mum stronger too, Nico thought. Things didn't scare her as much any more – she hadn't texted him once this evening even though it was late, and dark.

I've found my place, Nico realised. *I know exactly what I want to do with my life; Italy's given me that*. He thought with excitement of his plans for the future and was glad that Jade was in them.

'Oh look!' she said.

'What?'

'My first fireflies!' Jade was rapt.

Nico laughed. He leaned his arms on the parapet of

the bridge and the two of them watched the darting lights flickering above the night-black water until the evening turned chilly and they walked back to Via del Corno for the last time.

By the time I moved permanently to Italy Emily was four. She was a happy child who had never been afraid of my appearance and she loved her new home. She quickly endeared herself to my friends, particularly Ilaria who spoiled her scandalously. I bought a place in the hills and settled down as a farmer of sorts growing olives and grapes and later kiwi fruit, which surprisingly flourished.

Emily eventually spent some time at school in England and later at university. After a brief marriage she returned to Italy and worked on the farm. She also became my helper when I decided to begin writing the Alessandro Lupo novels. She was forthright in her comments on the stories and was invaluable as a secretary: I have no truck with IT and certainly not with social media. The success of the books took us both by surprise. I was unwilling to reveal myself but, unfortunately, this only seemed to inflame the curiosity of fans still further. However, times have moved on and there are now several reasons for coming clean at last.

Firstly, I had hoped that, as Alessandro doggedly pursues the serial killer who is systematically murdering ex-Fascists and informers, I would begin to make sense of what had happened to me during the war. Now Alessandro has solved his last case yet I know little more than when I began the books. Besides, writing them became much more important to me than mere therapy and I have been gratified at their reception.

Secondly, I no longer care about my appearance or how people might react to it. I have made new, young friends who are not in the least concerned with my looks. Their only interest is in the books and, by extension, the nature of the person who wrote them.

Thirdly, I wanted to write this memoir to pay tribute to the men and women of all nations who fought valiantly against such overwhelming odds to free Italy from the horrors of Fascism. I couldn't do this and continue to hide my face away.

Finally, I had hoped that in taking some of the characters through my own experiences I would find my way to that last, lost memory: what did the Black Brigade boy say just before he shot me? I have discovered that the question is no longer important.

The future is not mine; it belongs to the young. All I ask of them is that they do not forget the terrible things that happened during that dark period of history and work to ensure that they are never repeated.

LIST OF CHARACTERS

IN 2005

Nico Collier, on holiday in Florence with his mother, Hattie, and her boyfriend, James Crozier

Jade Thompson and her twin sister, **Amber,** on holiday in Florence with their parents, Luisa and Kevin

Signora Minardi, landlady of the apartments where Jade, Nico and their families are staying

Ornella, companion to Signora Minardi

Caterina and **Carlo Biagi,** who live near Borgo Sant'Angelo, a small town in the countryside

Lia, Valentina and **Dario,** Caterina and Carlo's teenage children

Davide and **Sofia,** Caterina's parents

Matteo, Caterina's brother

Nonno, Caterina and Matteo's grandfather

Nonna, Caterina and Matteo's grandmother

Emily Baxendall (Mrs Bax), an expatriate Englishwoman who has lived in Italy for most of her life. She lives with her elderly father, Alec, in a grand house in the countryside.

Edoardo Rossi, a picture restorer

E. J. Holm, a reclusive crime writer living in Tuscany

1933–1944

Roberto, Gaetano, Elena and **Ilaria,** four close friends

Jerzy and **Henryk,** escaped Polish prisoners of war who joined the resistance movement

'Il Lupo', a British SOE officer working with the resistance in Italy

Books by E. J. Holm
The Shattered Mirror
The Leopard's Kill
The Coloratura Assassin
The Prince without a Country
Murder in the Fifteenth Tower
Revenge unto the Fourth Generation

HISTORICAL NOTE

The SOE and the war in Italy

The Special Operations Executive (SOE) was a secret organisation founded in 1940 to 'set Europe ablaze' (Winston Churchill). The agents of the SOE – all volunteers – had a two-part mission: to carry out acts of sabotage, such as blowing up bridges and factories, and to help support rebel groups fighting against the enemy. The SOE became very active in Italy after its government agreed to an armistice with the Allies at war against Germany. The armistice was signed in September 1943 and Italy surrendered to the Allies. Germany retaliated by occupying Italy. The country then fell into civil war, with some Italians siding with Germany and some with the Allies.

The infamous Black Brigades were created after the armistice to rout out anyone caught supporting the Allies, including partisans and SOE agents. They were feared for their extreme brutality. The story of Tosca Buccarelli and her torture in the infamous Villa Triste is true. The building is now an apartment block.

The Primavera

The Primavera (Spring), the picture which features in this book, was painted by Sandro Botticelli (Alessandro di Mariano di Vanni Filipepi, c. 1445 d.1510) in about 1482. It depicts a mysterious woodland glade where approximately 190 species of flowers flourish; roughly 130 of these are recognisable and half of these are spring flowering. There are eight figures and a flying cherub in the glade. No one is exactly sure who the figures represent but one of the most likely interpretations is that they are Mercury – messenger of the gods – the three graces dancing, Venus, Flora (the goddess of spring), Chloris (a nymph), and Zephyr, the gentle west wind associated with spring.

The picture may have been commissioned by, or for, Lorenzo di Pierfrancesco de' Medici (1458–1503) in celebration of his wedding to Semiramide Appiani in 1482.

Other artworks

All the artworks mentioned in the book, except for the Esther cycle, are real and can be seen in the locations mentioned.

The Vincenzo Danti (1530–1576) exhibition took place in 2008, three years later than in this book. I have moved it to fit in with the plot. Likewise, the restoration of Donatello's *David*, which was undertaken from 2007–8. I have tried to ensure that all other dates are accurate. Any mistakes are entirely my own.

ACKNOWLEDGEMENTS

I am grateful to Arts Council England, East Midlands Arts, for their generous grant which enabled me to visit Italy and carry out valuable first-hand research.

Journalist Veronica Horwell first sparked my interest in Botticelli's masterpiece, *Primavera*, with her witty and perceptive article, 'Oh no it isn't', which she wrote for the *Guardian*.

Several friends with expert knowledge have given me valuable assistance: David Boulton advised me on medical issues and the uses of shotguns. The late Clive Beer-Jones of Black Widow told me many lively stories of roadie antics. Jane Weller was a fount of information about the military and modern military history. She also directed me to ANPI, the National Association of Italian Partisans (Associazione Nazionale Partigiani d'Italia). Joan Parker gave me many unique insights into daily life in Italy.

I am also indebted to friends and colleagues who were kind enough to read and comment on the manuscript. These include Mary, Jane, Fran, Lynne, Miriam, John,

Patricia, Linda and Helen Louise. My young beta readers were especially forthright! Thank you for your insights, Gary, Bea and Katie.

Italian friends were always warm and welcoming, especially Paolo and Cristina Badiali and Tina Avola. In Florence, Marco Germinale and Valentina Barbero kindly shared their knowledge of scooters while the experts at Florence by Bike were generous with their time and expertise.

In the town of Villagrappa, Dottoressa Elissa Massa and Bruno Conficioni organised a wonderful reception. The people of Villagrappa kindly shared many memories and stories of wartime. Thank you also to Bruno for his tour of abandoned farmhouses.

Naturally libraries have proved indispensable and I would like to thank the following: The British Library; The London Library; University of Leicester School of Education Library; Rugby School Library; Lutterworth Library.

My son-in-law, Chris Allen, has been a stalwart in ferrying me back and forth in search of information.

Finally: the person to whom I owe the most is my daughter, Elizabeth Allen. Thank you.